LIFE AFTER REDDY

BY

KAITLIN CAUL

Renaissance.
Diverse, Canadian Voices

Cover art, design, typesetting, and interior design by Nathan Caro Fréchette. Edited by Myryam Ladouceur, L.P. Vallee and Meaghan Côté. Legal deposit, Library and Archives Canada, April 2018.
Paperback ISBN: 978-1-987963-29-8
Ebook ISBN: 978-1-987963-32-8

Renaissance Press
http://renaissancebookpress.com
info@renaissancebookpress.com

This book is dedicated to my parents, who always encouraged my odd hobbies; to my sister Aimee, who inspires me to always reach for more; to my brother Marcus, who challenges me to have his enthusiasm for writing; and to my best friends Manda, Angela, Kim, and Helena, who still love me after enduring years of zombie talk.

I love all of you.

CHAPTER ONE

OAK RIDGE MENTAL HOSPITAL, TEXAS
August 22, 2032

Once upon a time, there was a little town called Redby that nobody cared about. Some evil pricks from Almesa Corporation built giant walls around the town, filled it with zombies, then sat around and watched all the little people run and scream and die. We lived that way for ten years, screaming and dying and starting all over again. Being immortal kinda sucks like that. Then my friend made a cure, we got out, Redby burned to the ground, and Almesa collapsed. That part all happened a little fast. Then I went nuts, and the rest of the world went back to being full of sunshine and rainbows and blissful ignorance.

The end.

On the inside of the glossy green journal, neatly typed out on a name tag, read my name and current residence. Cassandra Isabella Saratores, resident of Oak Ridge Mental Hospital. The doctor gave me the journal with my name tag already attached. I guess he figured I wouldn't remember my own name if I didn't see it every day. Some days, he wasn't far off.

Inside the journal, filling exactly half a page, scrawled the details Doctor Brown had asked me for. A quick summary of all the shit that had happened over the ten years I'd spent trapped in Redby, also known as Zombie Hell. I glossed over the part about how, a few days after getting out, I decided the free life wasn't my thing and opted to kill a guy. Insanity plea, lots of media attention, a year of court appearances that played out more like a reality fucking TV show, and suddenly I'm the newest resident of the biggest, baddest max-security nuthouse in the United States.

Welcome to Oak Ridge Mental Hospital. Would you like the blue pills or the red pills?

Setting the journal on the bed, still open to the first page, I shifted around to get comfortable. The mattress squeaked a protest and the cold stone of the wall pressed against my spine. There would be no getting comfortable in this room, and no escape from the reflection in the door's window.

Most of the details bled out beneath the hall's light, save for the ugly, dark lines stretched across my skin like puckered, jagged cobwebs. Mementos of all my failures.

A shadow passed through my reflection. The guard making his rounds. Inside of half an hour, the pill cart would be at my door. The nurse would smile and make small talk, waiting for me to finish taking my meds. She'd ask to see my mouth to make sure I'd swallowed them. Then she'd tell me how cooperative I was, not like the other patients, and leave. Same shit and same day for all I knew. I stopped caring about the days of the week years ago.

Except for that damn journal.

I kept a journal back in Redby to report on movement patterns and supply drops. Helped me keep track of important shit like how much longer we could stay alive. It wasn't my style to write down my feelings and all that mushy emotional stuff.

"Just a summary," the doc had said. "It doesn't have to be detailed. Just write down as much or as little as you feel you need to regarding what happened in Redby."

Right, easy. I did that. On to the next exercise.

Except it wasn't good enough. I never did anything half-assed. Wait, that was a lie. I did a lot of things half-assed. Just not when it came to important things, like Redby. Maybe it was the old military training kicking in, telling me to keep records of everything, telling me to make a good report. Or maybe it was just the damn shrink knowing I wouldn't be able to leave Redby as a footnote in my life. It didn't matter why.

I tore out the first page, crumpled it up and threw it into the far corner. Next I picked up the pen, growled something unkind regarding the doc under my breath, and started writing.

They say when you die, you see a light at the end of a tunnel. I've died plenty and I can promise you, there is no light.

I don't mean mostly dead either. I mean face ripped off, guts spilling out, all dead. It sucks at first, but you get used to it. In Redby, you had no choice. You either learn to live with cursed immortality, or you crawl into a corner and give up.

I never give up. I guess that's why I'm here. The Hunter in me never died. Even if my body did.

My name is Cassandra Isabella Saratores. I am thirty-two years old this month. At eighteen years old, I joined the military. At twenty-one years old, I became a captive of Redby, Nevada, otherwise known as Zombie Hell. For ten years I lived in a constant state of life, death, and undeath and if there is one thing I learned through all those years, it's this:

Dying hurts.

Every time.

CHAPTER TWO

There were seven of us stuffed into the back of a canvas-covered flatbed, supported by a truck with suspension made of stone. Seven suited up soldiers in a windowless trap, in the dead of summer, with nothing but our own hides as cushioning. Three days of that is enough to test even a saint's patience.

At least I had good company for the ride. Or passable company. I could've done without the endless chatter from Steve. Hell of a sharpshooter. Way too obsessed with his fiancée.

"Hey, did I ever tell you guys about my fifth date? Erin wanted to go to a lake she used to visit as a child. Her parents sold their cabin there when she was fifteen and she always regretted not being able to go back one last time—"

"She thought the cabin was torn down so she never bothered looking it up herself. Then you went and found out it wasn't torn down and rented it for the weekend. You had a magical, wonderful weekend full of love and puppies and rainbows. For God's sake, Steve, just shut up already." I put my head in my hands and tried to drive the headache out of my skull. If we didn't stop soon, Erin would be a widow before she ever got married.

"So what's out there?" Ace, my best friend, elbowed me in the side. His grating tone wormed its way into the space between Steve's rebuttal and my search for one good reason to end this boredom with a fistfight.

"Road and more rocks. Not so sure this town exists anymore." I didn't even have to look out the back flap. Since leaving Eureka, the Nevada skyline had been one endless parade of rocks and dirt.

"What's it matter if it does or not? Brass says go, we go." Ace shrugged.

"Getting tired of staring at your ugly mug." The words were muttered as low as I could manage, half trampled by the endless creaking of the truck bed and roar of the wheels. Ace still heard me.

"Says the Gutter Princess."

I answered with a middle finger flipped his way.

Gutter Princess came from my first day in Basic when the drill sergeant had singled me out as a lost cause. Tiny, scrawny, mouthy, and coming from a background that screamed trouble, but there I was, refusing to leave until he made something of me. Princess, he said, because I thought I could be better than the gutter I crawled out of.

"Hey, guys, I think we're slowing down." BigMac, my other best friend, had the sort of voice that would've put Barry Manilow to shame. Nothing seemed to move the mountain of a man. He took the same approach to life whether he was facing a spring breeze or the headlights of an eighteen-wheeler. Yet, with tempers starting to flare and no escape route, it wasn't surprising the thought of freedom sparked some excitement in the big guy.

The truck's engine dropped off to a sputtering purr and we all leaned forward to get a look. For the record, that many heads vying for twelve inches of space didn't work out too well. Being near the back of the truck, I could only catch glimpses past BigMac's head once in a while.

One solid wall of grey filled the windshield from end to end. I didn't connect the colour to steel until some leviathan gears let out a deep, endless groan and the sky appeared through a slowly widening crack.

The door peeled back into a much larger, darker wall beside it.. As the truck's engine roared back to life and took us through the opening, I felt the hairs on the back of my neck stand on end. I had to wonder if this was what cattle felt like as they were being herded into the slaughterhouse.

The chills running up and down my spine propelled me out of my seat. I reached across Ace to tug at the canvas behind his head, ignoring his protests and bony elbow prodding my ribs. There was a hole in the fabric. It had been buzzing in the wind throughout the trip. It'd just been an

5

annoyance for the last five aggravating hours, but now it became my chance for one last up close glimpse at the wall as we funneled past. The flap at the back of the truck was wider and easier to peer through, but the angle was wrong. By the time I saw anything, we were already well beyond it.

I didn't know what I expected to see aside from ten feet of reinforced concrete and steel. Walls tended to be pretty uniform and uninteresting wherever they were placed. They didn't often come with shiny brass plaques dedicating them to a company. The plate was hard to read at an angle. Harder given all the letters were embossed and unpainted. I caught a glimpse of a name and a circular symbol beside it before the truck drove past.

Ace shoved me back to my seat with a quick jab to my ribcage. I answered with a swat upside his head. Neither of us acknowledged the stinging after-effects. We didn't want to admit some kind of weakness. Still, I'm pretty sure his sullen glare matched my own.

"What'd you see?" he asked after he finished pretending I hadn't clocked him a good one.

"Plaque of some kind. What kinda city has a wall with a plaque on it?"

"What the hell kind of city has a giant, impenetrable wall?"

I gave an eloquent grunt. It was my way of saying he had made a good point.

"Anyone know what the Almesa Corporation is?" I scanned the familiar, road-fatigued faces of my troopmates. Not a single one of them showed a glimmer of recognition.

"What's that got to do with anything?" Ace again.

"Was the name on the plaque. Plus some kind of weird circle thing. Kinda like one of those ying-yang symbols, only it was on fire. And it didn't have any dots in it."

"Must be some kind of benefactor. I've heard of some companies that are so rich, they can up and buy any town they want," Steve said.

"Any of them ask the military to move in to the spare bedroom," I quipped. Maybe they had twenty-foot-tall bears up here. I'd never been to Nevada so it may as well have been another country. Judging by the unsettled looks on the faces of my friends, I guessed none of them knew what the deal with Siege City was either.

We drove on in silence for another few minutes until we came to another gate. When this one opened, we drove into a shiny new military base equipped with all the essentials; barracks, mess hall, garage, armoury, even a tiny medic office. The massive wall continued around the base and snaked off to the other end of town. It took me a moment to realize the hulking structure must have enclosed the entire town. The base attached to one end, like a bubble piggybacking on a much larger bubble.

We all piled out of the trucks to the sweet harmony of Captain Stone barking out orders. He stood in the middle of the dusty yard, hands clasped behind his back and face turned red with the effort of shouting us into order. A woman stood beside him. I didn't like her. I didn't like the way she struck the same pose as him, as if she had as much right to command us as he did. I didn't like her space age armour with its glossy black finish and impenetrable black mask. I especially didn't like the way she stood as motionless as a statue. No one stood that still.

"Who the hell is that?" I asked Ace.

Ace shrugged and looked at BigMac, who also shrugged.

"Base commander maybe? I don't know. She looks like she belongs on a spaceship or something," Ace said.

I grunted and swept a look around the base. More black-suited soldiers walked the perimeter, stood on the wall, and leaned against the buildings in small, tight-knit clusters. They made no effort to interact with our company. Though I couldn't see their faces, I got a distinct 'fuck off' vibe from them. The whole damn scene made me feel like the school reject trying to sneak into the popular crowd.

"Saratores, Montana, Hobbs!" Captain Stone's voice sent a jolt down my spine. "You three planning on setting down roots? Get your gear and grab a bunk. You've got one hour of down time, starting now."

We forgot about the black-suited soldiers in our haste to get out of Captain Stone's line of sight. We each grabbed our bags, then legged it towards the barracks. The second after we claimed our bunks, I turned to Ace.

"Burgers," I asked.

"The greasiest," Ace agreed. BigMac just smiled.

The gate between base and town was still open. Cargo trucks carrying our trunks and equipment trundled into the yard, kicking up dust storms as they moved from paved roads to hard packed dirt. We slipped past them with an acknowledging nod to the guards outside the gate and made for the centre of town. BigMac led the way. Guy was like a bloodhound when it came to fast food.

It took us fifteen minutes to find a spoon greasy enough to satisfy our cravings, right in the middle of what passed for the downtown core. We each ordered our meals, BigMac ordered two, then headed on outside to start walking off the long trip.

The sun pummelled us with enough heat to convince me it had a score to settle, and it wouldn't be satisfied until it had taken its revenge out on my skin. The only reprieve we got came in short bursts of hot air from passing cars that hit like a blow dryer blast to the face. Though we were pretty far up in the mountains, the heatwave which had been sweeping across the southern states didn't seem the least bit deterred by higher ground. If anything, the craggy peaks poking over top of the wall just helped to keep the hot air caged in. Ace and BigMac, what with their blond, pasty white genetics, looked to be taking the heat worse than I was. Though judging by the glazed look in Ace's eyes, the heat was the farthest thing from his mind.

Ace was a curious guy. Anyone who spent more than five minutes around him would be subjected to the murky depths of his mind via the non-existent filter in his mouth. He was a conspiracy theorist at heart, and I could tell the mystery of the walled-in town had gotten his motor running. Trouble was coming.

"Hey Cass, you ever think about the future?" And here it came.

"What?"

"The future," Ace reiterated. "I mean like, what comes after the military life. This isn't what you're going to do forever, right?"

"Maybe," I said with a shrug. I took another bite of my bacon cheeseburger and gave the amount of grease staining the bottom bun a suspicious glance. "Military life suits me."

"Yeah, but it's not forever. I mean, not unless you're planning on being a REMF."

REMF, for the uninitiated, meant Rear Echelon Mother Fucker. It referred to anyone sitting in a big, comfy chair at home while we did all the leg work. They made the plans, wore the shiny medals, and got all the accolades. They were the kind of people us uneducated grunts looked up to. Or at least we were supposed to.

"Hell no. But I ain't got nothing better waiting for me at home, so I might as well make it last," I finished with another shrug and cast Ace a wary look.

"Me, I want a career. Maybe in computer science," he said.

"Why? So you can make all of those games you keep on about? Fix up some new realistic type shooter that'll make all the young wannabes cream their pants." My self-amused chuckle was cut short by a jab from Ace's elbow.

"At least I got a goal," Ace countered. I responded with a jab of my own, which he blocked and answered with a well-timed French fry throw.

"What's the future matter anyway? It ain't like thinking about it is going to make it happen any faster," I groused.

"No, but most people have plans for their lives. Dreams they want to achieve. Goals to meet. Like this guy." Ace jerked his chin toward the wall. "Who the hell dreamed of putting a wall around a town in the middle of nowhere?"

I didn't answer. Birds sang, children laughed, but every ounce of joy was stripped from the day when we looked at the wall. I felt the uneasy chill creep down my spine again, forcing me to break the silence. "It's weird, isn't it? I mean, it's not just me, is it?"

"No, it's definitely weird," Ace agreed.

"So why put it there," I continued. The question of the wall snared my brain and I had trouble wriggling free. Dammit. Ace was supposed to be doing all the theorizing. "I mean, what the hell they got in the mountains around here to need a wall like that?"

"Maybe it's not what's outside they're worried about."

I gave Ace a sidelong look, then pointedly stared at the children playing in a sprinkler across the street. Yeah. That kind of monstrosity required caging.

"What was the name you said was on that plaque," he pressed.

"Almesa."

"Maybe they bought up the town. Then to make it clear that they own it, they built a wall around it. Maybe they plan on keeping these people here forever. Or kicking them out, because they're all technically trespassing now."

"Or maybe you're stupid."

"Maybe that'll tell us," BigMac cut in.

The big man didn't like to talk much, but when he did have something to say, it was worth hearing. Both me and Ace forgot our disagreement and looked over at what caught BigMac's attention.

A monolith of modern architecture sat across the street from us. It wasn't quite a skyscraper, but it towered over every other building in the town. One side of its multifaceted, glass exterior jutted up into the sky like a sword, while the other descended in gigantic, artsy steps toward the ground. In front of it, in the middle of a plain, paved courtyard, sat a monument the size of an RV. The same symbol I'd seen on the wall; a balance of shadow and relief swirling around each other within a circle while flames leapt from the outer rim, all of it done in solid brass. Another plaque decorated the cement block raising the symbol over the heads of all those passing through the courtyard. These Almesa guys liked their dedications.

Without a word, the three of us headed over to investigate the statue. I got there first and began reading the engraving.

"*On this spot on February sixth, two thousand and sixteen, the town of Redby became the building ground of the FUTURE.*" I had to pause and look at my two buddies. The plaque emphasized future in all caps and required a moment of appropriate awe. "*In cooperation with Melissa Chamberlain, CEO of Almesa Corporation, Western Branch, the mayor of Redby, Bernadette Adams, signed the document which enabled Redby to become the very first gated town in North America. By providing heightened security measures and an impenetrable wall, Redby has transformed into a place free of crime, suffering, and abuse. This monument will stand forever as proof that true peace can be achieved at any cost."*

"At any cost, huh?" Ace mused.

"Apparently."

"For some reason, that doesn't fill me with the warm, squishy feeling of safety."

"You're a warm, squishy feeling." Ha. Fear my razor wit.

Ace rolled his eyes and gave my side a nudge.

"Think that's why they called us in? Extra security?"

Ace's comment got me thinking for a minute. If this was some new government project, it would stand to reason they'd want to put a whole lot of muscle behind it to make sure it worked out. We were the Experimental Forces Company. Our job was to test shit. Although compared to some of our usual assignments, this guard duty business seemed kinda dull.

"Dunno," I answered with a shrug. "Maybe. Maybe not. Figure we'll find out at the briefing."

"Let's go look around a bit more. This building gives me the creeps."

We followed Ace when he struck off in a new direction. We always did. That was the way of things back then. Ace picked the direction, I picked the activity, and BigMac stood as the wall of common sense between us and disciplinary action. We were a good team.

CHAPTER THREE

OAK RIDGE MENTAL HOSPITAL, TEXAS
August 22, 2032

The nurse knocked before she entered. The familiar taptaptap-taptap of her cheery knuckles striking the Plexiglas window drew me out of my focus. She entered a second later, not waiting for my response, and greeted me with a twiddle of her fingers.

"Afternoon, Cass," Nurse Marcia Reynolds said, her tone all sing-song and sunshine and rainbows. She was a plump, rosy-cheeked little pixie of a woman. Not fat, but she'd taken Monroe's curves and dialled them up to eleven. Her short, red hair had the same buoyancy as her personality. You couldn't bring her down, even if you told her you'd run over her cat.

On purpose.

Four times.

"Oh! You're writing! Anything interesting?" she asked with a mischievous little giggle which made her seem more like a mom trying to get in on some schoolgirl gossip instead of the co-conspirator she was going for. "You know, I used to have a journal. I wrote in it until I was... ah... let's see... sixteen? Seventeen? Somewhere around there anyway. I think I still have the old thing too. I keep it tucked away in my keepsakes box. Oh, but listen to me going on. Here are your pills, darling. Drink up."

I did as I was told. Three pills, one after another. After each one, I stopped to show her the inside of my mouth, just to be sure. Hospital policy. I downed a small, paper cup of water to chase the taste of chalk out of my mouth. Meanwhile, Marcia pulled a small, black rectangle out of her pocket.

"Aw, come on, Marcy. I thought we were past this," I said.

Marcia gave me the look of a mother whose kid had just refused her medicine.

"No, Cass. We've discussed this, but there is no moving past it. This is mandatory. You know that."

I grumbled and held out my arm. I already had enough track marks to make a junkie jealous. Most of them were from this damn needle.

They let us out of Redby a year ago, but we never really attained freedom. The moment the first Red set foot outside our ten-year prison, the list of rules and restrictions came down like a goddamn gavel, sentencing us to carry the punishment for our own imprisonment for the rest of our lives. No travel outside state lines without government approval, no international travel at all, weekly doctor visits to be tested, time and time again, for traces of the virus left in our systems. For me, the tests were daily. Hell, they already had me locked up, might as well make use of it.

Marcia pulled the cap off the black rectangle and pressed a button on the base. The rectangle beeped and a green screen woke along its side, displaying a bunch of zeros. Nurse Reynolds smiled at me, pressed the needle into my arm, and stared at the screen. A second later, the rectangle beeped again and the screen flashed "CLEAR" in place of the numbers.

"Wow. No virus. Same as yesterday. How shocking." I tried to put teenager levels of cynicism into my voice. Marcia gave me the mother look again.

"What happened in Redby scared everyone very badly, Cass. The government had to declare a state of emergency across Nevada just to keep things under control. These daily checks assure people that there will never be another incident like Redby."

"You know what assures that? Dismantling Almesa and burning Redby to the ground. They did both. This," I held up my arm for emphasis, "is just paranoia. And believe me, I know paranoia."

"They don't want another outbreak."

"There can't be another outbreak. I'm vaccinated. Every Red is vaccinated. The zombie virus is completely wiped out. Like polio."

"Polio has made a comeback in recent years."

I rolled my eyes. "Okay, not like polio. Like some virus that got wiped

13

out and can never appear again. They made sure of that before they let us set one foot outside Redby."

Marcia sighed and placed a hand on my arm. I tensed. I hated being touched. I tolerated it from Marcia because I liked her. She took care of me the way a zookeeper might take care of a tiger; plenty of love, care, and attention, and a big old fence between you and the dangerous killing machine. Only sometimes she seemed to forget the killing machine part and treated me like a house pet.

"Cass, this is less about looking for the virus and more about peace of mind. People need to know that they are safe. Especially now that the Reds are walking freely among them. Many of the people who were trapped in that town had family on the outside. Those families deserve peace of mind."

"Free. Right. Permission slips for travelling outside state lines, locator cuffs for those that do, virus checks, parole officers, and that's all for the ones who haven't killed anyone since getting out. How many more have been locked away since yesterday?" I stared hard at Marcia, expecting the usual patient sigh and reassuring smile. Instead, she looked away. I leaned forward. "Marcy, how many?"

"Three since yesterday morning. And one... He had a bit of a breakdown."

"What kind of a breakdown," I pressed.

Marcia fussed with the needle. She cleaned the tip with a sterile antiseptic wipe and recapped it, then slid it into her pocket. The wipe got folded up, then crumpled into a ball, then stuffed back into its aluminum sleeve and shoved into her pocket. With nothing left to occupy her hands, she folded them on her lap and stared at her plain, snub nails.

"Cassandra, I think we should stop. You are getting far too worked up and you know that's bad for your recovery."

Shit. She'd remembered the claws. Given how I was sitting forward, practically leaning into her lap, I wasn't surprised to see sweet, understanding Marcia start to pull away. If I didn't ease up on the tension soon, I'd lose her. And with her would go the only contact I had to the outside world.

I settled back on my bed, pulling my legs up to my chest and wrapping my arms around my knees. I wanted my body to say 'don't fear me.' Took me a second to realize my eyes still said 'murder, death, kill.' I stared at the wall.

"I'm sorry, Marcy. Please don't go. I just want to know what's happening to my people," I said.

Marcia Reynolds wavered for a moment. She worried her lower lip with her teeth and rubbed her knuckles hard enough to turn her skin white. After a few seconds of internal struggle, she sighed.

"He killed his family. Shot them all with his father's gun, then shot himself. By the time the police got there, it was all over," she said in a small voice.

We sat in silence for a little while afterwards. I guess Marcia expected me to mourn the loss of another Red. Instead, I just drank in the silence. Not thinking helped me calm down.

"It's time to go. Don't want to miss breakfast," Marcia said a few minutes later. She gave me her motherly smile again, but her eyes remained sad. I waited for her to stand up before following her lead.

Marcia walked me out of the room, then turned the other way to continue her pill route. A guard waited for me and the other medicated patients to make our way to the cafeteria. Feeding time.

The cafe held as much visual appeal as the oatmeal they served in the morning; large, white, and bland. Five windows squatted along the western wall, all of them barred. Every step I took marched me from one patch of light to another. Some days I pretended each patch represented a tiny world outside of reality. Like the floor is lava, only for crazy people.

At one end of the room, a line of people in pastel outfits went through the mechanical motions of picking up an empty tray, passing it to a lunch lady behind the counter, retrieving the tray now piled with questionable food, and shuffling off to find a seat. I stepped into line, shut off my brain, and became part of the medicated merry-go-round.

I didn't start thinking again until after I'd found my usual seat near the exit and started eating. Then I noticed the second tray on my table.

A lot of people like to think they're cautious, or wary, or observant, or whatever. Me, I'm paranoid. I was paranoid before I went to Redby and when I came out... Well, they got a name for that disorder. My point is, paranoia leads to a certain awareness of one's surroundings. A mouse doesn't squeak without me knowing where it is and how many steps I'd have to take before I could squash it. People are bigger than mice, so it's damn near impossible for one of them to sneak up on me. This guy, I hadn't even heard him coming. A tall man sat across from me. His skin had the burnished copper tone of someone born to a heritage of sun and open, grassy plains. The blue hospital outfit hung off his whipcord frame, but when he moved his arm, tense muscle crawled over his forearms and biceps. Though he had a few scars, his collection didn't begin to measure up to my own. A long braid of glossy black hair hung down his back. Narrow, almond-shaped eyes of the same lightless black fixated on his plate. The guy didn't even glance at me as I took inventory of his appearance.

Okay. Weird.

Then again, I lived in a mental hospital, so I guess "weird" was relative. At least he wasn't screaming in my face about the end of the world. Still didn't like how he had appeared out of thin air, but I let it pass. In the grand scheme of things, having a buddy at breakfast wasn't such a terrible thing.

I finished my meal without any interruptions from the new patient and headed for the rec room. After breakfast came an hour of "quiet time" during which the calmer patients were allowed to socialize.

The white walls of the hospital gave way to a child's understanding of colour coding a room. Chairs and tables of varying pastel shades dotted the floor, arranged in a haphazard pattern as if they'd been thrown into the room and then simply righted wherever they landed. The floor itself bore a checkered pattern of grey and brown tiles. I think at one point they'd been burgundy and white. Painting easels lined one wall, facing off against the electronic entertainment section of the opposite wall. A ring of mismatched chairs huddled around the barred and chained TV, their occupants bathed in the glow of some ridiculously cheerful child's show about ponies.

They didn't let us watch the news out here. Too violent, they said. Too much potential to disrupt the delicate balance of our fluffy little nuthouse. While the other patients might have been happy living in obliviousness, I needed to know what was happening in the world outside. I had people out there; friends and family. Well, I had family. If Marcia hadn't agreed to feed me whatever tidbits she could get from her morning news feed, I would've gone crazy.

Crazier.

I wound my way around the chaos of tables and chairs, snagging an unused seat that wasn't a God-awful shade of pink and set it in a corner, next to one of the barred windows. I sat down facing the room with the window to my left, put the journal in my lap, and stared past the glass and iron for a full minute.

I didn't want to be part of the outside world. I mean, someday, sure, it would be great to go home again and see my parents. Tell them I got all better. I liked to think I could be rehabilitated. The entire point of being in the hospital was to make me a sane, functional human being again. Problem was, I knew enough about me to know not to trust myself.

Sometimes though... Sometimes I really missed the world.

I let out a long, relaxed breath and opened the journal. I had just set the nib of the pen against the page when a chair scraped across the ground beside me and set up in front of the window next to mine. Of course, I had to look up and check out who it was. Most days, my surly, 'piss off' expression drove people away. For the second time that day, someone had ignored some pretty damn clear signals and decided to get cozy in my personal space.

The intruder turned out to be the same one from breakfast.

What the hell?

I narrowed my eyes and gave him the suspicious staring of a lifetime while I tried to recall all previous times I'd seen him in the hospital. Aside from breakfast, there weren't many. He must've been a new patient. Which meant he didn't know me or my preference for being left the hell alone. Or else he was just really damn oblivious. I didn't make a point of being friendly with anyone. Which wasn't to say I went out of my way to piss people off. I got along with people just fine from a distance. Still, socialization was one of the issues Doc said I had to work on.

"Are you following me?" I demanded of tall, dark and intruding. Important facts first. If the guy was trying to suss me out as some sort of target inside the hospital, I'd have to find out quick and get him sorted before security could step in.

"No."

Oh, well that settled that.

I glanced around the rec room. Plenty of people occupied the far end of the room, either watching TV or sitting around one of the tables where games and crafts were set up. I'd picked a window seat, ten feet from the nearest full table of fellow crazies.

"You sure," I pressed him. "'Cause it seems that way. What with you coming to sit right beside me when there's plenty of other open spots all around us." The new guy turned to face me. For the first time, I got a good look at the near black depths of his irises.

"I'm sure." Then he turned to look out the window again.

Okay, ninja guy was starting to unravel my cool. He was toying with me and I knew it.

"Maybe you happen to be real thick. Let me spell this out for you; I came over here to be alone. Get it?"

"And here I thought it was because you enjoyed peace and quiet. As I do."

"Go enjoy your own somewhere else. This here?" I traced a wide circle around myself with an outstretched finger. "This is my personal space. You're in it."

He said nothing.

Toying with me. Even so, he didn't look ready to burst out in song, so I supposed I could put up with his presence for an hour. Once we headed out into the courtyard, I could lose him.

I settled back in my chair, gave him one last scowl, and put the pen to my journal again. Nothing came to me. I knew what I needed to write next, but the only damn thing I could think about sat less than two feet away. I wasn't going to be able to get anything done so long as I wasted my time wondering about him and his motives.

"Cass," I said after a minute of silence. I looked up from the journal and caught him staring at me with one dark eyebrow arched almost to his hair line.

"I'm sorry?"

"My name. It's Cass." I put down the pen and held out my hand to him, offering to be all civil-like. I had to hold it there for a good thirty seconds before his calloused, scarred, long-fingered mitt rose like the ponderous lift of a drawbridge and shook mine. He had more strength in him than his appearance let on.

"Ezekiel Okayama," he answered as he lowered his hand back to his lap. He had both palms resting on his knees. If the chairs had allowed for it, I think he would've been sitting cross-legged. As it was, he looked far too comfortable in a chair that was built for a person half his size.

"You don't say much."

"I find words to be inefficient."

I grunted. A man after my own heart. Maybe I could like the guy after all. After I got over his creepy teleporting, stalking gig.

"Nice to meet you, Zeke." I gave him a quick smile, then bent my head over the journal again. There, Doc would be so proud. I'd gone and made a friend. And we hadn't even had to throw punches first.

"What are you writing?"

Zeke lost a few friend points.

"A journal."

"About the zombies?"

That made me stop and look up at him. Everyone knew about the scandal these days. Redby had become a household name. Almesa was in a nosedive on the stock markets and the government was undergoing some serious internal investigations to figure out why the town hadn't been discovered sooner. Even so, not many people knew I had survived the city unless I outright stated it. Most people thought my scars were due to some horrible accident. Not wrong, but not on the money either. Redby hadn't been an accident. My being there when the walls closed up had.

"Yeah," I said when I saw the inquisitive brow start to inch up his forehead again. "It's...uh... Doc said it would be good for me. To write down what happened."

"Is it helping?"

"Just started."

"Ah." He gave me a knowing nod. "I wish you luck then." Zeke started to turn back toward the window, but I made a noise in the back of my throat. I didn't know whether or not I wanted to turn it into a sentence, but his eyes settled on me and I had to say something.

"Just out of curiosity, how'd you know? Most people just think I got burned or something."

Zeke lifted a hand and moved it toward my arm. Instinct screamed at me to tense. I don't like being touched. He must've picked up on the vibe because his fingers never met my skin. They hovered over my forearm and traced around a large, oval scar and the jagged fishtail trailing out toward my wrist.

"This is a bite mark. Size and shape indicates human teeth. I noticed you had a few of them."

I let the journal rest against my knee and moved a hand to rub at my forearm. The scar he singled out started to itch as soon as he moved his hand away. I covered it with one hand while his eyes bored a hole through my skull.

"Don't know of anyone who'd see that other than another Red." Red was our name for fellow Redby survivors. There weren't many of us left, but we all felt a kind of kinship after what we'd survived. The ones who could still be considered human anyway.

"I wasn't there, but I heard about what happened. I have a lot of experience in intraspecies altercations." He smiled. I think he wanted to take the creep factor out of his words, but the sight of his thin lips stretched across pristine white teeth left me with the impression of a wolf cozying up to a sheep.

Zeke got another sidelong look and nothing more. He seemed satisfied with the conclusion of our talk, because a few seconds later his face became a neutral mask and he set his eyes on the grassy field outside our window. I let the topic drop there too. Not much else to say and I couldn't shake the disquiet crawling along my skin. If I'd met him back in Redby, I would've stabbed him by now.

I glanced over my shoulder at the rec room guards and caught one of them eyeing us with a certain amount of interest. Now would be a good time to start acting inconspicuous again.

I picked up the journal and pen, folded one leg under me, and started writing.

CHAPTER FOUR

REDBY, NEVADA
August 5, 2021

We got bored with exploring the town after making a complete circuit of the market and ending up back at the fast food joint. BigMac wanted to stop in for dessert. Ace and I vetoed the idea, claiming it was high time we headed back to base. The debriefing would start soon and I still needed to shower. We enjoyed the meandering hike through rural suburbia. It gave us time to play our favourite game; Gun to Your Head.

"Okay, gun to your head," I said to get us started, "you gotta sleep with someone you wouldn't normally sleep with. Who would it be?"

"What kind of a question is that," Ace griped.

"The hell do you mean," I shot back.

"I mean you gotta give me parameters. Someone I wouldn't normally sleep with. Like a leper? A dude? Someone I hate? Cause I know some hot people that are absolute bitches. What the hell is my incentive for engaging in sub-par nasty anyway?"

I gave Ace a sidelong glance.

"Your incentive is the fucking gun. And if you're going to turn this into some fucking gay bashing-"

"Alright, alright." Ace held up his hands in submission. "My bad. Forgot you went both ways."

I grimaced but said nothing. One fucking night of drunken tell-alls, and suddenly the whole goddamn company thought I was bi.

Not that any of them gave me shit over it. Other than trying to hook me up with the new campus nurse.

She was smokin' hot too.

Fuck! Brain. I am not bi. I've only ever slept with guys.

I shook off the memory of a bikini tanline peeking from beneath a

22

white uniform and brought us back to the game.

"Fine," I said. "Let's say it has to be a famous person, but not one of your top picks. More like bottom of the barrel picks. Currently famous too. None of this time travel shit. And-" I held up a finger to forestall the quick response I saw building in the corner of Ace's mouth. "No proof that you two did it either. Just you, the gun, and the celebrity of your nightmares."

The smug smile on Ace's face curdled like sour milk. He made a displeased noise in the back of his throat and spit off to the side of the sun baked sidewalk.

"Fuck. Now you've gone and fucked up my answer," he said.

I rolled my eyes and barked out a short laugh.

"Whatever. It's not like you've got a better answer. Male, female, or something else, you don't give a shit what's between the legs so long as the outside is the right shade of brown."

The laugh died in my throat. I scowled, but Ace wore that shit-eating grin that I knew too well. He knew exactly what time bomb he'd armed, and he wanted to see it go off.

"The fuck is that supposed to mean," I snapped.

"Means all you Latino types keep together, Cass."

"Alright, fuck off. I was born American. That's all I'll ever be."

Ace raised his hands a little higher. He knew full well my dad's side of the family was a touchy subject, what with my dad being as Mexican as enchiladas. I'd grown up being told to take more pride in my Mexican heritage. The Saratores' were a strong, noble bloodline with a long history of blah blah blah. I didn't learn Spanish as a kid just to piss the old bastard off. It worked too. We hadn't managed anything more than an uneasy peace since I turned ten.

We settled into silence for a few seconds while I stewed over the idea of shoving Ace's face into the sidewalk.

"What about you, BigMac," I asked, trying to redirect the violent thought train racing through my brain.

"Gun," he said.

"You'd sooner die than go for one night of bad sex?"

23

"Yep."

I thought about his answer for a minute, then shrugged. BigMac never talked about his love life much anyway. For all I knew, he didn't have one.

"Eh, I couldn't picture anyone giving it to our good ol' Mackie anyway," Ace said.

"Why the hell would you want to picture that?" I smirked. The look on Ace's face gave me no end of amusement.

"Shut up, Cass."

"Gate's closed," BigMac reported. His own gates, I assumed. I was about to make a witty retort involving Ace and a key when I happened to look up. My witty retort turned into a confused grunt.

Sure enough, the gates to the base were locked up tight. This wouldn't have been an odd thing in and of itself, except for the lack of guards stationed outside to let us in. There used to be a guard there. I was sure of it.

"So it is," I remarked. I followed it up by staring hard at the wall. Sooner or later, it'd have to cough up some sign of life.

Or else it could continue sitting there like a big, stupid wall.

"Are we late?" Ace asked. I checked my watch.

"Nope. Fifteen minutes early. Guard probably just went for a piss break." I looked along the wall again as if expecting to see the guard detach from the shadows and retake his place like nothing had happened. Nothing moved save the steady blinking light over the intercom system. "Look, the intercom's working fine. We'll try that."

I strode forward with a confident step. Ace and BigMac fell into place behind me. When I got to the little grey squawk box attached to the wall, I pressed a finger to the buzzer and held it down ten seconds longer than necessary. Anyone within fifty feet of its counterpart would be too annoyed to ignore it.

And yet they did.

I held the buzzer down again, leaning on it like I could make it louder by pressing the little red tab right through the wall.

Still nothing.

24

The third time I started poking at the buzzer, pecking out a code that was half random button presses and half "Mary Had a Little Lamb." A voice with the tone of gravel and the patience of a rabid Doberman answered with a snarled, "Yes?"

"Captain?" I knew that whiskey hardened voice as sure as I knew my own name.

"Corporal Saratores? The hell are you doing on the intercom?"

"Looking to get back into the base, sir. There's no one out here."

The comm went dead for a minute. I could picture the grim-faced man who led our company cursing out some wide-eyed greenhorn for leaving a post untended. He never minced words. Not even with his superiors.

Our captain was a damn good soldier. Hard, unforgiving, and respected by every man and woman in the company. Though barely topping thirty, Captain Stone had the kind of rep expected of lone survivors and heroes of the battlefield. He'd gotten command of the Experimental Forces Company by request. Rumour had it he told the brass if there were tactics to be tested and soldiers to be trained, he wanted to be damn sure it was done right.

"No one's giving me any answers over here. Bunch of goddamn paranoid bastards." The captain's voice paused and my stomach dropped. Something in his tone sounded off. "I'm gonna find the base commander. You got Tweedle Dee and Tweedle Dum with you?"

Tweedle Dee and Tweedle Dum did not look happy. I had to cough to hide my laughter before I could reply with a simple, "Yes, sir."

"Good. You lot stay put. Keep an eye out for any others. Haven't heard from Miller yet either. I figure he's still out there too. A tenth of my goddamn company out on the town and the doors lock down. Fucking perfect."

I didn't have to say another word. The intercom cut out again, leaving me with the happy mental image of the base commander counting down the last few seconds of her existence.

Captain Stone was my hero.

"So what now?" Ace asked as I turned away from the wall. I put my back to the steel doors and gave him a shrug. Behind Ace's skinny blond head, the rural streets and sleepy neighbourhoods of Redby stretched away to the opposite end of the wall. God, I couldn't wait to put this place behind me. Rotation wasn't for a full year, but I knew I'd be counting down the days as soon as we found out what the hell we were supposed to be doing here.

"Boss says wait, we wait. What else is there?"

A truck veered onto the street a few blocks away. It fishtailed across both lanes before centering itself a little over the yellow line. One headlight looked as if it had taken a bird at high speeds while the other glared right at me. Drinking and driving in Hicksville must have been less frowned upon than where I was from.

"Why the hell would they abandon the gate?" Ace asked.

"I dunno, Ace. I just know what we got told." The truck made its way down the street, swinging back and forth as the driver chased the twinning vision of the yellow centre line. Even drunk, the guy would have to see us. No one would be stupid enough to miss the hundred-foot-tall wall in front of them.

"It just doesn't make sense, don't you think?"

"I think it don't matter."

The sound of Ace's voice started to annoy me. Not because Ace kept running his mouth, but more because what he said made sense. There was something fishy about the unguarded gate, and the way the captain sounded at the end of our conversation itched at the back of my brain. Private company or not, the base commander was military. She should've been telling the captain all the important details about her command. Such as when gates go unguarded and why.

The truck continued barrelling its way down the street. The longer I stared, the more I thought it was picking up speed. That'd be crazy though. Who drives toward a wall at full speed? I stepped a few feet away from Ace and eyed the oncoming truck a little closer.

Ace kept talking.

"Like shit it doesn't matter. We just get told to think it doesn't matter—"

"Guys..."

"—because we're at the bottom of the totem pole. I'm telling you, if we got some ranks, there'd be people pissing their pants—"

"Guys."

"—to keep us in the loop. They'd be scurrying all over trying to find the person they could pin the blame on for not telling us every little goddamn detail of their lives. They'd—"

"Guys!"

Ace stopped and looked at me. BigMac looked at me. I stared at the truck in dawning horror. It wasn't stopping.

"Move!" The sound ripped out of my throat like a mortar. Before I even finished saying the word, I twisted sideways and threw myself at the nearest pocket of open air.

There was a boom followed by the unholy shriek of ripping metal. Glass exploded over my head and against the wall, rattling off my exposed arms and back.

Then it ended. I surged to my feet as the debris settled and the truck gave a last death rattle. I remember yelling something, trying to intimidate the driver. I didn't have a gun. Not allowed to carry them into civilian space. I had my training though, and that was enough if I got the drop on the guy. I couldn't remember what I was yelling, but I stopped as soon as I ripped the door open.

The guy behind the wheel of the truck was dead. Not from the crash. He'd died sometime before judging by the huge chunk taken out of his neck. His shirt, arm, and one leg of his pants were all drenched in blood. The other arm lay over the twisted steering wheel, as if he'd just fallen asleep with his head resting against it.

"What the hell," Ace breathed over my shoulder. I didn't bother answering. I had nothing to say. Hell, I was thinking the same thing.

A dead body had no right to be attempting murder.

"What the hell!" This time Ace put a little more vehemence into his voice. I could hear the gears in his head turning, unable to find an answer for this random event.

The shit began to hit the proverbial fan in quick order. Before I could open my mouth to mimic Ace's question, we heard a boom from somewhere in the distance and a great mushroom of smoke shot up into the air. Then the screams started; distant and broken at first, then louder and longer and closer. I knew what terror sounded like, and there was a lot of it coming from the town.

"We gotta get out of here," Ace said, edging away from the truck. I stood my ground.

"No, Captain said stay. We stay."

"Cass, don't be fucking stupid. We don't got any weapons. We gotta clear out already."

"And what?" I snarled back. I wasn't angry at Ace, just scared. But you didn't get the luxury of being scared in my position. "Let him think we got something to hide?"

"Jesus, he drove the fucking truck into the wall! No one will blame us."

"He's dead. He couldn't have driven the truck." I gestured back at the open door and the bloodied man beyond. Something must've happened when I did, because Ace went white as a sheet and BigMac made a choking sound in the back of his throat.

I wanted to turn around. I wanted to know what the hell was going on here. I started to, but then the intercom screamed a single, galvanizing word in Captain Stone's strained voice.

"RUN!"

I ran.

Ace ran.

BigMac ran.

To this day, I don't know what they saw behind me. Not a one of us knew where we were running to. We found out what we were running from though. As we cleared the block and took off into the suburbs of Redby, the air exploded with the sound of gunfire from the soldiers positioned on top of the wall.

CHAPTER FIVE

OAK RIDGE MENTAL HOSPITAL, TEXAS
August 22, 2032

"Miss Saratores?"

Goddamn. This journal was going to take me forever if I kept getting interrupted.

I tried to ignore the woman hovering over me, but she wasn't going away.

"Miss Saratores, Doctor Brown wants to see you."

Dammit, dammit, dammit.

I growled under my breath and put the pen down. My shadow took a step back.

"Now?" I griped, making sure she heard the annoyance in my voice. "We're supposed to go outside soon."

"This is your scheduled meeting time for today." No forgiveness in her tone. She didn't care if she disturbed me. I was just cattle here.

"Goddammit. Of course it is." I let out another growling sigh and slammed the journal shut. The prick *would* take away my outdoor time.

My usual session time with Doc Brown took place after we went outside. He knew I needed to see the sun once a day to convince myself I wasn't trapped. He must've had a tighter schedule today. Had to fit in all those golf sessions and sitting on his ass seminars.

"Alright, let's get this over with." I stood up and motioned for the nurse to lead the way. She stood a good three feet away already and didn't glance back as I fell into her shadow. She had a very loose definition of the word escort.

Zeke didn't say a word as I left. Just kept sitting there, staring out the window. I think he was in a trance.

The nurse led me down the familiar halls. By led I mean she hoofed it ahead of me while I meandered to the doc's office, which I could have found on my own in my sleep. When she got to the solid metal door fronting his office, she stopped long enough to knock and let me catch up.

A glossy gold plaque on the front read "Doctor Francis Brown" all in caps, like bigger letters made his name all the more impressive. Below it was a smaller set of caps that read "Psychiatrist."

The door opened and the nurse took off. She'd done her job. Now she could leave me in the capable hands of good old Doc Brown and the bear-man-thing in the guard uniform at the end of the hall. I gave the bear-man-thing a bright smile and a nod, like I was greeting an old friend. His beady eyes never stopped staring through me, even as the doc poked his head out the door and beckoned me inside.

"Ah, Cassandra. Right on time." He smiled a fake smile, spoke in a tone of fake camaraderie, and beckoned me inside with a wide sweep of his hand that was all fake warmth. Inside his office were the typical trappings of a tenured university professor, complete with shelves of books behind his desk and a wall dedicated to his accomplishments. A picture of himself with a shaggy golden retriever sat next to his computer on the old oak desk.

No family photos. No paintings done by little children who loved their daddy. No flowers.

I guess I wasn't the only one who could see through the doc's fake front.

"You pushed my meeting forward," I said as I sauntered into the room.

"Yes, I apologize for that but it was necessary. I have an appointment at our usual time. Please, have a seat." The doc removed his glasses and used a corner of his shirt to wipe the lenses fastidiously. The man was a neat freak. He had every paper on his desk stacked in perfect order, every stitch of his tweed suit ironed into perfect lines, and every grey hair on his balding head combed down into a perfect semi-circle around his temples. I'd been seeing the man since being committed a few months back, and I'd never seen him leave so much as a dust bunny behind a bookshelf. Even his shoes were always glossy and black, never cracked, never scuffed.

"You know I like going outside." I took my usual spot in the squat, overstuffed armchair facing the doc's desk.

"I know, Cassandra, and I am sorry. You'll be able to go outside tomorrow. Now then," the doc rounded the desk and settled into his *educated man throne* while changing the topic, "in our last session, we talked about getting you started with a journal. How is that coming along?"

I held up the little green book and gave it a quick shake. My pen rattled against the spiral binding where I'd clipped it.

"Oh good." The doc's face lit up with a genuine smile. "I'm glad to see you've taken my suggestion to heart. Have you made much progress?"

"I got a bit done." I shrugged and looked as disinterested as I could manage. Couldn't let the guy's ego build up too much. "Just got to the good part when you interrupted me."

"Ah, and what do you mean by 'good part?'" Doc Brown picked up his own pen and held it poised over a little yellow notepad. He had a computer right beside him, all sleek and next gen and ready for use, but he was the old-fashioned type. Had it been in the hospital's budget, he would have bought one of those shrink couches for me to lie down on.

"The zombies." I looked down at his pen as it started scratching away on the paper.

"And you consider the zombies good?"

"No, but it makes for a good story."

Scratch, scratch, scratch.

"And this story, are you writing it for yourself or for an audience?"

"Well, I sure as hell won't be on the best seller list any time soon." The doc looked up from his notepad. I rolled my eyes. "It's for me, Doc. Just me."

"So where does your story begin, Cassandra?"

"Redby, obviously."

"Mm-hmm." Scratch, scratch, scratch. "So, then you haven't addressed any of the events that brought you here?"

I shifted in my chair, struggling to get comfortable. It could've been made of clouds and fluffy puppies and I wouldn't have been any better off.

"I told you, Doc, I ain't ready for that."

The good doctor put down his pen and folded his hands on top of his desk. He gave me a severe look over the gold rims of his glasses. I knew I was supposed to feel ashamed because I wasn't living up to his expectations, but I only felt irritation that he'd look down on me that way.

"I am not your enemy here, Cassandra. You have no enemies here. You haven't for a long time now."

"A year ain't that long. And it don't mean they aren't out there."

"You're afraid."

I looked at the wall o'success. A shit load of degrees, diplomas, and ribbons sat in neat rows side by side, all surrounding an old cuckoo clock. Doc Brown liked to be the best at what he did. I bet he was using some of those award-winning techniques on me right now.

"It's not about fear."

"No? How are you sleeping?"

My jaw hurt. I didn't realize I'd been clenching it until then. The pain got buried under all the nervous tension he cultivated in me. The man knew how to hit my buttons. He started talking again, all smug and secure, knowing he'd called my bluff.

"Look, the bottom line here is that I want to help you. I really do. Not just because it's my job, but because I think you deserve it. You deserve to recover from this and live your own life."

"Just so you can say you fixed a Red." I regretted the words the second they left my lips. They were true, of course. I just didn't want the doc to hear them. He took offence to being called out on his own bluffs.

The doc leaned back in his chair and rested his elbows on the soft leather arms. His steepled fingers touched his lips, almost like he was shushing himself as he stared me down. The wheels turned behind his eyes. A debate raged in his head. I didn't have to be party to it to know his intentions. Same as always. He'd pick just the right honeyed words to convince me I meant more to him than a pet project, then he'd smile and pat himself on the back for a job well done and send me on my way till next week.

One thousand, eight hundred and seventy-three people had lived in Redby. One thousand, eight hundred and eighty-one had been trapped behind the walls when the outbreak started. Four hundred and twenty-three walked out the gates. Now the suicide toll post-escape was over two hundred and rising fast. In another year or so, I might be the only survivor left. Assuming I didn't off myself as well. Not much chance of that happening given my stance on death, but I liked to keep my options open. If the doc could rehabilitate me, turn me into a productive member of society again, it would be the win of the century for his career. He'd done the impossible, they'd say. He'd be a hero, a prodigy ahead of his time, a frickin' Nobel candidate.

And I'd just be a footnote in his award-winning speech. Lucky me.

"Cassandra, why did you come here?"

"Because I'm not guilty," I threw back at him. "I thought he was a zombie. Papers say so."

"You killed a man in cold blood." The doc pulled open a drawer on his desk. He shuffled through some papers, brought up a folder, adjusted his glasses, then read off the details of the file. "Victim was found partially dismembered with multiple broken bones, crushed windpipe, punctured lungs, and dislocated joints. Eyes, ears, and tongue missing. Later found scattered across the bar. Four fingers removed and likewise found in other locations in the room. Remaining fingers broken at every joint. Manhood crushed. Sound familiar?"

God, the headache came out of nowhere. I closed my eyes and pinched the bridge of my nose to stop the pounding. Bad move. With each throb of my skull, a full-colour replay of my last night of freedom screamed through my head.

"Doc, I don't wanna talk about this yet," I ground out.

"You can't keep hiding forever, Cassandra. Sooner or later, you will have to face your demons."

I kept quiet. I knew damn well I had demons in my closet. They were throwing a party that very minute. Smart thing to do would've been to evict them, but they paid their rent and then some. They were there to stay as far as they were concerned. I was in no mood to argue. I hunkered down in my chair and stared at the success wall. I got through all my sessions that way, scowl and bear it until he released me.

The drawer opened and closed again. For a minute, I thought we were done.

"You are here because people believe you stand a chance of being rehabilitated." The doc's voice dropped to a quiet, persuasive murmur. "Important people. People that can decide where and how you serve your time for the crime you committed. They are not easy people to convince. If there is any hope at all for you, it is because you believe in yourself, Cassandra. They saw it. You need to see it as well."

I still didn't have anything to say to the man. He seemed pretty convinced he had me pegged. Couldn't say I blamed him. I was a pretty standard story.

Rough childhood growing up, poor family, mother in pain, father issues, authority issues, gang issues, then the military. Then Redby. It didn't take a genius to understand where I got my anger from. The doc had a better idea than most of what had happened in Redby, so he'd been able to give a pretty good diagnosis of what went sideways in my brain. There were stress disorders and anti-social problems and a couple of internal scars that had messed with my body's ability to deal with everything from processing food to processing emotions. I was a wreck when I arrived, but I'd always had one saving grace keeping people thinking I wasn't as far gone as most Reds. I still cared about life.

The day of the release from Redby, the media had been ravenous for any shots of us survivors. They'd taken interviews wherever they could get them. Third uncles twice removed were tracked down and hounded for life stories and tragic backgrounds. We were stars. When the Reds started killing themselves off, or landed in various forms of incarceration, we became superstars. My own story had been on the front page of every newspaper within a hundred miles for months throughout the trial and sentencing. Just a few days after getting out of Redby and there I was, dismantling a man like a plastic doll. I was "the Hunter who wouldn't quit" and I was everyone's favourite tragic hero.

In Redby I'd protected people. That was my job. Killing the guy in the bar, him being a known wife beater and all, had convinced people I was still just trying to do my job.

Sure. Whatever floats your boat. Problem being the good old doc had taken the incident plus my long history of being over protective and mixed himself up a nice little summary of my life. All it lacked were a few key ingredients.

Like the fact that I still sized people up first for how best to disable them and second for whether I should give them a minute to introduce themselves or just go for the throat. I wasn't stable. I wasn't going to get better. I wanted to, sure. What basket case doesn't wish all their problems would just up and disappear? But wishes and reality don't always get along. All the potential these important people saw just amounted to the death throes of the instincts of a better person. No magical spark of hope. No chance for recovery. Just a lame old horse that needed to be put out to pasture and forgotten.

Only I couldn't tell them. They'd pluck me out of the cushy mental hospital in a hot second and stick me in some prison to rot. I heard they were even starting to build one just for the Reds that were too crazy to release into the public.

And we'd just gotten away from the walls too.

The doc leaned back in his chair and steepled his fingers like an architect building a temple to his own genius. He looked at me over his fingertips while I sat there being all withdrawn and thoughtful. He must've been timing how long it would take me to break down and see things his way, because the next time he opened his mouth came a full minute after he'd last said something.

"Tell me how the medication is working."

"Good," I said.

"You are getting some sleep at night?"

"Yeah."

"And the voices?"

I winced a little and tried to keep the neutrality in my voice. The doc's eyes burned a hole through my head.

"Gone."

"Is that so?" He used the sort of tone parents use when they know their kid is lying about who emptied the cookie jar. I fidgeted in the chair and kept staring at the diplomas like I could set them on fire with my mind.

"Yep. I haven't heard from them in more than a week." While awake. "The pills are working." At not leaving me in a drooling stupor all the time. "I tell ya, Doc. I'm all cured." Hah.

In one of our normal sessions, we'd reached the part where the doc would chastise me about lying and tell me how important it was for me to commit myself to getting better. This was all for me, after all. I was the star of the show.

"Alright then. I'll get to work on your parole request forms."

My heart stopped.

"What?" I gripped the arms of my chair in a sudden panic. My pulse pounded through my skull as my heart tried in vain to make up for lost seconds by leaping out of my chest. I wasn't ready to leave the hospital yet. Not by a long shot. It took me a few seconds to realize the doc was smiling at me and hadn't moved an inch. Not even to pick up his pen. The prick had played me.

"Funny," I groused at him as I settled back into my sullen slump. I pulled my legs onto the chair and curled myself into as small a ball as I could manage. It wasn't the best protection, but it made me feel a little better about my chances of defending myself should something burst through the door behind me.

"I can lie too, Corporal Saratores." He let out a long sigh that I swear sounded boastful. "And I'm better at it. Now, either you can start talking or we can repeat this process over and over and over again. Just as we have in all our other sessions."

"Miss," I corrected. "Legally declared killed in action nine years ago. I thought the journal was supposed to take care of all this touchy feely talking shit."

"The journal is supplementary to our sessions. It is a place for you to write down your memories and emotions without fearing inspection. It is you helping yourself." He spread his hands and splayed his fingers, encompassing the whole of his cramped little office in one fluid gesture. "This is me helping you. The best way for me to do that is by understanding what you went through. Now, the voices."

36

I closed my eyes again to block out the sunlight. It made my headache worse.

"The voices are people I used to know." Resignation weighed heavily on my tone. Something leapt out of my subconscious and screamed at me to stop talking. I punched it in its proverbial face out of spite. Now that I had opened the floodgates, I wasn't going to shut them again.

"How did you know these people?"

"They were my friends. People I failed to protect."

The doc accepted this as fact and picked up his pen.

"Let's start at the beginning. What are their names?"

"Lots of names. Builds up over the years, you know."

"Just the first ones that come to mind."

"Sebastian Montana and Mackenzie Hobbs. My best friends, Ace and BigMac."

CHAPTER SIX

REDBY, NEVADA
August 5, 2021

We kept running for five blocks after the gunfire started. By the time we stopped to catch our breath, nothing remained but a distant rattle interspersed with the occasional pop of a grenade. They unloaded on the town as if we belonged to enemy militia. I hadn't seen my troop this active since the last time we went overseas. I put my hands on my knees and sucked in lungfuls of air like I'd forgotten how to breathe. Ace lost it.

"Jesus H. Christ!" he screamed, his voice high-pitched and panicked. He stopped once in the middle of the street to catch his breath, decided that was a bad idea, and started pacing. "What the hell? I mean, what the actual hell?!"

"I dunno. Something's real messed up and I don't know what it is. Were they standing on top of the goddamn wall?" I said between gasps. My lungs weren't burning anymore, but adrenaline still coursed through my body. Every brush of air against my skin felt like a thousand needles and the slightest movement of my legs threatened to take them out from under me.

"Standing and shooting at us!"

"Keep moving." The two deep, resonate words came from BigMac. He stood a few feet away, flexing his hands like he'd forgotten something. I think we were all missing our gear at that point. I sure as hell felt naked in just a tank top and camo pants.

"BigMac's right. We gotta keep moving. Captain said run so…so we find some safe ground."

"Safe ground?" Ace squeaked, each word gaining an octave of panic. "What safe ground? Our safe ground is back there. Behind a wall that we can't get through. There is no safe ground out here."

He had a point. A quick glance around revealed a bunch of houses with little picket fences and little stone gardens. We were in foreign land with no backup, no gear, and no way of communicating with anyone outside of town. This was the sort of situation where you just prayed for a rescue.

"Look, I know you're freaked out. We all are. That doesn't mean we can just sit out here pissing our pants like little girls. We find the other stragglers, we set up a base, and we figure this out," I said. Ace made a convenient target when my adrenaline and fear bubbled over.

"Jesus Christ. Who the hell put you in charge, huh? I say we make a break for the highway. They can't block off the roads forever."

"I'm thinking that since they have access to all the bullets, yes they can."

"Stop this." BigMac's voice rolled through our argument like a peel of thunder preceding a storm. We both stopped to look at the big guy. He was white as a ghost. "You can fight later. We go with Cass' plan."

I took my cue.

"Right, Okay. We know Steve's still out here. Let's figure out where he went. We regroup, find a safe house, then work on an escape plan. Captain's got to be chewing someone out for this fuck up already. He'll work on shit from his side, but he'll be expecting us to do something more than sit around with our thumbs up our asses."

"And where do we start, oh mighty leader?"

I had to bite down on my tongue to keep from taking up Ace's barb. It would be very cathartic to punch him square in the nose. Not helpful though. I needed all of us alert and coherent if we wanted to stand a chance of figuring out what we were up against.

"Starting with the strip. The restaurants and shit. He's got to be somewhere around there. Or heading back. We stick together. No splitting up. Clear?" I asked.

"Clear."

"Clear."

I gave a curt nod, relieved to hear them both report back like proper soldiers. Ace could be mouthy, but he knew how to follow orders. BigMac just wanted to get somewhere he could freak out in a nice, quiet little corner. I knew how the big guy operated. I only hoped I knew Steve just as well. I took point and started jogging back toward the market strip.

"Let's move."

Ten minutes later, we were back at the fast food joint. People milled about the street, banging on shop doors or hustling out of them to reach the main drag. Many of them stared at us with huge, pitiful doe-eyes until they realized we had no weapons. No way to help. I didn't give them a second thought until a blue SUV swerved around the corner and almost flattened me on the sidewalk.

"Jesus!" I cursed after my life stopped flashing in front of my eyes. The SUV kicked up a banshee screech as it dragged its tires across both lanes, then kept on chugging for home. My one glance of the driver was a frenzied looking blonde woman clutching the wheel tight enough to weld her fingers to the leather.

"This is nuts, Cass. Whatever's going on, there's more of it downtown," Ace snapped. The closer we got to the core, the more edgy he became. He was right though. I could hear the car horns and sirens from where we stood, and we still had a couple blocks to go.

Behind us lay nothing but a wasteland of suburbia. There were plenty of houses to be had, but houses contained unknown hostiles and no chance of support. We had no way to get back into the base. Not yet. The Captain would come through though.

In the meantime, I stuck to the plan. Me, Ace, and BigMac were a team, but we'd never operated without someone higher up the chain telling us what to do. Steve was a Ranger. If anyone stood a chance of getting out alive, it would be him. We just had to attach ourselves to him before he took off.

That sinking feeling turned into a yawning pit in my stomach the closer we got to downtown. Not an inch of space remained clear on the highway. Cars honked and swerved past to get to the gates, driving up on the sidewalk, through parking lots, and in some cases, straight through buildings. Any foot of space not stuffed with some part of a car acted as a funnel for the people hoofing it in the same direction.

The opposite direction offered the same flood of people and vehicles as those who reached the gates were met with a hail of gunfire from the soldiers on the wall. The two waves of panicked citizens met somewhere around the middle and turned into a chaotic maelstrom of bodies and metal that held no hope of being sorted out.

And all around them, the downtown core burned.

I didn't see the flames, but I saw the smoke. It curled in a lazy, drunken line over the rooftops. The higher the smoke rose, the more it spread out, turning the blue sky into a greyish smudge. Long, dark fingers drifted across the highway, lit here and there by a hellish red glow. The Almesa building, the big glass sculpture that could be seen from anywhere in town, was gone.

Just gone.

A jagged, lopsided hole stood in its place, belching black smoke in an endless river sweeping across the sky. The sculpted levels and fancy architecture were replaced by sharp teeth of twisted steel and glass poking at the sky, as if someone had lifted the entire building and smashed it against the edge of a table like a beer bottle. The angry glare of flames flickered underneath the smoke, lighting up the broken windows until their edges gleamed red, even with the waning daylight.

"Holy shit..." Ace drawled, summing up my thoughts in two drawn out words. He and BigMac stared up at the Almesa building too. In fact, damn near everyone who wasn't fleeing in terror had their eyes glued to that nightmare.

"I think they're blocking the exits." BigMac's voice rolled out like a drumbeat, steady and strong, but over the sounds of screaming people, honking cars, and wailing sirens, I could barely hear him. I tore my attention away from the ruins and tracked his pointing finger along the straight and narrow highway passing through town.

The press of bodies by the gate kept growing, turning back on itself, milling around in terror while the soldiers fired down from their lofty perch. Heads kept bobbing up and disappearing in the current of bodies.

I watched one man throw a child out of the way only to be shot down by a soldier a moment later. Other people turned on each other, tearing at clothes, skin, eyes, whatever they could grab. One person bit into a woman's face.

Through it all, the gates didn't budge. Not an inch. Not even when the people closest to them began to ram their cars into the steel over and over again, desperate to either escape or die trying.

A bullwhip cracked through the sky, chased by the rumble of an avalanche. I turned around in time to see a grey wall of dust and debris boil up into the sky from the Almesa building and turn the artistic smear of dark soot into a solid blanket spreading out over half the city. The sky dimmed, like someone turned out God's night-light. It spread fast and far, engulfing the horizon in a matter of seconds. An answering shadow spread over my insides, smothering the fire of adrenaline and hope. Something fundamental changed that moment, and I didn't want to know what.

It was the gunfire that got us moving again. The quick chatter of machine guns dancing across the walls never stopped. Even when I couldn't see the top of the wall anymore.

People scream when they're frightened or hurt or angry. It's a primal reaction to some great disturbance in our continued existence. We scream to call for help, to warn people that there's danger, to scare off whatever's hurting us. We all know what a scream sounds like. The fake ones at least. There's a different kind of sound you make when you know death is imminent and no one can save you. That scream, the shrill squall coming from the last rally against death, is unlike any natural sound a human throat can make. That sound stays with you forever if you're unfortunate enough to hear it. More than the rattle of gunfire, more than the boom of explosions, that death knell stays with you.

The people of Redby were making that sound as we turned and fled. I can still hear it in my dreams.

CHAPTER SEVEN

REDBY, NEVADA
August 5, 2021

We found shelter in the storeroom of a little mom-and-pop grocery store. The room was no bigger than a walk-in closet and had as much floor space as a coffin. No matter which way we turned, our backs pressed against shelves stocked to the brim with food and knickknacks. BigMac was a tall, thick blob opposite me, and Ace was a shivering beanpole leaning halfway out the doorway.

"Great plan," Ace griped as he pulled his head back in to the storeroom.

"Shut up. I wasn't planning on getting shot at. Again."

"I wasn't planning on getting caught with my pants down. Seriously, why didn't anyone bring a gun?"

I gave Ace a dry, unamused look which he failed to note. The shadows and dust consumed everything but the most basic of outlines. My voice made up for the lack with a heaping helping of disappointed monotone.

"Civilians, Ace. Not enemies."

"Oh yeah? Two of them nearly ran us down and I saw a bunch more tearing into anything that moved. These people are crazy. This whole town is crazy."

"They're not the ones shooting at us. The civvies are just running around scared." I leaned my head back against a bulk jug of some brand of soap, looking for a bit of head space. Ace made a point I didn't want to listen to.

"Yeah, it's our own goddamn people shooting at us! Doesn't that strike you as a little fucked up?" Ace asked.

"Look, it sounds like it's dying down. We could make a break for it."

The gunshots were intermittent now, muffled by smoke and distance. I could just imagine what that meant in regard to what was left of the population.

The rest of the Almesa building came down while we were busy scurrying for cover. It collapsed in on itself, like someone had opened a black hole at its centre and sent out wave after wave of billowing grey clouds. A swath of choking black smoke, dust, and debris engulfed the town. The shop windows had been blown out when the roiling cloud tore down the highway. Even though we were as far back in the store as we could get, the invasive dust clawed its way down my throat and into my eyes. There was no way we'd be moving around those streets without major breathing problems.

"We still have no goddamn idea where Steve is. Where are we breaking to, exactly?"

"Gotta find a way out." BigMac spoke up for the first time since we'd gotten off the street. The big guy must've been as scared as the rest of us. Fear stripped the boom out of his voice.

"We don't leave people behind," I snapped.

"We're not Marines, Cass. I'm with BigMac on this one."

"This ain't a democracy." Anger surged through my veins. If there was one thing that got me through Basic, it was not staying down. I didn't let others quit either. For me, the only way out was all or nothing. But I began to think nothing was the only route left.

"And you ain't in charge. Not officially."

"As official as you need." I thrust out my lower jaw in defiance of Ace, daring him to take a swing. Tension became a tangible force in the air between us, choking out the cloud of dust for dominance of our lungs. BigMac shifted his weight from one foot to the other, his boots creaking like the settling floorboards of an old house. For a minute, none of us moved.

"Okay, new plan. We get the hell out of dodge, we contact the brass, and we get some help out here. The wall is too heavily defended. We'll never get through with a frontal assault. Our best hope is to go underground. Sewers are probably undefended." Each word came out as its own clipped sentence ground through Ace's teeth.

Well miracles do happen. Ace wanted to avoid a fight. Too bad for him I wasn't on the same page. He'd struck a low blow when he suggested we just abandon ship.

"I don't like it."

"Alright, I'm sick of this!" Ace threw the first punch. I stepped into it, right into his reach, ready to beat the snot out of him. I got as far as balling one hand into a fist before BigMac's calloused palm landed on my shoulder and dragged me back. He slid between us, his hands pushing us away from each other with the inexorable force of a glacier cutting through waves on the ocean.

"Fine," I growled. The fight ended, at least for now. A quick, angry nod from Ace assured BigMac that we weren't going to tear out each other's throats any time soon. The big guy let us both go and I shook off what frustration remained. When I was good and settled, I jerked my head toward the door. "We'll try the sewers, but we're not taking a damn step out there until we find some masks. Won't last a minute in this smoke."

"I saw a shelf with some kitchen towels on them." Ace must've caught my questioning look, even through the shadows, because he followed up the suggestion with a shrug. "This ain't exactly a supermarket."

"Alright, yeah," I agreed. I still wasn't happy, but I'd rather be unhappy than dead.

Ace went out the door first. He checked the room, then gave us the all clear signal. We followed him over to the "kitchen wares" shelf, finding our way on hands and knees by feel alone. It was impossible to see more than three feet ahead through the thick, slate dust.

We each grabbed a dish towel and tied them around our faces while the smoke stung our eyes. The soot sat heavily on my tongue in a mix of burnt everything and iron, refusing to give me even one untainted breath. The taste of fire nestled at the top of my throat, a burning sensation right behind my tonsils.

The worst part was the smell though. Everything stank of charred oil and metal, and the sickening stench of burning flesh. They say burnt hair smells bad but not near as bad or as strong as a burning body. Like something you'd throw on the barbecue, except you know what's roasting out there is people, and it turns your stomach. It was thick enough to create a sludge that coated the inside of my nostrils. Even with the scant protection of my dish towel mask, the stench invaded every pore of my body, starting with my head and working its way downward. If we didn't get out of the smoke soon, it wouldn't matter whose plan we followed, we'd choke and die anyway.

We left the building in single file, tiptoeing across the field of shattered glass at the front of the store and ducking out the warped frame. First Ace, then me, then BigMac. There wasn't more than two steps left between us. I stretched out a hand to touch Ace's back, where a pool of sweat glued the fabric to his taught shoulderblades. BigMac rode shotgun on my shadow, his heavy breaths stirring the hairs on the back of my neck.

It was a good thing we kept so close together. When I pulled my arm away from my eyes to get a look at our surroundings all I could see was a solid wall of grey. Even the buildings were swallowed up by the haze once we got out onto the main street. Rubble replaced smooth pavement, and bits of still burning paper fluttered down from the non-existent sky. We passed an abandoned car, its broken headlights staring down the middle of the street while its broken windshield gaped at me like the open jaws of a shark. The engine still purred but no one sat behind the wheel. A body lay on the ground a few feet away, curled into the fetal position with a hole through her skull left by a bit of reinforced steel. We pressed on, now twice as eager to make our escape.

A few steps further on, another shadow loomed out of the murk. It crouched on the ground, tugging and grunting over some fixture on the pavement. The nearest sewer grate.

We all reached the manhole cover at the same time. The man who had been focused on trying to get it open let out a small shriek and jumped back when we dropped to our knees beside him. A large, dark smear covered half of the man's face, starting from a long gash made in his forehead and trickling all the way down to his ragged, plaid shirt collar. He stared at us with wide, bloodshot eyes for all of three seconds before beckoning us to help him out. A fit of dry, rasping coughs disabled him from pitching in as Ace, BigMac, and I struggled with the thick slab of metal.

At first, I was convinced my fingers were going to tear off before we could move it. We had nothing to lift it with. No handy crowbars or steel pipes to pry it out of its slot. Just our own hands and a vague idea that we all had to pull in the same direction to get it to budge. Up first, which I communicated to Ace by smacking him on the shoulder and thumbing toward the sky. Idiot had been hauling for all his might toward himself. Once we got that sorted out, sliding it on to the ground between me and BigMac became easy.

The old man went into the hole first. He hadn't stopped coughing since we'd arrived. It might've already been too late to save him with all the smoke he'd inhaled, but that didn't stop us from trying. Ace, for all his cut and run ideology, was on my side when it came to saving lives. Usually. When it was convenient. And when he got to go next.

The smoke congealed in my throat. It formed a thick, gritty coating starting in my nose and dripping down my esophagus like tar. Each breath took an increasing amount of effort, even with the help of my makeshift mask. I knew the sewers wouldn't be filled with spring fresh air, but it had to be better than the clay filling our lungs on street level.

The pitch-black hole swallowed up the man's legs and lower half. He tested his weight on each rung, boots shuffling across the rusted metal, before he took the next step. His hands wound around the top of the ladder tighter than a vice grip, showing off the white of his knuckles, even through the oil splotches. My own muscles tensed when his hands slipped and nearly sent him plunging into the lightless pit. A stumble, I thought, until his eyes turned up to me, brown irises lost amongst the bloodshot whites. All the blood drained from his face, leaving him looking like an ethereal illusion formed by the smoke.

I put my hand on his, intending to reassure him, then I felt the first tug from the other end of the old man. It felt like being a fisherman with the first nibble on the line inspiring a flood of excitement and mystery. But unlike the fisherman, I had no desire to reel in whatever had hooked into his legs.

The old man screamed and yanked on my arm. I stopped being the fisherman and became the bloody rope between two tug-of-war teams. The shock tore through my shoulder and ran right through to the other side, where BigMac held onto me like an anchor. The old man's grip wasn't as strong as whatever had him. His nails dug a furrow down my arm, trailing blood and black smears, and then he was gone, sucked into the hole without a sound.

"What the hell happened?" Ace wheezed through a cough. I looked from the empty, black sewer opening, which now reminded me of nothing so much as a hungry mouth, to my friend.

I didn't want to go into the sewers anymore.

I panicked. A low, rattling moan echoed up from the opening in the ground and I knew with the sort of awareness that only comes from instinct that whatever got the old man was coming for me. Instead of giving Ace his answer, I bolted to my feet and ran.

Ace let out a swath of curses and took off after me. BigMac followed on his heels. I didn't have to look back to know they were there. The steady beat of their footsteps matched my heart's rabbiting pace. In my head, I could see the thing crawling up from the sewer and joining the chase. Every whisper of the wind, every kicked pebble or distant, muffled shout told me it was closing in and drove me faster.

The debris-filled courtyard of the Almesa building yawned before us, its smooth, flat stone drowned under a sloping hill of shattered glass and steel. The statue that had once stood tall and proud in the centre of that courtyard was buried up to its immobile flames. The wavy prongs jutted up from the tangled mess like a hand clawing its way to freedom. At the base of that mess lay   several broken, unmoving bodies.

The unlucky ones who hadn't run fast enough.

A shout echoed through the grey wall of smoke off to my left. I veered in the other direction on instinct. Ace grabbed my arm before I got far, hauling me sideways in his rush to get me moving in the right direction.

Most of the buildings near the Almesa complex had been obliterated by the falling building. Those still standing had their windows and doors blown out, leaving them open to the mudslide of debris that came down in its wake. One of them, an old second hand store, braced itself against the onslaught of debris with boarded up windows. Two men stood in the doorway, caught in the midst of an argument.

"...still alive!" Their voices were muffled by the screaming panic pounding through my head, but I could make out a few words. One of the men held the other one back. The second man's arms flailed uselessly at something behind us. He had to have seen whatever chased us. I put my head down and ran like hell.

"My wife!" I was almost there. His voice carried over the pounding in my ears. "My wife is still alive!"

Shit.

I stopped dead in my tracks, no more than a dozen steps away from the open door, and pivoted on the spot. It took me all of three seconds to spot the one moving body among the pile of corpses. A woman in a torn sundress struggling to get up. One of her legs remained pinned under a block of cement. Ace had already pulled up beside me by the time I picked her out. BigMac was still a few paces back.

"BigMac," I tried to shout. Smoke sucked the moisture out of my lungs and started a coughing fit. I took several deep breaths with the rag pressed against my face and tried again. "BigMac, get the girl. She's still alive."

"I'm closing this door, Jim. I'm not waiting." The shorter guy had given up the fight. He stood in the doorway, one hand on the frame and one on the handle. He wanted to shut us all out and damn the consequences. Jim wasn't having any of it. He threw himself in the doorway, right up against the shorter man, and braced himself against the frame.

"No, you're not. Not until I have my wife," Jim hollered.

"We got her, now get inside. Everyone in," I shouted, or tried to. The smoke took the strength out of my voice. It didn't matter because a second later, Ace barrelled through the two men like a bloody quarterback. The rest of us flooded in after him with BigMac bringing up the rear, the injured woman cradled in his arms.

The door slammed shut behind us and plunged the foyer into complete darkness. Second by slow, agonizing second, my eyes adjusted to the tiny bit of light seeping in through cracks in the barricades. Boxes formed a pyramid up to the windows, and shelves pressed against them to keep the whole shoddy architecture in place. Someone had gone to great lengths to secure this store. Even as the shadowy outlines began to take on a hint of detail, one of our "saviours" grunted and shoved his weight against a crate to cover the door.

"Hey, you guys alright? Did you get her?" A new voice. I swiveled my head in the direction of the sound, but all I could see was vague, people shaped shadows.

Someone clicked a button and the room flooded with bright, filmy light cast by a little electric lantern. The lantern creaked on its wire handle as its owner leaned in to get a good look at us.

"Who're they?"

My thoughts exactly. After the spots cleared from my eyes, a tall, bald man with mahogany skin and bright amber eyes loomed into view. He looked a little worn around the edges, covered in dust from the waist down, but out of the lot of us, he seemed to be the most in control of his faculties. His eyes lacked the buggy, deer-in-headlights stare that the three people behind him held. I probably didn't look any better come to think of it.

"I dunno. They ran in—"

"They saved her, Jacob. Greg wanted to shut me out there with those creatures and these people saved her." Silence hung like a lead weight in the room after the devoted hubby's little tirade. He glared daggers at the shorter man as if hoping to pin him to the wall with guilt. "They're goddamn heroes, if you ask me. And they're welcome here."

"She was dead, dammit. What you saw was just an illusion. It was your own mind playing tricks on you. You risked our lives for nothing." So, Greg had some spirit in him after all. Hadn't seemed like it when he'd been willing to lock us out. I didn't much care for listening to their fight. Someone had taken the lead out of the air and poured it into my veins. Every part of me felt tired and sore and far too heavy to hold up. My hands shook, my eyes wouldn't focus, and each breath sent stabs of pain racing through my lungs. Shock seeped into the crevices of my mind. Jim and Greg continued spitting and hissing at each other and I put my back against the wall and tried to catch my breath.

"Hey, Cass."

Dammit, Ace. I just wanted to rest. I closed my eyes and put my head down. Maybe he'd get the idea.

"Cass?"

He didn't.

"Then how do you explain her being alive now, huh?"

Ace put his hands on my shoulders and I lifted my eyes to meet his gaze. His eyes kept darting left and right, always keeping the civvies in his peripheral vision. He looked like he wanted to be spooked, but hadn't quite worked out why yet.

"What the hell happened back there? Why'd we run?"

"Maybe she's one of them. They all look alive too."

"There was something in the sewer," I said with a shake of my head. "I dunno. It pulled him down."

"What was it?"

"Take that back. Take it back now or I'll—"

"I dunno," I said. I looked up at Ace again, a little more annoyed than usual. I really just wanted to let my mind go blank so I could pretend this was all a bad dream.

"You'll what? Say it. Tell everyone what you'll do. It's just like high school all over again. You bully anyone who says anything you don't want to hear. Well I'm sick of it and I'm saying what everyone's thinking. You risked our lives for a corpse."

"So, you didn't even see it?" Ace spread his hands, as if that would somehow pull the answer out of thin air. "It could've been a person. Or he could've slipped, did you think of that? Jesus Christ, Cass. That was our only way out."

"It fucking pulled him, alright?"

Two things happened then. Jim picked Greg up by the collar of his shirt and slammed him into the wall, sending out a boom that rattled through the entire store. BigMac outclassed them both, letting loose with a bellow halfway between a roar and a landslide.

"Everybody calm down!"

51

Silence followed. No one moved, no one breathed, while the woken giant glowered at the lot of them. Then the wisp of a woman in his arms gave a soft moan and all eyes went to her.

She couldn't have weighed more than ninety pounds soaking wet. Her limbs were made of twigs, not an ounce of fat on her body, and if she hadn't been dressed in the remains of a bright violet summer dress festooned with flowers, I might've mistaken her for a young boy. Even her short brown hair had a boyish look, though it had looked a lot more girlish and fashionable before being covered by a metric ton of falling building. One of her shoes was missing, but so was the foot attached to it. Blood drenched her leg from thigh to stub. Though her foot had bled a lot before being pulverized, that wasn't the source of the litre of internal paint. The pattern indicated it had flowed down her leg. Down from the long, jagged gash in her thigh. Messy as her wound was, I knew a deep cut when I saw one, and that one had severed her femoral artery.

You don't live long when your femoral artery's been cut. Assuming it isn't a clean cut, and this one wasn't, you got about thirty seconds of consciousness to realize you're screwed, and then maybe three minutes to get help. This woman's thigh had been gouged, almost like something had taken a big old bite out of her. Her artery had been shredded like tissue. There was no way she should've been alive.

Which explained why I thought I'd gone crazy when her head lolled back on her neck and her filmy brown eyes passed over the lot of us. She looked alive. She even made quiet moaning sounds. There wasn't a hint of understanding behind those blank brown eyes, but she moved of her own free will.

"Baby?" Jim whimpered, his voice wavering with disbelief. Jim's hands unclenched from Greg's shirt and let him drop, whereupon the skinny nerd sagged to the floor like a sack of flour. Jim turned and moved toward BigMac, those same hands now outstretched in supplication to his confused wife. "Susan, sweetie, I'm here. I didn't leave you. See? We're safe now."

For a second, it looked like the woman got her brain back in order. Her eyes locked onto her husband and something approaching a smile twitched at the corners of her mouth. Then she closed her eyes and lifted her head.

And then her teeth sank deep into the middle of BigMac's throat.

CHAPTER EIGHT

REDBY, NEVADA
August 5, 2021

Someone screamed. I was already across the room with my hands wrapped around the woman's twiggy arms before I realized it was me. Despite the fact that she should've snapped in a stiff breeze, I couldn't get her to budge. Her nails dug into BigMac's neck, burrowing deeper and deeper for every tug I gave.

Ace materialized beside me in an instant, one arm locked around the woman's throat and all his weight thrown into a neck-breaking yank. He managed to pry her gnashing teeth away from BigMac's neck for a few precious seconds before she whipped her head to the side and caught Ace in the temple with her own skull. He fell back with a strangled sound halfway between rage and shock.

People started shouting and moving around me, all of us working to separate the woman from my best friend. And BigMac just stood there, a dumb-founded expression on his face, while blood fountained from the place where his throat used to be.

It took thirty seconds to wrestle her off him. Thirty seconds of yelling, punching, and desperate fighting. The whole time the little witch's husband blubbered and screamed at us to stop hurting his wife. When our strength in numbers won out, the creature let out an ungodly shriek and turned into an eel with a dozen arms and legs. She twisted at impossible angles, fingers scrabbling at our clothes and teeth gnashing empty air. Ace had her by the waist by then and I held her by the throat. Together, we heaved her away from the other startled survivors and threw her against the barricaded door.

She landed with a thud and a sickening crunch that should have meant broken bones. Instead of huddling up into a little ball of pain like I expected, the psycho creature twisted onto her belly and started crawling toward us on bloody hands.

A gun barked not five feet from my ear. I hit the ground. Ace did too. When I looked up, Greg stood over me, holding a compact pistol with the barrel pointed over my head.

"No!" Jim cried out. "No no no no no. Susan. You killed her." The big, dark skinned guy had been holding him back, stopping him from interfering with us while we tried to save BigMac. Though the big guy looked like he had a couple pounds of muscle on Jim, it wasn't enough to hold the crazed man in place when his wife slumped to the ground. This time she looked good and dead with a bullet hole square between her filmy eyes.

Jim shoved the bigger man out of his way and threw himself onto the blood-slicked ground. He gathered her up in his arms and huddled against the wall, sobbing to himself. A second later, BigMac hit the ground.

"BigMac! Hey, hey buddy. You can't die on me, alright?" I scurried over to him on hands and knees. My palms slipped on the wet tiles, threatening to throw me to the ground beside him.

Jesus, there was so much blood. It kept pumping out of his throat, frothing around the edges and pouring down to soak the tiled floor beneath him. The stupid little kitchen cloth he'd been using as a mask turned into a necktie soaked through with his life fluid. His eyes track over to my face, but I don't think he saw me at all. He stared through me, like he'd already started down the road to his final destination and left us all behind. His lips parted to suck in each gasping, gurgling breath and though they quivered every now and then, he never managed to form a full word.

"Oh Jesus. BigMac, you're gonna be alright. It's not that bad." Ace refused to cry in public, but I could hear the tears in his voice. His brash, grating wit wore down into a mousy whisper as he stared down at his best friend. His hands tugged at his own kitchen towel, fumbling with the simple knot as if it had transformed into a padlock when he hadn't been looking. He ripped it off and pressed it against the gaping wound. Soon, that too had soaked through.

People say your life flashes before your eyes when you're about to die. What they don't say is that the same thing happens when you watch someone else die. Especially when it's someone you care about.

I sat there watching BigMac bleed out and all I could think about was the first day we'd met, back in Basic. Ace had been trying to heckle me all day and failing at it. BigMac had been following him around, quiet and solid as ever. Even though I hated Ace from the moment I laid eyes on him, I never had a bad feeling about BigMac. He was the sort of guy that you couldn't hate.

I'd never seen BigMac face an enemy he couldn't beat before either. The guy was a big, silent puppy dog, but when pushed, he could tear a man's head clean off. At some point during our history, I'd just assumed he was unstoppable. Nothing ever phased him. Nothing ever kept him down for more than a few days. The weak, wounded man staring up at me with blank eyes couldn't have been BigMac.

It couldn't be.

"Somebody get a bucket of clean water. Is anyone here a doctor? Come on, he's dying!" Ace bent over BigMac as if he could make the blood stop flowing if he came at the wound from the right angle. His fingers were smeared with the big man's blood and the cloth had stopped functioning as a sponge within the span of a single heartbeat. Around me, the other survivors moved but said nothing. The lamp spilled a steady stream of yellow light down on BigMac's face. When it filled his glassy eyes, I knew he'd left us.

"Ace…" That couldn't have been my voice. It cracked on the single syllable, making me sound like I was about to cry or something. I swallowed hard, cleared my throat, and tried again. "Ace, he's gone."

"Fine, I'll do it myself. I need a—a needle and some thread and— Christ! Where's that water?"

"Ace, come on," I pleaded. I put my hand on his shoulder. He jerked his arm away.

"He's stopped breathing. Cass, keep pressure here. I've got to start

CPR."

"No, Ace." I looked down at the big, quiet man. Now even more silent. The light had fixed in his eyes and glossed them over. He wasn't making that hideous gasping, gurgling noise anymore. He wasn't making a sound, or moving, or breathing. My unstoppable force had been stopped. "He's gone."

"He's not. He can't be gone. He got hit by a car for me. Broke three ribs and both his legs, but he got back up. He's always gotten back up. He survived a fucking IED with us, Cass. He can't be gone."

I waited. It was all I could do at that point.

"Fuck. Oh fuck. BigMac... buddy..." Ace moaned. As the realization set in, he lost the ability to hold himself up. I watched as Ace slumped over BigMac's chest, burying his head in his bloodied hands. "He's my best friend."

I left Ace alone when BigMac began to cool and my friend still wouldn't remove his hands from the cloth pressed to his throat. BigMac was dead. Gone. Never to fight by my side again, or be the shield between Ace and I when we came to blows, or eat another burger. It was that last thought that caught at my heart and made me want to move. I couldn't stand the thought of the big guy not having another moment of childhood delight in his life.

I knew death was a risk in our line of work the way someone knows that any day they might cross the street and get hit by a car. Maybe the average citizen did't spend as much time walking in front of cars as we did waiting for people to shoot at us, but the possibility existed. Over the years we'd been shot at, bombarded, even pelted with grenades, but the three of us survived. I'd felt like we were invincible so long as we stuck together. Now I didn't know what to think.

I took a look around the room, hoping a change of scenery would clear the fog numbing my mind. It was the first time I'd tried to take stock of my surroundings.

There wasn't much to see in the dim glow provided by the camp light. Elongated shadows crawled over the grimy, tiled floor and got lost amongst the clothing racks not ten feet beyond the first cash register. I could make out the silhouettes of bookshelves beyond the racks of outdated bell-bottoms and flannel sweaters. This was the sort of place fashion came to die.

Greg and the other survivors huddled around the electric lantern in the middle of the floor. Their shadows lanced across the tiles and melted into the pitch-black void. The light stood as the only barrier between us and the unknown monsters lurking in the darkness, but even the glimmer of safety was an illusion. Funny how quick humans are to regress when our routines get interrupted.

Jim, the bereaved husband, huddled close to the barricaded door with his wife's remains. Every now and then a choked sob drifted up from his private hell.

"I need some answers. What the hell is going on here?" I asked as I approached the five people talking in hushed voices around the lantern. Their conversation came to an abrupt halt. I pulled up a few feet short of joining their little pow wow and eyed all of their upturned faces with the same sort of wariness I saw staring back at me. I didn't trust them and they sure as hell didn't look like they trusted me.

"We were hoping you could tell us," the big guy said. What was his name? Someone said it once. Jack or Jake... Jacob! I gave Jacob a suspicious once over.

He looked young, barely out of his teens, but big enough to make some pro-footballers jealous. Despite his build, he had a smooth, calming voice. The sort of voice that could've done stand-in work for Morgan Freeman's dulcet tones. He could've told me everything had been a bad dream and I might've believed him.

To Jacob's immediate right sat a young woman, maybe in her early twenties, with long, blonde hair and a tiny t-shirt which read "Contents Under Pressure." She looked at me once, then looked down at her lap like a scolded child. Beside her, the gun clutched between his hands like a safety blanket, sat Greg. Completing the circle were an older man and woman, maybe in their late fifties. The man wore a simple button-down green shirt and beige pair of slacks. A badge clipped to his front pocket read "Technobabble: for all your electronic needs! Floor Manager: Ted." Ted looked like he was still caught in the midst of the chaos outside, his eyes distant and his mouth agape. The woman beside him looked like a poodle. A snobby, curly haired poodle in a pink pantsuit. She stared at me past her gold-rimmed glasses like she wanted me to burst into flames. I decided to avoid her.

"Me?" I looked back to Jacob as his words percolated through my brain. "Why the hell would I know what's going on?"

"Well obviously you're in on it. You're military, aren't you?" Miss Poodle snapped, her voice full of intellectual superiority.

"What gave it away?" Couldn't be the camo uniform or dog tags I was wearing.

"You don't have to be a bitch about it. We all know you people are the cause of this."

A nerve twinged inside my brain. The military had provided the only source of stability I had in my life. I did not appreciate some snippy little city bitch turning down her nose at them. I sucked in a breath to give her a verbal smack down, but Jacob beat me to the punch.

"Katherine—"

"That's Miz Gladestone to you."

"Ms. Gladestone, please calm down. We're all scared and we're all confused. Attacking each other isn't going to help us. We need to work together." Jacob held eye contact until the fight retreated from her face. He was like a goddamn beast tamer, only with people. Once the snippy poodle was under control, Jacob turned those big, brown eyes of his back to me. His voice eased away the tension still gnawing at my nerves. "We would appreciate it if you joined us."

I hesitated for a moment, debating who I could sit beside. Then Jacob made a spot for me on his left and I relented with a brief nod of my head. Regardless of how uneasy I felt, these people were civilians. They weren't out for my blood.

"I'm Jacob." The big guy put his hand against his chest, then began gesturing around the group, starting with Contents Under Pressure beside him. "This is Mindy, my girlfriend. You've already met Greg. Ms. Gladstone was—"

"Is."

"—Is an executive for Almesa. That's Ted, from the computer store across the street."

"Cass," I said when the circle came back to me. I then jerked my chin in the direction of my friends. "That's Ace. The big guy is— was—BigMac. And yeah, we're military. Got into town little over an hour ago."

"Can I ask how you came to find us?"

"Well gee, me and my evil military buddies were just waltzing along that big old wall you've got around your town when we plumb fell off and lost all our weapons, ammo, and body armour. We thought this'd be a great opportunity to go strolling among the locals and see what kind of damage we'd caused with our inexplicably diabolical, government sanctioned presence here." I turned a withering glare on Gladstone. "Is that what you wanted to hear?"

Maybe I could've used a bit more rationality. Whatever. They had me cornered.

"We were fine until you showed up."

"Katherine—"

"Miz! Gladestone! And for the record, I am telling the truth. Almesa's security detail was doing fine until the military got involved. I'm telling you, this is the government's attempt to grab a piece of the action before we revolutionize this country. They can't stand the thought of not being in control."

"Does it look like we're in any kind of control right now," I snarled.

"Both of you, please, calm down."

"She's right though. All of this started after the military showed up. What if it's their plan?" Greg looked up from his precious gun and cast furtive glances around the rest of the group.

"What the hell kind of plan is this? I don't even know what's going on. If you ask me, the only suspicious thing in this town is Almesa."

"The Almesa Corporation is a perfectly legitimate business. We are here to protect people," Ms. Gladestone squawked, her voice rising a few octaves in indignation.

"Maybe you're just covering yourself. Maybe you're lying." Greg again. His fingers twitched on the gun. My instincts went into overdrive. I leapt to my feet while Jacob kept trying to get a handle on the situation. Greg scrambled to get up too. Before he got both feet under him, Ace hit him from behind like a rage-fuelled freight train.

The struggle between my friend and the skittish gun nut lasted less than a few seconds. Ace hit him with two quick jabs, breaking his jaw and bloodying his nose. Mindy screamed and scrambled away from the scuffle. Ms. Gladestone did too. Ted sat there like a vegetable who happened to possess a heartbeat, and Jacob froze in shock. When Ace straightened up again, the gun in his hands, a familiarly cold look occupied his eyes. He pointed the muzzle of the gun between Greg's eyes.

"I believe," Ace said in a slow, measured tone, "my friend asked for an explanation."

"Ace." My throat strangled his name. The way he looked at Greg, all calm and still, was the same way I'd seen him face down insurgents. He saw an enemy, not a scared civilian. I realized in that moment how far from controlled this situation had gotten.

"Quiet, Cass. Let him speak." Ace placed his free hand on the butt of the gun to steady his aim and moved his finger to the trigger. "What the hell is going on in this town?"

"Ohb Ebus! Ohb Hckt!" Greg moaned, a mixture of pain and pant-wetting fear mangling his words. He cupped his hands over his nose to catch the copious amounts of blood pouring out of him, but more leaked through his fingers. That didn't deter Ace's aim.

"We don't know! We don't know! We were coming downtown for some lunch when people started pouring out of the Almesa building. Some of them looked sick and then they started chasing people down. Biting them. Then the building exploded!" Jacob had his hands out before him like he could force some kind of barrier between Ace and Greg. Mindy cowered behind his shoulder making quiet sobbing noises. Despite her earlier bravado, Ms. Gladestone cowered behind me.

"The Almesa building, huh? Sounds like you owe my friend an apology." Ace gave Greg a sharp nudge with his boot. He screamed, and so did my nerves. I jumped forward to put myself in front of him.

"Jesus, Ace, calm down. These people are civilians." I caught his hands with one of my own and put the other on his shoulder. My aim was to get the gun away from him, but he didn't want to oblidge.

"BigMac is dead because of them, Cass. My best friend. This is a war zone now. It's time we started looking out for ourselves."

"Listen to yourself," I hissed in his ear. I took another step forward but Ace didn't relinquish an inch. The gun pressed between us. Now if he pulled the trigger, he'd only shoot one or both of us. "I get that you're upset about BigMac. I am too. But taking it out on civvies? We're here to protect them, Ace, not kill them. Get a hold of yourself."

"They killed him," he bellowed in my face. He tried to wrest the gun free, but by then I had him in a position where I could counter any move he made. When his fingers tightened and twisted on the metal, I put my shoulder forward and turned my wrist so the gun ended up facing the other way.

"Something killed him. It wasn't—"

A blood curdling scream ripped through the air. Something moved in the shadows by the doorway, and then the scream drowned into a gurgle, followed by the sound of tearing flesh.

"It's that thing," Ms. Gladestone shrieked. "It's alive again. And it's eating Jim."

I shouldn't have looked away. Ace needed me to stay focused. I failed him.

My friend lurched to the side, trying to throw me off balance. I grabbed onto his shoulder for support. And onto the gun.

The gunshot was a deafening crack of thunder in my ears. I knew I'd taken the hit. At that range, there was no way I could avoid it. The barrel became a hot spear pressed against my midsection. When I looked down I saw the blood spattering my white tank top. It spread in a thick, dark stain from my sternum, but it wasn't coming from me.

I looked up, into Ace's eyes, and saw the shock reflecting in his bright blue irises. He opened his mouth to speak and ended up with a bloody cough.

"Ace. Oh God, no." I wrapped my arms around him as his legs gave out, lowering him to the floor. His head settled in my lap, his hands shakily reaching for my own. The other survivors disappeared to help Jim. I was alone while the only friend I had left in the world died in my arms.

"Ace, I'm sorry. I didn't mean to. I'm so sorry," I choked out. God, the blood wouldn't stop. I pressed my hands over the wound but that just gave me a very real idea of how quickly he approached the last few moments of his life. Ace pressed his lips together and worked his throat, trying to force out a few last words. He managed a garbled whimper, and then a sigh.

Ace's body went limp in my arms. I kept holding him, waiting for him to wake up and tell me he was joking. Waiting for all of this to be some nightmare I would wake up from.

Waiting.

Then BigMac sat up.

I snapped. I'm not proud of that moment. Hell, all I can remember of it was a burning in my muscles and a voice screaming in my head to get out. I took the gun and broke for the back of the store. I stumbled through racks of clothing and over boxes until I found the back exit. It stood unlocked, untouched, and unbarricaded. It probably hadn't even factored into the thoughts of Jacob and his friends when they'd picked this shelter. I burst out into the back alley, turned toward the main street, and started running.

I ran for a long time. Don't know how long. Any time I saw people, alive or dead, I turned in the opposite direction and kept running. Some time later, I ended up in a three-storey apartment building. I found a room, locked myself in, put the dresser in front of the door, and curled up in a corner to cry myself to sleep.

CHAPTER NINE

OAK RIDGE MENTAL HOSPITAL, TEXAS
August 22, 2032

The cuckoo clock on the wall hit two o'clock and released a tinny chime. No more outside time. I didn't care. I wanted to go back to my room and curl up under the covers. Maybe hide for the next few days. Maybe lose myself in drug-induced oblivion and hope my history would fade back into my nightmares.

"Cassandra?" Doc Brown sounded almost concerned as he called my name. I hated the false sincerity in his voice.

"I don't wanna talk about this anymore, Doc." Damn. When did my voice get all choked up? Yeah, it had been a long time since I'd last thought about my friends, but I'd put all those issues down. I mean I'd put them to rest. I mean... Damn. I lifted a hand and passed it over my eyes, hiding my grimace behind a forced yawn.

"Time's up for our session anyway. We'll resume this next week. Don't forget that you have group therapy tomorrow." Doc scrawled a few final notes on his little pad, finished with a flourish, and tucked both pen and notepad back into his desk drawer in the exact same place he'd taken them from.

"I thought I wasn't allowed in the sharing hour of power."

"We're going to give it another shot. Just..." the Doc paused for dramatic effect and gave me a stern look over the rim of his glasses, "no zombie talk this time."

"Well then what the hell am I supposed to talk about? Zombies are kinda my thing."

"It upsets the other patients. You can address your issues with the rest of the group, but I would prefer it if you would use less provocative language."

"Fine. I'll tell them I got my face chewed off by puppies."

The Doc deflected my sarcasm with a sunny smile.

"Licked, not chewed. That would be preferable. Thank you, Cassandra. You may go now."

I showed myself out of the doc's office and gave the bear-man-thing at the end of the hall a cheery smile of my own. He scowled and folded his hairy arms over his chest, which to anyone else would have been intimidating. I turned around and walked the other way to stifle my laughter. An orderly cut me off and corralled me back to the rec room.

Mr. Ninja, aka Zeke, had made himself scarce before I recovered my spot by the window. I felt a little disappointed until I remembered that the guy irritated the crap out of me and set off a few warning signals. Then I was happy.

I sat down, put the journal in my lap, and stared at it.

I had locked away my memories of Redby for a reason. Playing word games with the doc instead of giving him straight answers let me keep them in their cozy little closet. I didn't want to remember, but I'd forgotten why. The journal seemed like such an innocent waste of time when the doc had given it to me. My own bloody defences let me down.

"You could just stop writing it."

Oh, Jesus Christ. Not now. Not after I'd had peace for so long. I put my head between my hands and told myself to just ignore the voice. It would go away.

"Not so fun anymore, is it, Cassie?" the irritating, incessant voice chortled in my ear.

Go away, Ace. You're not real.

"Nope! Just a voice in your head. You dreamed me up. So why don't you just poof me away?"

Fine. I will.

"...Still here, Cass."

Fuck.

"Just pick up the book and start writing again. You're committed now, aren't you, Cassie? Can't give up now that you've started something.

Unless you get scared. Then you run off like a little girl."

It wasn't my fault.

"It never is."

Fuck you, Ace.

"So what's next in your little autobiography? Gonna talk about how you came back for us?"

I'm not writing anymore. I'll tell the doc I lost it or something.

"Lying?" Ace tsked three times in slow succession. The sound hissed through my skull until it became a perpetual background noise, like steady rainfall. "Why, that's downright rude of you. Not to mention bad for your recovery. Don't you think you owe it to yourself to get better? Maybe owe it to us? You're the reason we're here, after all."

I didn't respond to him. Having voices in your head is one thing, but talking to them really makes you crazy. It's worse if the voices happen to belong to people who have good reason to hate your guts. The best way to deal with Ace was to pretend he didn't exist. The more I pretended, the less I heard him. I could will him out of existence. I just wasn't trying hard enough the first time. I could do it.

"That's it, darlin'. Never give up."

You know what? Ace wasn't that bad of a guy. I could deal with his ghost hanging around in my skull. I preferred him over Tommy.

"Now that ain't very nice. What happened to us, Cass? We used to be close," Tommy drawled.

You're not real. You're dead. You're all dead. Just leave me alone. The pills are supposed to make you go away. I am the master of my own thoughts. I am in control. I repeated the mantra inside my head in an effort to drown out the voices. Ace laughed.

"You were never in control, Cass."

"Miss Saratores, are you alright?"

Something warm and solid landed on my shoulder. I jolted upright in my seat, one hand snapping to my left hip. The other landed on the thing on my shoulder, ready to twist it out of its socket.

I looked up into dark, chocolaty brown eyes. A little name tag swung inches away from my nose. Nurse Ripley, it read. The thing on my shoulder was her hand, now trembling beneath my tense grip. Out of the periphery of my vision, a big guy in a guard's dark blue uniform headed my way. Nobody else stood near us. No Ace, no Tommy, no voices.

I am the master of my own thoughts.

"Uh, yeah." Damn, that had been close. I released the woman's hand and gave her a weak, apologetic grin. I guess it looked just as scary as the look of death I'd just had in my eyes, because she drew back a few feet before waving off the security guard.

"You looked like you were in pain. Do you need to see the doctor?"

"No," I spat out. I passed a hand over my face and forced my heart to climb back down from my throat. "No, just a mild headache."

"I understand." Nurse Ripley smiled. She was better at pretending to be sincere than the doc, but the fear remained behind her eyes. She knew well enough that the people she worked with weren't the harmless kind of crazy. I doubt she'd ever let herself get that close to an unaware patient again.

"Say... uh... are any of the craft tables free? I think I'd like to do something different today."

"There's a free one over there." Nurse Ripley pointed out the vacant table on the other side of the rec room, then gave the floor a curious look and bent down to retrieve my journal. It must've fallen off my lap when she touched me. I pummelled my instincts into submission to keep from snatching it out of her hand. She held it out to me with a smile, and my emotions flip-flopped. I didn't want it anymore.

"Is it... uh... Can I put that back in my room? I think I'm done with it for today," I said.

"I'll take it back for you. Go ahead and get settled. I'll let you know when it's time for the movie."

I didn't want to let her leave with it. I didn't own anything here, not even the clothes on my back, but I still felt possessive of what I'd been given. You spend enough time scraping and scrounging for every comfort of life and you learn to keep your stuff close at hand. But that was the exact sort of habit I needed to break.

"Yeah," I forced out. "Yeah, thanks."

I smiled at Nurse Ripley until she walked away. I wanted to be sure she didn't see the suspicion in my eyes. It wasn't that I didn't trust her but… No wait, that was the problem. I just knew better than to make a big deal about it. That always ended with guards and sedation. Even if she stole it, I wasn't losing much. Just a few bad memories I was better off without anyway.

Hell, maybe it would be better if she ran off with it.

I pushed myself out of my chair and headed for the empty craft table. The distraction would get me through the rest of the day, but no more than that. I just wanted a handful of minutes and some peace and quiet to stitch my composure back together. The pills would take care of the rest.

The next morning, Marcia came by my room as per the usual routine. She gave me my morning pills, jabbed me with the needle, confirmed my lack of a virus, and gave me a brief run down of the news. Three more dead, all confirmed Reds. I got the feeling one might've been murdered, but Marcia deflected my questions by talking about the economy.

I followed Marcia out into the hallway as I always did, the journal tucked under one arm. Ace was right. Once I started something, I couldn't walk away.

"Oh! Happy birthday!" Marcia called out as I merged with the breakfast crowd. I stopped and look over my shoulder, just to make sure she'd been speaking to me and I wasn't making things up as I went along. Again.

"What?" I called back.

"Your birthday is today. I'll be out of town for the next few weeks. Finally got myself a vacation. Wanted to wish you a happy birthday before I left." The short pixie woman beamed at me as if she'd just told me I'd won the lottery. "Happy birthday!"

"Thanks," I said, only half convinced it was the right thing to say. I didn't favour the prospect of Marcia being gone for two weeks. I also wasn't fond of getting older.

"Take care now." She turned the cart in the opposite direction and continued down the hall to finish her rounds.

I stared at the spot where she'd been for all of two seconds, musing on how the little things got to me the most. Like the fact that I wasn't going to be able to celebrate my birthday with my friends this year. First time in five years. Damn, that sucked.

Oh well.

I turned around and made for the cafeteria. The pills always made me hungry.

Zeke waited for me at "our" table. I sat down across from him with my tray of cold cereal and orange juice. We didn't talk as we ate. Not even when Harry the former clairvoyant interrupted our little corner of solitude. He used to read fortunes for rich suckers. Then he predicted one too many endings to the world and started believing they were true. All the wealth he'd accumulated by feeding off people's fears had gone into sticking him in the hospital. Poetic justice in my mind.

Harry told me I would bring about the end of the world. Again.

One sedative later, we went back to eating breakfast in peace. Zeke and I had a comfortable sort of quiet, not that I was ready to admit I enjoyed Zeke's company. He still creeped me out. I just enjoyed having found the one other person in this place who didn't need to fill every second with random blather.

I finished first and didn't bother saying goodbye before I left the table. Zeke never even noticed.

Outside time came faster than usual, nipping at the heels of my first group session. The session bored the crap out of me, filled to bursting with more emotional admissions than I could handle in a day. Stepping out into the searing, noonday light was like ripping off a fresh scab; a little bit painful and a whole lot satisfying. I would've liked something more breathable than my pale blue hospital pyjamas for my sunbathing, but you take what you can get. The fact that I could walk around without chains on my arms and legs compensated enough for my lack of wardrobe choice.

The summer heat had taken its toll on the flat, grassy fields of Oak Ridge Mental Hospital. More brown than green decorated the lawns and the gardeners had all but given up on maintaining the meagre flower beds. Even the trees sheltering the administration building looked parched and brittle. The guards kept moving, walking the perimeter and shuffling across the guard towers, like little wax men that longed to melt into nothing.

There was a bench by the gardens where I liked to sit and mind my own business. I took my journal and headed on over, hoping the sunlight would burn away enough braincells to convince me to start writing again.

Zeke sat in my spot.

I stopped walking and stared at him for a minute, debating whether this was coincidence or design. Redby had taught me coincidences didn't exist and everything was part of some design to get you killed. Everything.

This wasn't Redby though. Zeke was just another crazy person in a hospital built for crazy people, doing his crazy person thing. While Harry the former clairvoyant might tell you coincidence was a sign from God of the end times, weird shit happening here usually turned out to be plain old, non-meaningful weird shit. Then again, Zeke and his shit happened to be weirder than most.

I decided to chance it. The bench had room enough for both of us and so far he had been doing all the stalking. I wanted a turn to sneak up on him.

Zeke sat facing the fenced perimeter, away from me. My slippers didn't make a sound on the brown grass. Even if they had, the air buzzed with summer insects and chatter from our fellow inmates. Sometimes a car passed in the distance, which left me feeling a little like a zoo attraction no one would pay money to see.

Mr. Ninja wore the same outfit as me. Same V-neck t-shirt, same elastic band pants, same uniform faded blue. Even the same slippers. His hair hung in a straight, black braid down the centre of his back. Somehow, he made it look like the sort of casual wear you might put on for the country club instead of my rumpled pyjamas look.

"Hello, Cassandra," he said before I'd gotten within two feet of him. I scowled and dropped onto the bench beside him, facing the other way. I could still see the smug little smile tugging on his thin lips out of the corner of my eye. The know-it-all jerk.

"Zeke," I greeted him. I opened the journal and took out my pen, trying not to look too put out by his awareness of my approach. Seriously, the guy had to have eyes in the back of his head or something.

"Is it your turn to follow me now?"

"You're in my spot."

Zeke made an exaggerated show of looking around the bench. He even leaned over me to check the far side and ran his fingers underneath the solid granite to check the bottom.

"I cannot find your name anywhere."

"This is where I sit. Same place I sit every day I come outside."

"Is it? Hm, I hadn't noticed." He smiled a stupid, smug smile again. I didn't have to be a genius to figure out his intentions.

"What's your deal?"

His attitude got under my skin. I tried my best to let the craziness of the place wash over me, but I'd been living off a healthy diet of paranoia for years. The way this guy acted like he had all the answers to every question ever asked bugged me. Smugness of that calibre was often a sign of bad things to come. People only became so cocksure when they either knew what was coming or had enough fire power to tilt the outcome in their favour anyway. Of course, he feigned innocence.

"What do you mean?"

"You've been here a day at most and you've done nothing but follow me around."

"Did you ever stop to think that this isn't about you?"

A tiny, petulant voice in my head wanted me to just say no. He had a point though. Maybe I was being a little too paranoid, what with the persecution complex and PTSD and all those other labels the doc had slapped me with. Maybe he just liked the same bench as me, and had the same reasons for taking the table in the cafeteria closest to an exit but far away from most people. Maybe he just liked the same angle of sunlight.

Or maybe he wanted to throw me off the trail by messing with my head. Words had a lot of power if you knew how to use them. A few well-placed words could distract someone from the truth by presenting a new, false target. Words were what they'd used to keep Redby hidden for a decade.

71

"So you're following someone else that is always conveniently close to me?" I reasoned, not bothering to hide the sarcasm in my tone.

"Yes."

"Huh?"

"Why do you think you're here, Cassandra?" Zeke squinted at me past the midday light. No clouds interrupted the blue of the sky and the sun had taken the opportunity to turn up the heat a couple notches. Zeke's narrow-eyed stare fit for the sunny day, and yet I couldn't shake the feeling he wanted to see more than the look of dubious interest on my face.

"I know why I'm here. I went crazy. Killed a guy. Same story you'll find for a few people around here. We're like a club, just with more guards and happy pills." I waved in general at the smattering of patients wandering the grounds around us. No one who got put in this campus was considered harmless. We'd all done something bad enough to warrant a trial, sentencing, and jail time. Which made me wonder why a guy like Zeke, who had just shown up out of the blue and didn't seem to be attracting the usual new guy on the block attention from the guards, took an interest in me. I gave him my own squinty-eyed stare and decided to get some answers. "Why're you here? You don't get in just so you can follow someone around."

"True. I am here because I am dangerous."

"Yeah. And the rest of us are all fluffy little lambs."

Zeke let out a laugh. At least I think it was a laugh. His lips curled up at the corners as if attempting to mimic someone else's example of how to smile and a breath caught in the back of his throat. Short enough that it could've just been a hiccup, yet it sounded mocking.

"Your problem, Cassandra, is that you only see one way in which people can be dangerous." Zeke paused and swung his attention out over the grounds. He inclined his head toward a corner of the building, where Harry the former clairvoyant stood with a guard, trying to convince him he needed to remove his pants to save the world. "That man over there, why do you think he is here?"

"He tried to burn the world down." More like his apartment building. He'd intended it to spread to the world, but the sprinkler system had other ideas. The list of casualties included his personal possessions and his freedom.

"Yes. And that woman over there. Why is she here?" Again Zeke inclined his head, this time to a woman crouched over the wilted flower gardens with a watering can. She had long, dark brown hair bound up in a loose braid and decorated with some of the dying flowers. Her face, what I could see of it from my angle, looked as serene as a sleeping babe. A nurse hovered nearby while the woman made the vain attempt of bringing life back to the deceased daisies.

"I don't know. She probably tried to cut off some guy's junk or something."

"You see? Even when you don't know the answer, you assume it is violence."

I tilted my head to the side and gave Zeke a quizzical look. Violence was the answer to everything around here.

Oak Ridge only took in one type of person. You either had to be insane, stupid, or too incompetent to sit through your own trial to land behind these bars. Not everyone had dismembered some guy to earn their golden ticket here, but we all had one thing in common; we'd all committed a crime. We'd all screwed with the status quo and in doing so, had earned the ire of the establishment. We were all here ostensibly to get better, but we all knew it was just a front for making the good, normal folk of the world sleep better at night knowing the crazy murderers were locked away.

"I'm not following," I said after Zeke proved to not be forthcoming with answers. The way his smile twitched and his eyes drifted away to a far-off point led me to believe he enjoyed his little game. Each time he baited me, I was too stubborn not to pick it up. He knew how to catch my interest, how to goad me along when I grew wise to his scheme and refused to follow, and how to keep me coming back for more. A smarter person would've walked away then and there. Too bad I could out-stubborn a mule.

"There are other ways to be dangerous than to cause physical harm," he said, his voice as smooth and confident as if he'd rehearsed the lines a hundred times before. "Political, for example."

"Are you trying to tell me that you're here because of some kind of political agenda?"

"Not me, Cassandra. You."

He had me going for a while there. Too bad he had to throw in the conspiracy theory. I blew him off with a scoff. "Yeah, okay. So, you're the one who spiked the punch, huh?"

"That woman I pointed out before? She is schizophrenic. Relatively harmless. She could be in a normal mental hospital making pretty finger paintings and getting better. Instead she is here, surrounded by guards." He paused for dramatic effect, the smile stretching his copper skin. "She is here because she is the daughter of a very important senator."

"So what? Daddy paid to put her in the bad hospital? That doesn't make much sense."

"It does if you think about the danger she poses. Imagine if the media discovered the mad daughter of a senator. Imagine how his competitors could use that against him. Would he not then want to keep such information closely guarded? Perhaps surrounded by walls and fences and guns?"

I mulled it over for a minute and imagined what I'd do in dear old dad's situation. I admit I had trouble following Zeke's logic. If it were me, I'd have just shot anyone who tried to use my own family against me. Can't say that's good for a senator's career though. My conclusion was I didn't understand the deep, inner workings of a politician's mind. There were plenty of nicer hospitals employing staff who could be paid to be discreet. Her dad had to be one hell of a jackass to put her here. Yet the fact that true, black-blooded, snake-oil dealing assholes existed in the world gave a shred of credit to Zeke's theory, and that kept me hooked.

"Alright, so maybe that makes sense for her, but I'm not the daughter of anyone important."

"No," he said with a wolfish smile, "you are just a survivor of a government experiment which was not meant to have any survivors. Why would anyone want to keep you somewhere safe and guarded where they could always keep an eye on you?"

My brain stopped cold in the middle of a thought. I'd been lending a little less than half my attention to Zeke's wild conspiracy theory up until then, having already dismissed it as just more crazy talk after the whole thing about a secret political agenda. The rest of my mind had been occupied with the way my seat didn't feel quite as comfortable as usual when I had the whole bench to myself, and how the heat of the sun made my skin itch beneath the loose cotton of my hospital clothes. Every other thought stopped when he said the one thing that made his theory click.

Almesa hadn't wanted us to get out of Redby alive. Their hand had been forced by an opportune explosion of media interest after one too many slip-ups being exposed. The first reporter to find us was called crazy and written off. Same as the second and the third. But after a while, there were too many of them. Then the cure happened and their entire scheme fell apart. I don't know what they had planned to do with us in the beginning and I don't think I want to know. I already wanted them dead for what had been done. I'm sure they felt the same way about me.

I drew in a breath and the walls closed in around me. The guards watched me, not to ensure my safety, but to wait for the perfect shot. The nurses gave me medication not to aid my recovery, but to keep me sedated. I looked past Zeke to the towers standing sentinel at each corner of our enclosed courtyard. Each one housed a guard trained to shoot first and ask questions later. The guard could see me just fine, though I could barely see the edge of his silhouette and the long, sleek rifle he carried. I had no cover. Running would be as good as putting the gun to my own head and pulling the trigger. I drew in another breath, trying to keep my cool, and responded to Zeke with a shrug. Inside my head, my senses screamed for a hiding place.

"There's still hundreds of other Reds out in the world. Keeping me locked up won't do much good."

"It will keep you alive and accounted for while their numbers are slowly whittled away. Tell me you don't see it happening."

I could see it happening. Marcia brought me news of their deaths every day. Feeding my anger, driving me. She must have been a plant. They knew I would break soon. If I went out in a frothing rage, they'd have all the evidence they'd need to point fingers at the other Reds and say we were all dangerous monsters who needed to be put down. By taking out the Reds, they could regain some of their respect. Maybe claw their way back to life. I had to get out from under their thumb. I could run. I knew I had friends on the outside. Maybe...

I glanced back at Zeke's face midway through forming my escape plan. He stared at me with undisguised glee, white teeth gleaming in an elated, cadaverous grin.

"You're fucking with me," I growled.

Zeke laughed.

I balled my fist to smack him one in his stupid, smug mouth, but thought better of it a second later. Even if the conspiracy theory had just been a story to get me riled, there were still guards. They still had guns and they were still dangerous. I had to force myself to unclench my hand and look away, snarling one last insult under my breath. "Asshole."

Zeke stood up, gave me a mocking bow, then strolled off toward a shaded patch of grass a few feet away. The rage boiled inside me, wanting a release. Preferably on his face. I could do nothing to express it. Nothing but stab at the journal with the pen I crushed in my fist. I didn't realize it was possible to put so much anger into the written word.

CHAPTER TEN

I sat in the same room for three days, too scared to move. Once upon a time, it had been some student's bedroom, but I'd transformed it into a mini fortress barricaded by shelves and a dresser. I did my business in the far corner of the room and covered it up with old towels. They did nothing to mask the stench. I took shallow breaths until my senses adjusted, then tried not to think about what I was breathing in. I ate chips and pop from a stash under the bed and used pages from a politics textbook as toilet paper. Posters turned into wallpaper plastered over the windows, leaving only a small corner free so I could spy on the street below.

After the first day, the power went out. After the second, the food and water ran out. By the third, I was so delirious with hunger and fatigue that I couldn't distinguish between dreams and reality. I woke up once convinced Ace had come back to life, found a jetpack, and crashed into the wall in an insane bout of self-sacrifice while I looked on, frozen by my own fear.

No one disturbed me while I hid away in my little bunker. No zombies, no survivors, not even a stray cat. Outside, the undead shuffled through the streets paying attention to nothing at all until something alive and frightened caught their eye. Then they moved with a possessed fury to hunt down and tear apart their prey. I watched one of them lunge after a man with a baseball bat. The man beat the thing until nothing remained but a pulpy mess of blood and brains, then took off running. The zombie lay outside my window for an entire night, but as the sun began to rise the next day, it twitched and groaned. Before noon, the thing had pulled itself back to its feet, still dripping bits of itself over the pavement. It shuffled off in search of more food, not minding the fact that half its head remained behind.

I waited for several hours after the last zombie cleared my line of sight before coming to the conclusion that I needed to get out. I was no less scared than I had been the day of the attack, but scared did not equate with dead. So long as I drew breath, I had a chance to make it out alive.

I had suffered through hunger before.. I learned from a very young age to get by with what little I had. When I left the room, a little woozy and too scared to piss, I took with me only what I had brought in; myself and the gun. Maybe it would have been smart to get a change of clothes, but I didn't know who the room belonged to and I still felt some sense of social responsibility. Whoever owned this stuff would want it back someday.

Maybe not so much now since I'd made a mess of things, but one could only feel so much concern for one's fellow man when said fellow man might be interested in eating your brains.

I made my way downstairs and outside without incident. The gun stayed in my hands, gripped between my sweaty palms and ready to fire at a second's notice. A merciless sun beat down on the pavement, baking the remains of the twice dead zombie into the ground. I caught a whiff of rotted, overripe flesh and felt the bile rise in my throat. And here I'd thought my stench had been bad.

A little mom-and-pop store sat on the corner across from me. Perfect. The door and windows still looked intact. Good chance it still had food inside.

Good chance there were still zombies on the street, even if I couldn't see them.

I took off running and dove through the open doorway. A little brass bell chimed as I threw my shoulder into the door, shoving it shut against its old frame. A nearby stack of old newspapers became a barricade and not until after I had them piled waist high in front of the door did I feel safe enough to turn around.

My hopes for a plentiful stash fell short as I surveyed the store. Every shelf, every bin, even the hanging racks behind the counter, all cleaned out. I tiptoed down the middle aisle, checking each shelf for so much as a scrap of nourishment. Hell, I'd have taken protein bars. Even the melted ice cream was gone, leaving nothing but a dried yellow stain to show where it had been. I didn't find anything until I reached the end of the aisle and turned to the next one.

There, on the floor between two aisles, lay a shrine of glorious food. All piled together nice and neat. Bread, veggies, cereal, and even some bottles of water filled one bag while the one beside it contained an avalanche of candy bars. It must have been the last haul this store had to offer.

I didn't think. I just dropped to my knees in front of the pile, thanked God for His mercy, and ripped into the first candy bar I got my hands around. The gun sat forgotten in my lap while I inhaled the chocolaty bliss, pausing long enough to breathe between bites. A bottle of water jostled loose from the pile and bumped against my knee. I tore the cap off with my teeth in my eagerness to get at the refreshing liquid. It dribbled in little rivers down my chin, soaking into the front of my sweat stained shirt.

I was transported to heaven. The feel of cool water on my skin, washing away days of filth and fear, the taste of the water as it trickled down my throat, semi-sweet thanks to the chocolate still coating my tongue, these were the gifts of God Almighty. I felt renewed. I could survive this. I could find a way out, back to civilization. Back to my company and some semblance of sanity. I could get through this.

Then I heard the click of a gun.

An old, six-shot   stared at me from the entranceway of a room labelled "employees only." A young man with thick sausage fingers and a body that made potatoe sacks look slim held the pistol with an aire of petrified confidence.

Stupid. I should've checked the entire building before thinking I could drop my defences. I hadn't even thought to look for a storage room.

"That's mine. That's my food," the boy squeaked out. Any attempt to look menacing was thwarted by the stylishly long cut of his brown hair and the black paint on his nails. The pockets of his khaki pants were stuffed to overflowing with more goods. His hands shook as he pointed the gun at me.

"Easy now. I was just hungry. I'll leave now, alright?" I tried to ease myself up to my feet. My assailant jerked a single step back like a frightened deer and centered the gun between my eyes.

"No! No, you can't go now. If I let you go, you'll tell people you stole food from me and lived."

"Buddy, I don't even know who you are." I looked him up and down. He couldn't have been much younger than me. Maybe just leaving his teens. Pimples still covered his forehead and cheeks. Though he weighed a few solid kilos more than me, I could rush him if I had to.

"You'll tell people and they'll think they can steal from me too. It's everyone for themselves right now. I have to protect myself. I have to make sure you don't tell anyone."

Shit. Emo Wonder wanted to grow up in a hurry. He put a finger over the trigger and tensed from head to toe.

"Well well well, what've we got here? Looks like an old-fashioned Mexican standoff," a new voice drawled from the darkened back room. I had a clear line of sight to the figure strolling out of the shadows, but my would-be attacker had to shuffle to the side and look over his shoulder. I snatched my gun off the floor the second his eyes left me. The new challenger sauntered into view, shotgun hung between his hands like he just happened to be walking in our direction and hadn't meant to point the long, double-barrel nose at us. A self-assured grin tugged one corner of his mouth up and put a glint in his grey eyes, shadowed as they were by the wide-brimmed cowboy hat tipped over his forehead.

"Hello, folks. The name's Tommy. And what might yours be?"

"You set me up! He's with you, isn't he? You distracted me so he could kill me," my attacker squeaked. He took another step back, putting his back to the wall, and kept jerking his gun between me and Tommy. I took careful aim at the kid's kneecaps without taking my eyes off his face.

"No! Jesus, calm down! I don't know who either of you are," I said. The six-shot swung around to point at my head.

"That's a pity. I'd like to get to know a pretty girl like you."

I... wha? Was new guy seriously hitting on me in the middle of a standoff? The sixshot swung around to point at Tommy.

"Look, we're all a little worked up here. Why don't we put down the guns and walk away, alright? Everyone lives," I said. The gun turned back on me.

"It's my food!"

"Far as I can see it, the young miss is closer to it right now, which makes it hers. Plus, you're outnumbered." Tommy used the barrel of his gun to point in the younger guy's direction even as the old pistol wavered somewhere between his face and his throat. Tommy waved the shotty around like a kid with a harmless stick.

"The hell are you doing?" I hissed at the cowboy. I didn't want to steal the other guy's food. By the rules of finders keepers, he was the fair owner.

"You want food and water? Cause you won't find another supply this good anywhere else in town. This here is the last big haul. What say we split it? Fifty-fifty."

Uh, well that threw a wrench in my good Samaritan thought process. Maybe the emo had found it first, but I was starving and Tommy made a very convincing argument. Maybe more food could be found elsewhere, but I wasn't elsewhere. I was here, almost sitting on this stash.

"I found it first! It's mine!"

"He's right." Dammit. Ace would've just told the kid to shut up. I never thought I'd wish for Ace's sensibilities.

"You wanna eat or do you wanna play fair?" Tommy cocked his head to the side and focused on me. The shotgun remained pointed at the emo's midsection. The six-shot juddered between Tommy and myself every few seconds. Its owner couldn't make up his mind about which of us posed the bigger threat.

Dammit. Dammit. Dammit.

"I'm taking some of this food. Not all of it." I took one hand off my gun to gather up the plastic bag of candy bars. I shoved in a loaf of bread and a few water bottles just to be safe. That left most of the veggies and healthy shit for the emo. He'd stand a better chance of surviving if he had a decent diet.

"You can't do that! It's mine!" Emo Wonder pointed the gun at me and took a step forward. Tommy stepped in and hefted his shotgun, turning himself into an impassable wall with nothing more than a shift in his position and a clicking of his tongue.

"You're outnumbered. Be glad I'm leaving some for you," I said. I hated myself for saying it. The kid had no survival training, no combat training, and no idea of what to do. He didn't even move as I stood and backed toward the door. He stood perfectly still and made little sounds of protest in the back of his throat, like he couldn't believe his own eyes.

"Get the door," I told my new partner. Tommy didn't hesitate. He scooted around me when I stopped a good two feet from my temporary barricade and kicked the newspapers until they collapsed in an avalanche of old headlines. The bell chimed and I stepped backward until I stood in the street, Tommy at my side and a bag of stolen goods hanging from my arm.

The door shut and gave me a few seconds of utter silence. I breathed a sigh of relief and looked down at the bag of candy bars and water bottles dangling from flimsy plastic handles over my elbow.

What the hell had I just done?

I stole from the store, something I sworn to myself I'd never do again, and then I'd also taken food away from a scared boy just looking to survive. By the looks of it, he didn't have another soul to rely on in this town. Maybe they'd all been killed already. I was supposed to protect people like that, not steal from them.

"My truck's this way." Tommy's words jolted me out of my spiralling guilt trip. I had almost forgotten he still stood beside me.

"Why the hell would I want to go to your truck?" I asked.

"Because half of that stuff is mine," he said with a nod toward our plastic bag of loot. "And I figure a steady gun hand like yours could be useful. Wanna team up?"

"No." Like hell I trusted this cocky cowboy. I did owe him half our haul though, so when he shrugged and started walking, I followed.

"What's your name?" he asked as I fell into step beside him.

"Cass."

"Just Cass?"

"Just Cass."

82

Another shrug. The shotgun slipped over his shoulder on an old, worn strap. He kept one hand resting on the butt while the other disappeared into the front pocket of his jeans.

Once we were out in the sunlight, I had a chance to get a decent look at him. Pale brown hair that could've almost passed for a dark shade of blond swept back beneath his cowboy hat, save for a few errant strands which dangled over his forehead. His features were soft and rounded, like he'd decided to stop aging after high school. Even his attempt at a beard looked like little more than stubble that surrounded his mouth and faded on the way back to his temples. He wore a popped collar flannel shirt with the sleeves rolled up to his elbows and a faded pair of blue jeans which added to his Old West chic image. Sneakers covered his feet instead of cowboy boots. I guess the city life still had some hold on him.

Tommy stood a good foot taller than myself, though he looked to be about the same age. Those bright, steel grey eyes of his and the way he kept smiling like he hadn't a care in the world made it hard to pin his age. He could've said he was seventeen and I'd have believed him, except the way he swaggered with each step said he had some life experience. Not much. Just some.

"Like what you see?" he asked when he caught me staring. I looked away and didn't answer him.

His hand flickered in the corner of my vision, coming toward my chest. I snatched his wrist out of the air with my free hand and twisted it around backwards just hard enough to make him feel the strain.

"Try to touch me again and I break your arm."

When I released Tommy's hand, he held it up in a show of surrender and chuckled.

"Alright, alright. I was just trying to get a look at your tags." His hand fell into his pocket again and he nodded at my dog tags. "They real?"

Oh, uh... I guess he could've been reaching for those too. I glanced down at the little rectangles of metal hanging from a chain around my neck, then tucked them beneath the cover of my shirt.

"Yeah, they're real."

"So you're military, huh? I thought all of them were up on the wall."

"They forgot to do a head count," I muttered, venom dripping off each word.

"Lucky for me. You sure you don't wanna team up? I've got a nice little apartment all boarded up. Just needs a few stockpiles of food and ammo to make it feel like home."

"No. No offence, but I don't know you and I don't trust you." I had already done a stint in a walled off room anyway. I didn't want to hole myself up in some apartment again and wait for someone else to save me. I was going to save myself. I just had to figure out how.

"You could get to know me. Wouldn't mind the company."

Again, with the random flirting. He even had the cheesy, ain't-I-cute smile making dimples in his cheeks.

"Or I could shoot you and take all your stuff for myself."

"You won't do that."

"The hell makes you think I won't?"

"Because you're not that kind of person. You wanted to leave everything for the kid back there. Killer doesn't do that. Someone who wants to protect people does."

I gave him a sideways glance as we came around the corner of the grocery store. His truck, an old, rusted mud-crawler, was parked half on the sidewalk and half in the alley outside the back entrance. The door to the storage room hung wide open.

"I'm not here to protect you. I've got shit to do and I don't need some civvy with a hero complex slowing me down. If it comes to it, and I know it will, I will cheerfully leave you behind to save my own skin." I dropped the bag of stolen goods in the bed of his truck and began to sort it out. I knew anything I kept for myself I could make stretch for as much as a week. That meant protein bars and non-perishables for me, and the good stuff for the cowboy. Even when I couldn't stand someone, I went out of my way to keep them alive. I would have to sort through my priorities if this thing lasted longer than a week.

Tommy kept quiet for a while, leading me to hope he'd gotten the picture. He strolled around to the driver's side of the truck and threw the shotgun in the back of the cab. Then he rested his arms on the door's open window frame and stared at me through the back window. When he spoke, his voice had lost the all-too-confident drawl which made his every word that much more annoying. There was a seriousness to his tone that made me stop and look up.

"Listen, darling, we've woken up on the wrong side of the apocalypse here. Everything's changing and unless we change with it, we're gonna end up like those creepy crawlers back there." He paused and thumbed down the alley at—

I did a double take. Oh hell, I hadn't even seen them while I'd been so preoccupied by my new friend.

Three of the walking dead shuffled our way through the grey shadows separating the grocery store from the hardware store beside it. One looked like the thing I'd seen take a pummelling outside my window. The other two were fresher, still oozing dark, clumpy blood from the gaping wounds on their arms and necks. As I switched my pistol to my free hand for a steadier shot, one of them took notice of us and let out a low, raspy moan that sent a shiver down my spine.

"Now," Tommy went on, "I'm no expert in surviving disasters, but I know what I'll need to stand a fighting chance." He lifted a hand and began to tick off points, undisturbed by the slow shuffle of hungry brain eaters headed our way. "Weapons, ammo, food, shelter, and eyes in the back of my head. We'll both survive longer if we partner up."

Tommy opened his door and hopped in the cab of the truck. With a flick of his wrist, the old beater growled to life. The undead were on the opposite side of the truck from me. All the cowboy had to do was peel off and save his own hide. I might survive these three, but I had no idea how many more lurked about.

"Choice is yours, beautiful."

I looked from Tommy to the undead and back again. I still didn't trust him. It would be ridiculous to think I could after knowing him for a few minutes. Just because he'd helped me get some food didn't mean he'd be my friend through thick and thin.

He had a point though. I had no idea what was going on in this town and until I did, I had a snowball's chance in hell of making it out alive. I still had people to find and plans to make. All of which would be easier if I had someone at my back. If I still had Ace and BigMac, that wouldn't be an issue.

They were both dead because of me though. Three trained, battle hardened soldiers, and we'd all fallen to pieces in a day because of this stupid little redneck town. Tommy had lived through the first four days and seemed to know his way around a gun. He was ready to do whatever it took to survive. I didn't have to trust him right away. I just needed to work with him.

The undead stood three feet away from the truck when I let out a series of curses under my breath and yanked open the passenger side door. I snatched our haul of goodies out of the bed of the truck before I slid into the seat and hauled the seatbelt across my chest. Tommy hit the gas.

The truck snarled a protest as its tires screeched in reverse. It thunked into the trio of zombies with an impact that I felt from my toes to my teeth. They went down under the back end of the truck, leaving a smear of blood and fleshy bits over the bed's back flap. Tommy throttled the gears into drive and tore off into the street before the three undead could crawl their way back to their feet. I waited until my teeth stopped rattling before I turned to my new partner and held up a hand, ready to tick off a few points of my own.

"One, my name is Cass. That's all you'll call me. Two, you ever try to screw me over, stab me, shoot me, or save your own hide by leaving me behind, I will find you and kill you. Three, everything we find, we split fifty-fifty. Deal?"

Tommy grinned from ear to ear, cocky cowboy confidence back in full force. He took one hand off the wheel and held it out to me. I traded grips with him, making sure I squeezed just as hard as he did.

"Deal."

CHAPTER ELEVEN

I thought I did well with my little apartment. I'd used all available furniture to shore it up, which didn't amount to much more than milk crates given it had belonged to a student. The makeshift barricades served to keep me locked in nice and safe and it could have held out a long while had I needed to withstand an attack.

My one room fortress was nothing compared to the castle of horrors Tommy had made.

Tommy lived in what used to be the upscale part of the residential area back when living residents populated the area. It towered a grand five storeyss high with flowering shrubs in front and wrought iron fences around the balconies. The entrance had a two-door buzzer system to make sure no unsavoury types entered the building proper.

Not that the buzzer worked anymore. Or could even open the door given that Tommy had gone to the effort of boarding up both sets of doors then reinforcing them with every bit of furniture on the main level. I dedicated a full minute to boggling over how he got two full couches to fit into the tiny space.

After he parked the truck and hid it under a tarp, we climbed the fire escape and slipped in through a fifth-storey window. He barricaded up the window after us, then set out an honest-to-God bear trap beneath the windowsill. When we got out into the hall, every door but one, his own, was either nailed shut or outfitted with enough traps to trip up an army.

"Welcome to Casa del Grayson," Tommy said as he escorted me over the threshold.

"Jesus, you've turned this place into a fort," I muttered. I stepped where he stepped and kept scanning the walls, ceiling and floor for more traps. After what I'd seen and heard from him, I didn't want to take any chances.

The traps disappeared once we were inside his apartment. Though I had a hard time noticing their absence while navigating a mountain of boxes, plastic containers, and random junk spread throughout the living room. The town had been locked down for no more than four days, but it looked like Tommy had been saving up for the end of the world since the beginning of the year.

A pathway wended between the piles of food and survival supplies, snaking from the front door to the kitchen, making a stop at the balcony, then bee-lining down the hall to the bedroom and bathroom.

"You could protect the whole damn town with all these defences," I said. Too many seconds ticked past without any words passing between us. The silence started to feel awkward. At least for me.

"Could, but don't want to. More people means more mouths to feed and more chances for things to go wrong. Speaking of, you want something to eat?" Tommy disappeared into the open kitchen.

"Yeah, sure," I said. The candy bar hadn't done much to tide me over. Nervous as I was in Tommy's fortress of doom, I couldn't ignore the basic urges. My stomach felt like it wanted to claw its way out of my throat at the mere mention of food.

I headed out to the balcony while I waited for Tommy to make us lunch. Wind pushed at my face, filled with the smell of burning city, spiced here and there with the reminder of death. Just looking down at the town gave me a full-colour replay of the last four days of my life, starting with fear and ending with more fear and confusion. The town itself wasn't all that broken up. It just looked asleep, save for the spot in the horizon where the Almesa building used to be. The empty hole kicked out a steady stream of smoke, though not nearly as much as it had when it came down around my ears.

"How the hell did this happen?" I asked the empty air.

"Dunno, but I know it came from Almesa."

I nearly jumped out of my skin when Tommy came up behind me, two plates of ham sandwiches in one hand and a bottle of scotch in the other. He offered me one of the plates. I couldn't speak for Tommy's tastes, but my stomach growled in appreciation of the food. I sat down with my back to the apartment wall, sandwich already halfway to my mouth.

"How the hell does a security company go about bringing on the zombie apocalypse?" I asked after mowing down a few quick bites.

Tommy shrugged and sat across from me, cracking open the scotch and taking a long swing from the bottle.

Priorities; this guy had them.

"They only showed up a couple years ago. When they mayor signed the deal with them and the wall went up, they came out with some big speeches about how Redby would go down in history. The first city to eradicate crime. Kept the people feeling uneasy about the whole thing from packing up and heading out. They never bothered mentioning the medical lab they built or the weird way dissenters kept disappearing around them."

"How the hell do you know all this?"

"My mother worked for them. Was in the main office building when it blew. Dad had just gone to pick her up for a late lunch." No emotion. Not even a pause between bites. Tommy told his tragic tale like a news anchor reporting the weather.

"Oh. Sorry to hear that," I said. Tommy just shrugged.

"Everyone's going to have one of those stories soon enough. You lose anyone yet?"

"Well, I'm down here while everyone I know is up on the wall trying to kill me." My commanding officer, my friends, everyone I trusted. People in my life were too damn quick to stab me in the back.

"Good point," he said.

"If you don't mind me saying, you don't seem too shook up by what's happening." I finished my sandwich in three more bites. Best ham I'd ever tasted in my life and the scotch burned like wildfire all the way down my throat.

"What's the matter? Afraid I'm one of the crazy ones?" Tommy gave me a lopsided grin that would've been disturbing if not for the rugged charm offered by his cowboy hat. He looked young, unshaven, and tired. His eyes had been the colour of polished silver when I'd first met him. Now, even though he smiled, they were flat and dull. Tommy kept talking when I didn't jump to answer his trap question. "You wouldn't be far wrong, I guess. I mean, I don't think I'm crazy, but I don't get sad when I think of my parents." He paused and looked down at the bottle of scotch that now sat between us. "I don't think it's really sunk in yet."

Which didn't surprise me in the least. I was still processing the fact that I'd lost Ace and BigMac and… Hell. I'd lost my life to this town. I bet they'd already written me off as dead. My stomach contents began to sour.

"Thanks for the meal. I'm going to head to bed." I stood up and took my plate inside. When Tommy started to follow, I abandoned my plan to put it in the kitchen and just placed it atop one of his many boxes. I made my way down the hall while Tommy looked on.

"That's the bathroom, beautiful."

"Yeah, I figured that out." I opened the door anyway, revealing a tiled floor, bathtub with shower, sink, and toilet all crammed into a space the size of a closet.

"Well you don't wanna be sleeping in there. Bedroom's one door down," Tommy called out.

I stuck my head out the door and thumbed down the hall to the other door. A sliver of light crept in past the inviting shadows and dark, sultry colours, revealing an unlit room with a bed hidden in a sea of survival equipment.

"You mean there? Where you sleep?"

"Bed's big enough for two." Tommy grinned from ear to ear. I willed his head to explode, and when that didn't work, I started to shut the bathroom door.

"Wait! What if I gotta take a piss?"

"Use the balcony. Aim for the zombies."

The door shut. I locked it, then rattled the handle to make sure it would stay locked. Then I stepped back and turned around to face the cabinet mirror hung over the sink. I turned on the water, splashed some on my face, then stared at my reflection and wondered what the hell I had gotten myself into.

This was real. There was no point in denying that. I hadn't ever been the type to cry about the surrealness of a bad situation. I knew some people took comfort in pretending that bad things never happened. Especially not to them. To me, all the time. My life had been one big, long bad situation. I got used to dealing with it. This, though, this was new.

I turned to look at the tub, which would be my bed for the evening. A shower head hung from one tiled wall, partially hidden behind a colourful, patterned curtain. The tub looked just big enough to sit it with my legs almost stretched out. Tiny, secluded, and perfect. Just what I needed to collect my thoughts.

I stripped down and climbed into the tub. Icy cold water jetted over my face. I turned the taps all the way to scalding, but the water never warmed. No power, no heat. Oh well. Cold would be better for me anyway. I sat down to let the cold droplets wash away the grime that had built up over a week of sweating and sitting. First in a truck, then caged up in a bedroom.

Old, dried blood dribbled off my hands. It skittered toward the drain in dark clumps, revealing the long, ugly scratches that would become scars along my forearm. I hadn't thought about the man who had been pulled into the sewer since Ace's death. Now it looked like I would have a permanent reminder of him.

Ace's blood covered my clothes. Some of it had gotten onto my skin, and as I watched it wash down the drain, a sudden panic gripped my heart. The last pieces of my best friend were disappearing down the drain.

I took a deep breath and closed my eyes.

These were the things I knew: Ace and BigMac were dead. No amount of watered down blood would change that. I was trapped in a town overrun by the undead. The people I had once called friends and family were my new wardens. Chaos ruled and government died in a hailstorm of bullets. I had to survive by whatever means necessary. To that end, I had teamed up with a man that convinced me a little more each time he opened his mouth that he was off his rocker. He was well equipped though, and I hadn't gotten more than a ping on my creeper detector. He could be useful. Not trusted. Useful.

On the plus side, I now had a fortified place to stay, food enough to last a long time, and weapons to keep myself safe. As far as I knew, there were no rivers or lakes within the town limits, having running water was a good thing.

The shower head made a sudden and loud thumping noise. I scrambled back on my hands as the noise continued, staring at the sputtering stream of water. My back hit the far end of the tub. The shower head groaned and gave one final gasp of watery breath. Then it fell silent.

No more water.

Great.

CHAPTER TWELVE

REDBY, NEVADA
August 9, 2021

I fell asleep in the tub sometime after sundown. A loud pounding on the door snapped me out of my nightmares minutes later.

"Rise and shine, angel! Food's not going to find itself!"

Christ. It could not be morning yet. I craned my neck up and ignored the protests of my muscles as they were forced to move for the first time in eons. Light spilled in through the small window above the tub, stabbing me in the eye.

I groaned as a new noise assaulted my ears. Strings thrummed from the hallway, the prelude to a slow but cheerful guitar ballad. Maybe if I just pretended to be dead, he'd leave me alone.

I waited a few minutes, but the song didn't let up. Then Tommy began to sing.

Dammit, dammit, dammit!

I started to hate this guy.

I could kill him, reasoned a small yet clear voice in my head. I dubbed the little voice Lack of Coffee and told it to get stuffed. I wasn't going to start killing random people just because I woke up on the wrong side of the tub.

It took a few minutes more to pull myself upright and work the kinks out of my muscles. The fact that I expected them to move and work so soon after yesterday's activity was just an appalling affront to their existence. Tommy warbled through the chorus as I finished my morning stretch, tucked the pistol into the belt of my pants, and unlocked the door.

I stuck my head out first and fixed him with a glower that could have melted metal. He smiled, sunlight in his steely eyes, a hand poised over the neck of a wooden guitar.

"Morning, beautiful. Ready for a fun filled day of pillaging?"

"I hate you," I growled at him.

"You'll get over that." Tommy ducked his head under the strap of the guitar and lay the instrument against the wall. The shotgun replaced it, slung over his shoulder with the ease of a backpacker going on a hike. He cocked his head toward the door, tipped the brim of his hat, and raised an eyebrow at me. "Coming?"

Well I sure as hell wasn't going to sit around all day. My nightmares itched at the back of my mind like a bad rash. Staying in would just give them a chance to fester.

"Where are we going?" I asked as we made our way out to the parking lot.

Tommy shrugged and turned toward the street, completely bypassing the truck.

"Dunno. Around. Why? You know some place we can find food?"

"You expect me to know my way around?" I didn't even know North from South in this new hellhole.

Tommy shrugged again.

"I was expecting you to be useful."

I ground my teeth together and tried to keep my cool. Yeah, I couldn't tell Baker street from Barker street, but I was alive and not crying in a corner. Anymore. That had to count for something.

Undead filled the street outside Tommy's place. They stood in clusters or shuffled down the middle of the road, oblivious to everything around them. A bird flitted past a small group of them. The sound of its song caught their attention and sent them moaning and scrambling after it. A shiver ran down my spine as their gaping maws snapped after the bird's tail feathers.

God, I wished I was that bird. I wanted to fly out of this place and just keep on going.

I told my fear to get stuffed and drew in a deep breath.

"You want me to be useful?" I whispered to my companion. He stood stock still beside me, cool expression firmly in place. For all his bravado, the sight of walking, hungry corpses scared him as much as it did me. "Pick a place. I'll get you there alive."

Big words coming from me, even by my own estimation. My hands still shook just thinking about those creatures. I didn't want to get up close and personal with them again.

"Chocolate bar says you don't," Tommy countered.

I looked up at him, peering deep into his eyes. I had to be sure. He had not just bet against himself on a candy bar.

"Yeah, alright," I grunted. Why the hell not?

"There's a coffee shop two blocks down. Still has some baked goods that haven't gone stale yet."

"Coffee and chocolate, the breakfast of champions," I muttered to myself. "Alright, here's how this works. I go first, you follow when I signal you. When I do this," I held up my hand and balled it into a fist, "it means—"

"Yeah, yeah, I've seen all those military hoorah movies. I know the hand signals. Just lead the way," Tommy quipped, waving off my instructions.

"Right. This'll be fun."

Fifteen minutes later, I dragged Tommy through the front door of the coffee shop with one hand and smacked the crap out of a zombie with the butt end of my gun in the other hand. Tommy gave the creeper a solid kick to the face, caving in its nose and snapping its head back at an awkward angle. The desiccated corpse shuddered and released its grasp on his leg. I took the opportunity to yank him in by his shirt collar and slam the door shut before the damned brain muncher could get back up again.

"What the hell was that?" I demanded of my partner as I shoved a chair in front of the door. "What the hell military movie has a raised fist meaning run into the street and scream like a little girl?"

"I did not scream," Tommy huffed. "I was surprised. It came up out of nowhere."

"It was lying down and you tripped over it."

"Yeah well... what the hell was with you going all caveman on its ass and not shooting it?"

"There were five others standing across the street. I told you that. Remember the hand signals?" I lifted my hand and repeated the signal. I really shouldn't have taken him at his word. Hollywood never got the little details right.

"Oh... I thought you were waving."

My hand moved of its own accord and smacked against my face.

"Don't feel so bad. You'll do better next time," my partner said.

I drew in a deep breath, contemplated murder, then sent the thought out with the air from my lungs.

"Alright, whatever. Those things are going to be moving around out there now. We need to get what we came for and get out."

"We got some time," Tommy countered. He grunted and pushed himself to his feet, snatching his hat off the ground on the way. "Door's shut up tight. There's a back door, but it's always locked from the inside."

Pretty specific knowledge.

"Old hangout of yours?" I asked.

"Job." Tommy gave me a sidelong glance and a shrug, looking almost embarrassed to admit he used to have a life here. "Summer job. Before college."

I grunted acknowledgement. His body language said he didn't want to continue on the topic any longer and I was not one to argue with a stubborn torso. I glanced around the store while Tommy made for the baked goods behind the front counter.

Fickle sunlight streaming in through the tinted front windows provided just enough illumination to see by. It ghosted across the lavish setup like a spotlight shining on a museum piece of ancient history. Here lies civilization as it was just before the collapse: extravagant, wide spread, all colours muted and dark as if to forewarn of the end. The overindulgence that led to its final days can be seen in the amount of stuffing used to fill the poorly made, faux Swedish chairs. Marvel at the ignorance of their own impending doom.

A lingering sense of illegality prickled along the back of my neck as if the ghost of the shop's former life sat on my shoulders. I shook it from my thoughts and cleared my throat.

"I'm going to check out the back. Make sure we're alone. Yell if you see anything," I said to Tommy. He answered with a wide-eyed stare.

"Down," he roared.

I dropped.

I hit the ground on my shoulder, already turning to face whatever threat had caught Tommy's attention. I lay on my back when the cowboy swung a fancy bar stool at the head of a zombie looming over me.

He missed. The thing stood two feet away and he missed.

I didn't though. My foot connected with the rotter's knee. It cracked like a brittle twig, snapping back at an impossible angle. The zombie had no sense of balance. The moment I disabled its leg, it went to the ground. This time, Tommy didn't miss. The stool drove downward, smashing into its head and showering me with bits of splinters and brains. I rolled away as fast as I could to avoid retching on myself.

"How the hell did you survive so long on your own?" I demanded after wiping zombie bits off my face.

"I was good at this before you showed up. You're like a bad luck charm or something." Tommy punctuated his words with a wild gesture. He made a disgusted noise in the back of his throat and kicked at the broken stool. "Damn, good thing you're pretty. Don't think I'm much in the mind for breakfast anymore."

"Good. Let's get the hell out of here then. Before that thing gets back up." The sooner we were out of this neighbourhood, the sooner I could relax.

"What the hell do you mean gets back up?" Tommy picked up piece of broken bar stool and prodded the zombie's oozing skull. "This thing is all kinds of dead."

"I mean pulls the chair out of its head and tries to eat us again," I enunciated my words like as if speaking to a child. It didn't matter either way, because Tommy stared at me like I'd just spoken French or something.

"What the hell have you been smoking?"

Understanding hit me in a sudden cold wave. Tommy had been out on the streets three days longer than me. He'd been moving around, killing these things with his gun or his truck and never looking back.

"You don't know, do you?" I asked in a small voice.

"Know what?"

"They don't stay dead. You shoot them and they just get back up an hour later."

"Bullshit." Tommy frowned, the gears whirling in his head.

"I saw it happen. Back before we met, I watched a guy beat one of them down. A few hours later, it just got back up again."

"You think you might've been seeing things on account of not having eaten recently?" "I know what I bloody well saw," I snapped. Then a new idea slapped me upside the head. "A bet."

"Huh?" he grunted.

"A bet," I said again. I yanked the rest of the stool out of the zombie's corpse. "We wait right here for this thing to get back up. When it does—"

"If."

"*When* it does," I repeated, and then I stopped. What the hell did I want from him? I already had a roof over my head and a gun at my back. Any supplies we picked up we shared equally, or so I assumed. "You owe me half of whatever you take. That's three-quarters to me, one-quarter to you." And for good measure, I added, "Forever."

"That— You're— That's robbery!" Tommy sputtered. "You're robbing me! I take mine and you take yours. That's the deal."

"Chicken," I goaded him.

That changed his attitude in a quick hurry. Tommy's expression went from hot indigence to stone cold in a second.

"You're on. But—" he held up a warning finger, "if I win, I get a kiss. From you. On the lips. One minute of bliss. Deal?"

A tense moment hung between us as I waited for him to say he was kidding and back down, and he just kept on grinning like an idiot.

"You know I can kill you, right?"

"What's the matter?" he cajoled with the same sing-song tone as a nine-year-old egging on a playground fight. "Chicken?"

"You're on," I snapped. I didn't have to stress. The zombie would be up and trying to gnaw on our brains in minutes.

I glanced down at the unmoving corpse.

Come ooooon zombie. Move.

It didn't. Not for an hour after we finished securing our betting grounds. Every open space got covered up save one small spot on the front windows so that I could watch the street. If the crowd got too rowdy out there, I'd have to call off the bet. Every zombie shuffling past made me hold my breath. I didn't want to kiss Tommy.

Mostly because he wanted me to.

"Alright, I'm calling it," Tommy announced. He stood up from a overstuffed leather chair, adjusted his hat, and gave me a rakish grin. "Beautiful, you owe me a kiss."

Yeah, no.

"I told you, I don't know how long it'll take. Just wait," I answered through ground teeth, speaking each word carefully to make sure they all got through his thick skull. Tommy just shrugged.

"I've been patient. We've been sitting here pulling our poles for an hour. Daylight's wasting and I'm getting tired of stale muffins. It's time to move on."

"It'll get back up," I shot back. I didn't stand as he took a few steps forward. I didn't even twitch a muscle other than to watch his languid approach.

"He's not. Look, he's dead, alright? Everyone knows you bash in a zombie's skull, it's dead. Look, here," he stepped closer to the zombie and pointed at the mess that remained where half the rotter's face used to be. "This here? That's skull bits. It's dead."

"I know what I saw."

"For crying out loud. How long are we gonna have to sit here before you admit that you were wrong? A dead zombie is a dead zombie and this guy is de—aAARGH!"

Tommy nudged the corpse with the toe of his boot to prove his point. The second his foot connected with the body, the zombie wheezed out a moan and lifted a hand to catch the cowboy's ankle.

I lifted off the floor less than a second later, flying across the two feet between us to tackle Tommy to the ground. The undead creature latched a hand around my calf. We hit the ground and I twisted around to plant my free foot in his face. A snarling stream of curses poured out of my mouth as I pulled my foot back and kicked the zombie again and again, each time turning more of the monster's wrinkled face into hamburger. After the fifth kick, I caught a bit of luck. The zombie drew his head back, stunned or attempting to get his teeth around my boot. It didn't matter which. The second his chin came up, my boot slammed forward, snapping his head back with such force that his spine split halfway down his neck. The zombie loosened his grip and slumped to the ground.

Note to self; next time you want to win a bet, don't do it by locking yourself in a room with something you know will try to kill you.

"J—Jesus. That thing... he..." Tommy stuttered. One shaking hand rose and pointed at the remains of our experiment. I wiped my hands off on my stained pants and felt a little bit of smug enjoyment at his reaction.

"Yeah, he did. Just like I said he would," I reminded the stunned cowboy.

"How is that even possible? I killed it."

"I don't know. Hell, I don't know how any of this is possible." I threw a gesture out to the side, encompassing the zombie, the blood stains, and the world beyond.

"There's got to be... What was that?" The sharp bark of a gunshot rattled through the air. Tommy and I froze, waiting. When the gunshot came again, we both scurried over to the tiny patch of window I'd left available and pressed our faces to the glass.

On the street directly in front of us, three figures ran toward the end of the block. Two of them carried overflowing grocery bags over their shoulders, food dropping to the ground like breadcrumbs. The last, a man with greying hair and a trench coat, shot haphazardly behind him. Two more men came charging down the street after them, returning a few quick shots when the trench coat man paused to reload.

"Damn, that's not undead they're shooting at," I said during the interlude.

"That doesn't make sense."

I watched as the trench coat man took down one of his pursuers. He turned and ran after his two companions. The other pursuer stopped to check on his fallen partner. More figures began to shuffle into view, crawling out front doors or over fences. The pursuer hesitated a moment, his body jerking back and forth as he struggled with what to do. One of the undead let out a long, rattling moan, quickly picked up by the rest. The pursuer turned and fled, leaving his companion to the hungry corpses. The bleeding man on the ground struggled for a bit, but when the undead overwhelmed him, I turned away. I didn't want to watch what came next. I slumped down, out of sight of the window, and shrugged at Tommy. He still looked confused.

"People get desperate. If killing someone else means staying alive, you can bet they'll do it," I said. Then a thought hit me. "Besides, you were ready to kill that emo kid back at the store."

"No I wasn't. I was bluffing." Tommy cut a hand through the air, as if to clear it of the distraction. "I mean I checked that place just the other day. The store they came out of. It was empty."

"So... maybe you didn't check it well enough?" Things got missed when you were busy watching your own back.

"When I left, there wasn't so much as a bottle of acetaminophen left. They shouldn't have found anything, let alone a few bags worth."

"So, what're you trying to say here?"

"I'm saying... Come on." Tommy didn't give me a choice. He took me by the wrist and pulled me toward the back of the shop. Before I knew it, we were sneaking out the back way and edging our way toward the main street.

"Tommy, let it go. They were probably just taking a short cut," I hissed at my partner. He stood inches away from the open, unsheltered street. The small horde following the duellers still huddled over the dead man. I didn't trust our chances of going unspotted.

"Through the store? With people chasing them? I don't buy it."

"If you get us eaten because you decided that now's a good time to turn into a super sleuth, I swear to God I will haunt your ass forever."

"I'll be dead too. You can't haunt a corpse."

"Watch me."

We made it into the store with no time to lose. The zombies made short work of their meal, leaving nothing but bones and bloody tatters in the street. No sooner had we slipped through the door than I turned to block it off with anything large, solid, and liable to make a lot of noise if it fell over. I didn't trust the dead heads to be full. They never were.

Tommy went immediately for the aisles. I didn't see him for five minutes after finishing my blockade. When I did find him again, he sat in front of a pile of goods, sifting through it like an archaeologist sorting out bone from rock. From what I saw of his stash, he'd stumbled across the T-rex of last ditch hauls.

"I would've seen this." He offered me a bottle of antibiotics. In terms of survival value, that little bottle was worth as much as a mansion. Even a complete nitwit would not have passed up something that good.

Unless they were in a hurry.

I weighed the bottle in my hand and eyed the rest of his findings. In five minutes time, he found us a day's worth of supplies. He could've missed a store. Maybe overlooked it on his route. Yet a place this close to his apartment, this full of goodies?

On the other hand, taking Tommy at his word meant that someone had left this stuff here on purpose. Someone had provided enough stock to fill up three grocery bags and still leave us a decent pile. That could only mean one thing in my mind, and it was not a conclusion I wanted to admit.

Someone was restocking the town.

Someone wanted us to keep living down here.

"So you see it, huh? I'm not crazy?" Tommy pressed.

"I think we need to investigate more," I told him. I jerked my chin toward the door, already stuffing my pockets with what he'd found. "Take me to another store you hit recently."

God willing, it would be empty.

CHAPTER THIRTEEN

We hit three more stores that day, all of them restocked. The last store, the same general store in which I'd met Tommy, did me in. I knew from personal experience what had and hadn't been there before. The emo boy had cleared out the shelves.   The same shelves now stocked row upon row of goodies.

With no doubt left in my mind, I silenced Tommy's conspiracy theory babble and told him we had to make a plan. Redby's purpose reached beyond simply making us suffer for someone else's amusement. These zombies had a use. I'd been so focused on getting the hell out that I hadn't even considered why we were being kept in until the problem tried to eat my face.

On the upside, if someone could get in with supplies, that meant there was also a way out.

We decided on a stakeout. Well, I decided on a stakeout. Tommy opted for blowing up buildings until our mystery delivery man showed himself, but there were issues with that plan. We needed those buildings, and the supplies they held, and we lacked a large number of explosives. Tommy said he could make them. I insisted on stakeout.

We chose a spot not far from a grocery store that had been stocked up and emptied the day before. We had no idea when the next stock up would come, but we'd be ready for it.

A week went by while we watched from the bedroom of a house overlooking the store's backdoor. We split our time into shifts. I took the nights and Tommy took the days. He'd go out hunting for supplies while I watched, and I'd clear the streets so our front door remained unmolested while he watched. We had a good system, but by the end of the second week, I started to think that letting Tommy build explosives might be a better idea.

I had just settled in for my watch that evening when Tommy came back early. I heard him slipping in through an upstairs window in the master bedroom. We'd booby-trapped everything on the main floor and most of the second-storey windows. The master bedroom, accessible by a tree outside the window, and a bedroom that used to belong to a kid with a spaceship obsession, were the sole access points left untrapped. If he'd come in any other way, I would've heard screaming instead of his muted footsteps.

"Brought you something," the cowboy whispered as he tiptoed into the room. A small, black backpack slipped from his shoulder and thumped to the ground. He unzipped the bag and dug around inside, upsetting an empty chip bag. After pulling out the offending crinkly wrapper, he reached a hand in a second time and pulled out a pair of thick, black goggles.

"Happy birthday."

"Night vision goggles," I said with a hint of approval.

"Yeah, gen four. That's about as good as you can get," Tommy said with a big grin on his face. He looked like a kid who'd just won first prize when I gave him a compliment. Especially when it came to his tech. Tommy loved his electronics.

"How'd you know it was my birthday?" I fitted the goggles to my face. The world outside turned green and sharp. I could see every detail of the backyard, the action figures left forgotten on the grass, the fence surrounding it, and the dents on the back door of our grocery store. Broad daylight could not reveal as much detail as these goggles.

"Uh... I didn't."

Well, crap. I tried to play it off with a casual shrug.

"Not a big deal. Never been much of one for celebrations." I drew in a breath and changed the topic before he could answer, "Thought you'd gone back to base to rest."

"Sweetheart, you gotta stop calling it that. Call it my castle or the apartment, or even home. Base makes it sound like we've gone to war."

"We have and I'm not calling it home," I countered. Despite my firm stance, I smirked and flicked a glance down at my companion. We'd gotten a little closer since we'd started the stakeout.

Not that kind of close.

… Alright, maybe a little of that kind of close.

"Figured I'd rest here. If you don't mind, that is."

"Scared of sleeping alone again?" I teased.

"Only if you're offering to make use of that bed." He peered at me with one questioning brow raised to his hairline. I shook my head and turned my attention back to the general store.

"Don't snore."

"Never do."

Liar. He always snored.

I had two minutes of peace before he spoke up again.

"Truck's almost empty."

"Nothing at the pumps?" I gave the conversation a mere fraction of my attention. The goggles allowed me to zoom in and focus, meaning that even the insects scuttling across the grass were visible. I was a neon-green hawk and the delivery man was my intended prey.

"Can't get at it. All the old ones have been sucked dry."

"Jesus. Those things can hold lakes worth of gas," I muttered under my breath.

"People are stocking it up. Or driving around. Saw a guy earlier today try to take an eighteen-wheeler through the front gate."

"Did he make it?"

"Nope, but he made a pretty awesome fireball."

I bet he did. I bet he'd thought a truck like that could easily punch a hole through a solid steel gate. Or else he'd just wanted to make sure he left nothing behind to bring back.

I bet they hadn't even bothered shooting at him.

"Better if we don't have it anyway. Too loud. Draws too much attention."

Tommy didn't respond right away. That bothered me. He should've seen the risk we were taking with the truck. He wasn't stupid. Hell, he'd survived much better in those first few days than I had. The truck would have to go sooner or later if we wanted to stay alive.

"It was my dad's."

Well, crap.

I pulled my attention away from the backyard for a second to glance down at him. The goggles migrated to the top of my head.

His position hadn't changed, stretched out on the floor with the cowboy hat drooping over his face. Moonlight filtering in through the open window picked out the blues of his shirt and pants and gave his face a silvery sheen. The long shadows of the night traced along his nose and filled in the edge of his mouth where it turned down. Beneath the shelter of his hat, I knew his eyes would be cold and hard. Anything to help disguise the pain.

I decided to ignore his comment and let the silence settle over us again, hoping the conversation would end there. Thinking about what we'd lost and who we'd left behind happened daily. It got old pretty fast.

"Cass, who did you lose on Day Zero?" Tommy asked after a minute. I bit back a sigh.

"Why do you ask?"

"I told you about my folks. Hell, I've told you a lot about me. All I know about you is that you still got that military stick up your ass and you're not from around here. Oh, and it's your birthday."

I chewed on the inside of my lip and considered my answer. This was the part where I should have told him to mind his own business. Unfortunately, that whole bonding thing we'd been doing had the annoying side effect of making me want to open up.

"I came in with my company. They're stationed up on the wall," I said in a short, terse tone. I tried to hold onto it, but the memories refused to let go. "I lost my best friends. One died because I was too slow and one… I shot one."

My stomach coiled into knots. I hadn't acknowledged Ace's death out loud before. The words, the admission, made all the guilt come rushing back to suffocate me.

"Remember how I said my parents died in the explosion?" Tommy asked.

How could I forget? The half destroyed Almesa building was like a bone shard in my brain, always jutting up through every thought I had. Tommy kept talking, not waiting for my answer.

"I lied. I saw them walk out.—Shamble out. They were undead.—Came out of the building right before it blew. So I shot them. With my dad's own shotgun."

Jesus, what a pair we made. Tommy with the shotgun that killed his parents. Me with the pistol that killed Ace. The guilt I felt over the death of my friends wasn't just my own then. I knew, somewhere in the far recesses of my mind, that other people had lost loved ones in this town too. Which got hard to remember when they were the ones shooting you for the food you just stole. Tommy was different though. He was real and right beside me. He lost his parents and...

And I could do nothing about it. Even condolences seemed useless. Saying I'm sorry wouldn't make Tommy feel any better about what he did, and the words sure as hell wouldn't bring his parents back. At least his kills were to save his own life. I shot Ace by accident.

Whoops. Sorry you're dead, buddy. My finger slipped.

Yeah, that was useful.

"You did what—"

"Don't," Tommy interrupted. "Don't tell me I did what I had to."

That caught me off guard. Just for a second.

"Well then what the hell do you want me to say? Sorry?"

"No," Tommy muttered, "I don't know. I just needed to say it, I think."

I let it go. What else could I do? This was not a subject I wanted to talk about and—

Movement.

There, at the back of the store. A man hid in the shadows. He crept along close to the ground, which had rendered him almost invisible until he'd been right under my nose. A shoulder bag pressed against his back, bulging with mysterious goodies.

"Got him," I whispered to my partner.

Tommy rose to my side in a flash, pressing his face to the glass like a child at an aquarium.

"Where?"

"Back of the store. Come on."

We hit the ground a few minutes later. The mystery man had disappeared into the store seconds earlier, giving us just enough time to clear the backyard and get over the fence.

"Alright, here's the plan," I whispered as we stood outside the store. "When he comes out, I'm going to punch him. You grab him, then we bring him back to base."

"For the last time, it's not the base."

"Just shut up and get in position," I hissed. Tommy obliged, but not without an eye roll that could be seen from space.

We didn't have to wait long. Every little movement in the store came to me through the sliver of an opening left in the door. No night noises disturbed us. My nightly clean ups made sure of that. I tensed when the shuffling within the store grew louder.

The door gave a low groan and slid open a few inches. A head emerged, black as the shadows around it, and I didn't hesitate. My fist snapped out and connected with what should have been the soft tissue of his nose.

My fist cracked. The delivery man's mask did not.

The masked man reeled, but not as much as he should have from one of my punches. Instead, he was only dazed when Tommy appeared from around the other side of the door and tried to lock his arms around his chest.

Delivery Ninja moved with stunning speed. He slipped out of Tommy's grasp like a greased eel and knocked him to the ground with one well-placed kick. I was still recovering from the aftershocks of punching a brick wall when he took off down the street.

"Son of a bitch!" I didn't wait for Tommy to get back on his feet. I took off after our target, tearing through the dark alley.

His shadow darted left and right, then disappeared into a hole in the ground. A sewer. Fantastic. I did not want to be revisiting that nightmare.

The old man's face flashed before my eyes, contorted in fear as something dragged him into the darkness, and then I threw myself down the ladder after Delivery Ninja.

Many heroes in many types of fiction and non-fiction have claimed to be fearless in the face of danger. All of these people are either stupid or liars.

Fear is an ally. Fear tells you that you are alive and you want to stay that way. It warns you when something threatens your longevity and encourages you to either fight or flee. Fear is an extremely useful tool. As I descended further and further into the cool darkness of the sewer, I felt terrified.

Darkness engulfed me. Even looking up only gave me a faint glimpse of the moon before it disappeared behind a cloud. Water sloshed below my feet, babbling and rippling against unseen edges. The closer I got to the bottom, the more active it sounded. I remembered the goggles, now dangling around my neck, and slid them up over my eyes. A second later, I wished I hadn't.

I wasn't alone in the sewer. All around my feet were the bloated, rotting corpses of the undead. They filled the water and pushed up against thick steel grates separating the sewer tunnel into segments. Every one of them in my section was down for the count, but there were plenty more in the other sections that heard my movement and clamoured at the bars to get at my tasty flesh.

I put my back to the wall, wanting to place myself as far from the corpses as possible. A handle dug into my kidney. A door. That explained where Delivery Ninja had disappeared to. I slipped through the door and shut it behind me. One close encounter with the dead rising while I stood around unprepared was enough. I needed all my focus on what lay ahead, and not what crept up behind me.

The door opened onto a tunnel, thick with the stench of mildew and the sweet odour of rot. Steel pipes and heavy wires stretched along the walls like overgrown vines. Small, fragile lightbulbs dangled overhead, fruit hanging off the vine, overripe and long forgotten. A thin pool of water covered the ground, hiding any footsteps left by my target.

Couldn't hide the sound though. The unmistakable splish-splash of running footsteps echoed from an adjoining tunnel. I took off after him. Every question I wanted answered, everything I needed to know about this place and why I had been left behind, was in the head of that delivery man. If I let him get away now, there was no telling when I'd get another opportunity like this.

I caught up to him in a matter of minutes. Guess he hadn't been listening for my footsteps while I'd been chasing his. He stood stock still in the middle of an intersection when I found him, poise relaxed and arm raised toward me in a fencing position. A small, black device the size and shape of a generic stun gun pointed toward the middle of my chest.

My mind screamed a warning and my body twisted instinctively to the side. Not fast enough though.

I charged full tilt at the man in the black suit. The next second, a crackling blue light filled the tunnel and I flew backwards, slamming into the wall behind me with enough force to knock the wind out of my lungs. I lay gasping on the floor a few seconds later, wondering why stars popped in front of my eyes.

"You're lucky this tunnel is as long as it is. A few feet shorter and that impact would have turned your insides into jelly," the delivery man said in a perfect English accent.

I gasped for air. I wanted a quick retort. My lungs weren't rebooting fast enough. The delivery man loomed over me.

"I'll be taking that gun now, thank you—"

My turn to interrupt. My foot swept out, connecting with his ankles. The slick ground came to my aid and threw his weight off balance. Soon he was the one on the ground, and I stood over him with my gun trained on a spot just between his large, glossy black goggles.

"You're lucky I need you alive. Otherwise you'd be dead."

Whoa, that took more breath than I thought it would. I sucked in a few more lungfuls to make sure I didn't fall over.

"Oh, very nice. Why, I might just die from the cut of your razor wit."

Jerk.

"Shut up. I've got questions for you."

"Well, which is it? Am I to remain a silent prisoner or answer your questions?"

I—Goddammit! I hated smartass prisoners.

"Just tell me what I want to know," I snapped at him. I should've been more specific. The list he rattled off a moment later left me as lightheaded as getting body-slammed against the wall.

"Fine. Yes, Almesa arranged this town's incarceration on purpose. No, I don't know why. Yes, I work for them. No, that does not mean I am privy to all the details of their grand plan. Yes, your American government is involved in some way, though I have no idea why or how. Those soldiers they sent are not the most talkative of co-workers."

Okay, that was... uh... informative. He'd answered questions I hadn't even thought of yet. All of which boiled down to three disturbing facts; government involvement, my company cooperating with these Almesa jerkwads, and one hell of a cover up conspiracy. Exactly the sort of information I'd been after. Except now that I had it, I didn't know if I wanted it. The days to come looked bleak. I still had one hope though.

"What about the captain? What's he say?" I demanded.

"Which captain?"

"I could always kill you and look for one of your buddies. I don't doubt there's more like you. Stop being stupid and answer the question. Captain Stone. What's he saying?"

"How do you—" The delivery man tilted his head to the side. I couldn't see his face, but it wasn't hard to imagine the lightbulb going off beneath his mask. "...Oh. Oh, I see. You're one of them. How did you get stuck down here?"

"That's what you're supposed to tell me."

"Well, I'm afraid you're barking up the wrong tree, as it were. We were told to limit our interactions with your company and, like the good little employee that I am, I've been doing just that. They're not exactly my kind of people anyway."

Not the answer I wanted. I needed to know what Captain Stone was up to. How he planned on getting us out of this.

"Why the hell are you here? What's all this about?"

"As I said, I don't know. They pay me to do a job and I do it. Menacing me with that gun is not going to make the answers magically appear in my mind."

I was getting frustrated.

To hell with that. I got frustrated. I had been frustrated since the walls locked up. I'd lost everything important to me and replaced it all with a man who confused the hell out of me every time I looked into his steely eyes, zombies, and this damned English dandy who possessed the answers I needed, but refused to give them up.Hell, I wanted to kill him just for that pompous accent of his.

Yeah, I could kill him. No one would care. But first, I'd get my goddamn answers out of him.

Just as a side note, justifying murder is all well and good, but it should not be done when facing down an opponent who has already proven to be fast and capable.

I hit the ground. At some point between me holding the gun on Delivery Ninja and landing flat on my back, my opponent managed to knock the gun out of my hand and kick my feet out from under me. I rolled toward my weapon, fingers out-stretched. His foot came down on my wrist. My legs whipped around and caught him below the knee as he bent to retrieve my weapon. I brought him to the ground with me and sent the gun skittering out of reach.

We rolled across the floor, each of us trying to gain the upper hand. I knew I was damn good at hand-to-hand, but so was he.

Everything came to a screeching halt when his fingers closed around the butt of the gun. I made one last, desperate grab for my weapon. Then I found myself sitting perfectly still while he pointed the muzzle of my own weapon between my eyes and a single thought screamed through my mind; Basil. All English pricks needed a properly English name, and that one suited him according to my mind. Why my psyche deemed this to be the most important information at the time, I have no idea. Coherent thought patterns were never my strong suit.

"Ah-ah. That's enough play time for today," Basil huffed. He rose to his feet and took a few steps back, out of my reach. Damn. I should have done that. "Now then, I am on a schedule and this little distraction has already taken up far too much of my time. I am going to tell you something very important, and then I am going to walk away. You will not follow me. You will go back to your fried-bean-swilling friend and we will never see each other again. Are we clear?"

I nodded, because when someone has a gun kissing your forehead, there's not much else you can do.

"Good," Basil chirped. "On to business then. I am a gambler. Or rather, I should say I am a winner. Gambling implies a risk of loss and I don't lose. Recently, I took a bet on how long it would take for the survivors, meaning you and all the little ants hiding in their homes upstairs, to start phase two. It can only be started from the inside, you see. I have one day left on my selection and since you seemed so determined to catch me, I thought I'd take the opportunity to better my chances."

"Bets," I snarled. I couldn't help myself. My blood boiled. "You take bets on us? Is this just some kind of sick game to you? You think it's funny watching us die down here?"

Basil answered with an exaggerated sigh.

"Oh, stop being so overdramatic. You would have done the same thing if you hadn't gotten yourself stuck down here."

"The hell I would!"

Basil cut my rage short by pressing the cold metal of the gun against my skin.

"That is enough," he said in a firm tone. "Time is short, as I mentioned. I don't care for your sense of justice unfulfilled. Justice doesn't belong in our society anyway. All I need from you is to go to seventy-five Gilford Street and retrieve the package there."

"Why the hell would I want to do anything you asked?"

"Because it will benefit you as well. There is an end to this misery. A final solution. That is what waits at seventy-five Gilford Street. Do I need to write the address down?" Basil leaned in close, the smoky black glass of his eyes reflecting the light.

Light that shouldn't have been there.

"Down!"

I flattened myself to the muddy ground, hands clasped over my ears just before the boom. A few seconds later, a hand gripped my shoulder. I followed my first instinct and lashed out with a punch, wanting to get myself some distance. The flashlight shone on Tommy's face, stopping my wild blow a few inches short of his nose.

"Cass! *Cass!*" he shouted, waving his arms to get my attention.

"*What?*" I shouted back. White noise filled the world. Shotgun blast in an enclosed space will do that.

"He's dead!" Tommy pointed at a black lump on the ground that had once been Basil.

I stood up, prying the goggles off my face along the way. A ringing filled my ears, and I wasn't sure it was all due to the effects of the gun.

"You killed him."

"I just saved your ass and all you can say is 'you killed him'?" Tommy gave me a disgusted look.

"You killed him! He wasn't a zombie. He was a living person! And I had it under control anyway."

"Right. That's why he had your gun."

"That was a strategic move. I was cleaning his clock until you showed up," I countered. I shuffled over to the corpse and retrieved my weapon, plus that little doohickey he'd shot me with earlier. I had no idea when I'd have use for something that could paste people to walls, but it seemed like a handy weapon to have around.

"Well I just cleaned it better," Tommy retorted.

"No, you didn't. You smashed it to little bits. We needed that clock in one piece." I crouched down beside Basil and nudged his shoulder. Didn't look like he'd be collecting on his bet now. Nor would he be explaining what he meant when he said there was an end to this misery. Goddamn timing.

"Well, you could always…uh…" Tommy faltered, the abused metaphor falling apart mid-sentence. He propped the shotgun on his shoulder and scratched at the back of his head. I used the quiet time to finish cleaning out Basil's pockets.

Empty for the most part. Whatever he brought with him he'd left behind in the store as far I could figure. Other than his fancy energy weapon, the only thing I found on him was a smartphone and a key card.

"So, what was he yammering about before I... yanno..." Tommy gestured at the former delivery man with his flashlight.

"Before you splattered his insides all over the ground?"

Tommy scowled, then nodded sheepishly.

I shrugged. "Something about a final solution. Said it was at seventy-five Gilford Street."

"Gilford, huh? That's not surprising."

"Why's that?"

"Almesa has one of their facilities on that street. Bet you anything that's where they made the virus."

I waited. So did Tommy. I didn't want to give in, but I would've had better luck staring down a wall than out-stubborning Tommy.

"Because that's the way it works in the movies?"

"Because that's the way it works in the movies." Tommy smiled from ear to ear.

"You know, there's a lot of shit they make up in movies."

"Lies," Tommy protested. I waved off the rest of that topic as a lost cause.

"Hey, if you're so sure these places had some kind of information we could use, why didn't we hit them up earlier?"

"Bit of a distance. We'd have to take the truck. Besides, it's outside of our neighbourhood."

Our neighbourhood. It still felt weird to call it that, but at the same time, I knew exactly where our borders ended and what counted as our turf versus the next gang's turf.

Day Zero introduced the zombie problem. Day One introduced the gang problem. I'd teased Tommy about being more paranoid than me with his excessive traps and alarms at first. As the survivors started banding together and launching planned raids on restocked buildings and other groups, I started to understand. The zombies didn't worry him the most. The people did.

"Let's hit it up now."

"What, like, right now? I thought the whole point of tonight was to figure out a way out of here," Tommy said.

I swept a hand toward the remains of Basil. His blood mingled with the pools of stagnant water littering the floor, steadily expanding a bubble of murk around him that claimed more and more of the narrow hallway.

"There's our guide, Tommy. You want us to get some bread crumbs instead? Maybe some string? Hey, if we just stick to the left wall, I'm sure we'll be through this maze in a decade or two."

Tommy scowled down at Basil, then in the direction he'd been running. He took two steps forward, stopped, and turned to face me.

"Tunnel splits into three directions ahead."

"Yeah," I said.

"He... uh... he didn't happen to mention which way to go, did he?"

Tommy stared at me, and I stared right back.

"So, seventy-five Gilford then?"

I turned around and started walking. At least I knew the way back to the surface.

CHAPTER FOURTEEN

OAK RIDGE MENTAL HOSPITAL, TEXAS
August 23, 2032

I knew it would be a bad day when I woke up to find Ace sitting on the end of my bed.

The nightmares kept me up half the night. Mostly memories mashed together turned ten times worse by my own sick imagination. I got to watch my friends die over and over again, always failing to save them. Now Ace sat on the end of my bed, grinning at me, reminding me that those images were more than just nightmares. I rolled onto my side and pulled the pillow over my head.

"Cassandra," he cajoled.

Nope, not listening.

"Cassie, Cassie-coo."

Goddammit, Ace.

"Cass, I'm in your head. You can't block me out."

I tried anyway. I squeezed my eyes shut and pressed the pillow against my ears until my skull ached. I thought of numbers and flowers and happy memories. All the things Doc told me to use when the voices grew too loud. The flowers and happy memories made sense. They calmed me down. I think the numbers were just to confuse me and get me focused on something other than my personal ghosts.

Ace slammed into my consciousness. His rotting lips peeled back in a snarl and his voice roared through my body like a freight train. "*Wake up!*"

I jerked upright, slamming my head against the back wall. Ace cackled.

"That's it. I'm telling the doc to change my meds," I growled at the chortling spectre. The sound of his laugh rebounded through my thoughts, aggravating the headache threatening to break out of my subconscious. The knock on the skull dislodged it from the back of my head and sent it spiralling straight to the front, where it throbbed with a vengeance.

I only had a second or two to nurse it before my door opened and a large, portly man in blue scrubs pushed a cart into my room. Glowering, he put together my daily pills and handed them to me with a glass of water.

I knew this one. His name was Joey Masters. He did not like me.

Joey worked with people like us so he could throw his weight around, knock us into place when we got out of line, and get to feel superior. I suspect he'd tried to be a guard at one point, but hadn't been able to stomach the physical exercise involved.

Tommy materialized out of thin air as I obediently downed my pills. He strolled around Joey, sizing him up like a customer at a butcher shop. A feral grin tugged at one corner of his mouth, lifting his lip to reveal the barest hint of teeth. Tommy was on the prowl and Joey was his target. The orderly would feel nothing, but I'd have a front row seat for just how messed up my mind could get.

These days were the worst. I called them ghost days. No matter how many pills I took, I couldn't block out the voices.

Tommy stepped within two inches of the surly man and my chest tightened. He couldn't talk, punch, breathe, or otherwise interact with the real world. He existed in my head alone, and yet my instincts screamed at me to get between them, protect the survivor, kill the crazy ghost.

"What?" Joey snarled. My eyes snapped up to his face, reading the suspicion there. It must've looked like I was staring at him the entire time.

"I don't even get a hello, Joey? It's been a while since we've seen each other." The snark came out of nowhere. Yeah, I knew the guy didn't like me, but I didn't want to start a fight.

"Shut up and finish your pills."

I did, and then I opened my mouth like a good little crazy person so he could make sure I swallowed them all. He grabbed my jaw in a vice grip, squeezing hard enough to make my teeth hurt. I resisted the urge to break his wrist while he jammed a wooden stick down my throat to check if I had fooled him. I had to remind myself that I didn't want a fight.

"You know, normally my days start with a nice chat. Shouldn't break the routine, Joey. It's bad for my mental state," I said when my jaw came under my own control again.

My jaw, but not my head. Ace slid around the outskirts of my thoughts, poking and prodding my headache. His slimy touch infused everything I heard, felt, and smelled. It infuriated me that I couldn't block him out. Whenever he was around, whenever the pills stopped working, he made sure I became constantly, painfully aware of his presence.

"I'm not here to be your friend."

Of course not. No one wanted to be my friend. Everyone else just pretended they could be though. Figured it would make us more compliant. Joey was unique in his honesty. He handed out pills, cleaned up messes, and hated his life. Joey in a nutshell. It made him both the easiest person to deal with and the hardest. Whenever he came near me, I wanted to fly off the handle. I wanted to push him, just to see how long it took for him to start pushing back. And then I'd break him just like I'd broken the guy at the bar.

"What a loser." Ace laughed. He hopped off the bed and joined Tommy's prowl around Joey. Tommy went clockwise and Ace went counter-clockwise, walking through the cart whenever they came to it. Together, they circled Joey, their eyes locked on the orderly, glinting with a feral hunger that made me uneasy. They wanted to tear him apart, which meant I wanted to tear him apart on some level. My battle for self-control took a nose dive.

I am the master of my own thoughts.

"No you're not, Cass. So whaddya think? Should I peel his face off?" Tommy grinned from ear to ear. Joey would feel nothing. I would see everything.

"Stop staring or I will put you down," Joey growled.

"I bet you'd love that, wouldn't you, Joey? Tangle with the dangerous Red. You could go home and tell all your buddies that we're not that tough after all. Assuming you lived that long."

The words tumbled out of my mouth before I could stop them. I examined them and found I didn't care. Joey was a cocky son of a bitch anyway. I should take him down.

"Do it," Ace hissed. He stepped behind Joey and reappeared on the other side while Tommy passed in the opposite direction. Both of them fixed their fever bright eyes on me.

"Come on, Cass. Have some fun," Tommy added.

Joey drew the little black rectangle from his pocket and removed the cap. The needle glinted in the room's fluorescent light. Held in Joey's hands, the familiar tool looked menacing. Joey grabbed my arm and twisted it straight out from my body. He jabbed the needle into my forearm and, when his eyes moved from my face to the light up display, my brain went in to overdrive.

One jab to the throat to silence him. Another to the chest. Break his solar plexus. Kick to the groin to bring him down, then another shot at his throat. Collapse his wind pipe. Three seconds and I could kill this man. Tommy and Ace hissed encouragement in my ears, their words trickling down my spine like a hot shower. I tensed, ready to strike.

BigMac materialized out of the wall behind the orderly. He didn't say a word. He never had to. The consequences of my actions shone in his eyes. Go ahead and take another life, they said. Kill the hope of another family. The fight drained out of me in an instant and I dropped my gaze.

Joey looked up and seemed to inflate with self-worth. He yanked the needle out of my arm, leaving behind a small trail of blood, and smiled as if he'd won a victory.

"You're clean. Today at least."

I remained silent. To do otherwise would invite Joey to do something drastic. I didn't need to touch him to end up in solitary. My reputation was damning enough that one word from Joey would convince everyone I'd lost it again.

Joey swaggered out of the room. A few seconds later, I followed.

BigMac waited for me in the hall. He stared, empty of expression, and made me feel like the worst monster that ever walked the Earth. I looked at the floor to avoid meeting his gaze and started down the hall for the cafeteria.

"You've gone soft," Ace whined in my ear. He appeared by my left elbow, Tommy by my right. The headache stayed right in the middle of my forehead. Yeah, today would be a very bad day.

Not soft. I'm trying to get better.

"By getting soft," Ace said.

Goddammit, I am not getting soft.

"Oh yeah? They why didn't you break that guy into little pieces? You know you could," Tommy insisted.

Because breaking people is bad for my recovery.

"Right, your recovery. How's that going, Cassie? Forgiven yourself for murdering us yet?"

Shut up, Ace.

"Ooooh, that's not very nice. Doesn't sound like your anger management is going very well," Ace continued.

"Why, that sounded downright hostile. I think you owe Ace here an apology," Tommy added.

God, save me from wise cracking spirits.

"There is no God, Cass. Remember? He abandoned you in Redby. Or you abandoned Him. Which is it you tell yourself again?" Ace grinned at me.

I abandoned God.

He'd been my salvation once. He'd kept me alive when everything around me wanted me dead. He carried me into Redby, but I didn't carry Him out. I buried Him there, along with my self-respect, restraint, and sanity.

I entered the cafeteria hoping to find Zeke waiting for me. He would be a much better conversationalist than my two invisible shadows. BigMac stood in the corner. People shuffled through the food line. No Zeke.

Breakfast. Cold cereal and orange juice. Harry the former clairvoyant stopped by to predict my doom. Again.

After breakfast came the rec room. Still no Zeke. Tommy and Ace continued to pester me. I sat by the window and wrote. Or tried to. Every time I figured out where I needed to start, Ace or Tommy would do something to distract me.

Outside time. Zeke still didn't show. I started to get annoyed. The one day I wanted to see his stupid face and he didn't show. I suspected this was another one of his games. Then I remembered that he was not psychic, despite his spooky routine, and couldn't know I wanted to see him. Unless he'd been following me the entire day and watching how I looked around for him. I checked over my shoulder but unless he'd shrunk to the size of a dead rose bush, he couldn't be hiding behind me.

I wrote some more. Ace prattled on about how I skipped all the good, gory bits. Tommy agreed. BigMac stared at me.

Time to go inside again. Time for another one of my appointments with the doctor.

By the time I got to his office, my headache had suffered a nuclear meltdown. My skull wanted to tear itself apart and my eyes had transformed into little stinging balls of nettle. I felt grumpy, in pain, and tired of dealing with my tag-alongs. I just wanted the day to end.

I stomped into Doc's office and threw myself into the overstuffed, over priced chair he reserved for his patients. He stopped scratching away at his note pad instantly, which he never did. The doc did not stop mid-thought for anything.

"Cassandra, what's wrong?" he asked in a voice that oozed with false concern. I wanted to slap him hard enough to snap his fake gold glasses in half and tell him to stop pretending he cared about my health. He was just in this to get paid.

"I need you to change my meds." Changing my medication had helped with all the other ghost days. The doc recognized them by now, so I wasn't surprised when he made an understanding noise in the back of his throat and switched to a new notepad.

"Tell me how bad it is."

For fuck's sake, just give me the new meds. It's bad enough that I need to ask for them. You don't need to know that Tommy is studying your book collection right now.

"Maybe he does, Cass. Maybe that's a crucial bit of information. Tommy studying the books. Could be your mind telling you that you've got a deep, unacknowledged fear of learning," Ace said. He mimicked the

122

doc's fake concern, which only irritated me further.

"Oh! Or maybe I'm representing some new problem like..." Tommy paused and looked up at the book shelf. He pointed triumphantly at a little red volume on the second row. The title had something to do with memory. "You can't remember why you need the pills!"

Of course I remember. I—Christ, why am I talking to you two idiots?

"It's bad," I snapped.

The doc put down his pen and gave me a severe look over the top of his glasses. "Cassandra, I am trying to help you. Adjusting your medication is a delicate process and I need to know exactly what has happened in order to make the right changes. Now, are you seeing them or just hearing them? And for how long now?"

"Forever and ever, Amen!" Both of my spectres broke down in riotous laughter.

"Both," I answered.

The doc gave me another patronizing look over top of his rims. He kept his voice calm and patient, but a hint of force ran beneath it. "And for how long?"

"Be honest, Cass. We never went away. You just tried to forget we were around," Ace whispered.

"Shut up," I hissed. I could barely hear the doc over their stupid prattle.

"Excuse me?" Doc Brown stared, steely eyed, at my face. My stomach dropped out of my body.

Oh shit. I'd said that out loud.

"A day," I blurted, hoping to redirect him. I don't know if it worked or not because he just nodded, stared at me a little longer, then wrote something down on his note pad.

"How many are there?" the doc continued. He wasn't looking at me anymore, but I could still feel his attention boring into my head. Right into the headache, forcing it to swell.

"Two," I said. BigMac appeared out of nowhere. One minute the space behind the doc's chair held nothing but his impressive book colleciton, and the next he stood there, staring at me, blood pouring out of his neck.

I squeezed my eyes shut and rubbed a hand over them as I corrected myself. "Three."

"And are they in the room right now?"

Jesus, of course they were. I wouldn't have corrected myself otherwise. Use your head, you bloody idiot.

"Look, Doc, I'm not feeling well. Can we reschedule this for later?"

I played to his sympathy. He always acted like he gave a damn about me. Now he could show if he meant it or not.

"I know this is hard, Cassandra, but you have to try working with me. Believe it or not, this is progress. I know what you're going through."

No, you don't. You don't have a fucking clue what it's like. How could you possibly know what it means to see everyone you ever cared about die every night? Over and over again? How could you possibly know how it feels to know that the only way you can make that tight feeling in your chest go away is to tear into someone? How could you possibly know that sometimes, when I wasn't careful, when the days got bad enough, I caught myself missing the taste of flesh.

I ground my teeth together and struggled to put my head back in one piece. Tommy sat on the arm of the chair beside me and warbled out a few lines to an old cowboy tune.

Progress. Doc said I had made progress. This was bloody torture, but if it led to days without voices whispering in my ear, I could grit my teeth and get through it. Hell, I'd lived through worse. Just because this pain was mental and not physical didn't mean I could give up.

"That's right, Cass. Never give up the fight. Even if you have to leave good people behind." Ace stood beside BigMac now, his face as blank as his buddy's. Then a little smile quirked the corner of his mouth. He just wanted to push me over the edge.

I took a deep breath and stared at them; my ghosts, my regrets. I didn't care how it got done. I just wanted them to go away.

"Are you ready to talk now, Cassandra?" Doc Brown asked.

I nodded. My headache split my skull right down the centre, spots danced before my eyes, and Tommy and Ace played havoc with my emotions, but I would not give up. Fuck 'em. If it killed me, I would get past this.

"Well then let's start with your journal progress. Perhaps that has something to do with how you're feeling today."

Sure. Yeah. Let's dive right into the thick of things. That's how I like to deal with problems. Head butt it at full speed and hope you still have a head after you're done.

I started talking, because not talking was not an option. I told him everything, and I did it all while staring into Tommy's bright blue eyes, knowing he hated me for it.

CHAPTER FIFTEEN

We ditched the truck a few blocks back when it started attracting too much attention. Gilford Street lacked for action, but inviting it in with a big, noisy truck seemed like a stupid idea. Also, making our way on foot meant Tommy couldn't talk my ear off for fear of attracting even more attention.

Hah. Sucker.

"Seventy-five Gilford Street. Here we are," Tommy announced.

We stopped on a corner bordering the hospital and looked across the street to a large, red brick building. Dark windows and a locked door prevented us from getting a glimpse beyond the stocky exterior. If you ignored the lifeless corpses on the lawn, it looked almost like the place had shut down for the night. Tomorrow, the lights would come on and people would go back to work. The ones that hadn't jumped to their deaths out the windows anyway.

No sign marked it as a super secret research facility, or a lab, or even a faculty building. Nothing special. It was just seventy-five Gilford Street.

"So, what's the plan?" Tommy asked.

"Plan?" I hadn't thought we'd need a plan beyond find building, raid building, get final solution, win at life.

"Yeah. I mean like, how're we gonna find this thing? You know what you're looking for?"

Uh... good question.

"Kinda," I said with a shrug.

"What's 'kinda'? Your buddy did give you a general description of it, right?"

"I didn't have much time to grill him. I got what I could. At least we know what building it's in."

"Well what the hell good does that do us? There's six floors there. It could be on any one of them. You gotta at least know what this final solution of yours looks like." I swear to God, the man loved the sound of his own voice. He never shut up.

"No, Tommy. No, I don't. I've given you all the information I got. Final solution, seventy-five Gilford Street, that's it. I would've loved to ask him more, but you went ahead and shot him."

Tommy drew back, a look of shock on his face. Those damn eyes of his made me feel like I'd just smacked him across the nose and told him he couldn't have dessert. A knee-jerk apology rose in my throat and caught there when his face transformed into a petulant pout.

"At least I didn't lose my gun."

Tommy strolled past me and entered the lightless building. I looked skyward, begged God for the patience to get through the night, and followed after him.

The moon served as a light source on the street. With no electricity in the town, nothing dimmed the cloudless night sky. The bright and numerous stars turned the horizon silver while the moon served as a flashlight for the whole neighbourhood. The moment we walked through the door, the moon, stars, and all their glorious light vanished. I lifted the goggles and settled them over my eyes. Green light flooded the empty hall and washed away my unease.

"Hey... uh... I'm blind over here. Toss me those goggles," Tommy called from a few feet ahead. I bathed in the warm glow of smugness for a few seconds before strolling up beside him.

"Nope. My birthday, my rules."

Tommy cursed under his breath and dug into the pack slung over his shoulder. My vision lit up with searing, pale green light as blinding as the darkness. Then I clapped my hand over the flashlight and yanked it out of his grasp.

"Hey!"

"No flashlights. Not here. Flashlights are like dinner bells for the undead."

"And me stumbling around blind won't get their attention?"

"Just hold on to me. I'll guide you through. Keep your shotgun up and shoot only when I tell you to. And where I tell you to. Goddammit, Tommy, if you shoot me, I will bite your face off. We'll start with the rooms facing west so that we'll have some moonlight for the search. Ready?"

"Yeah. I guess."

I understood his hesitation. Being blind in an unknown building in an unknown part of town didn't sound like a fun prospect. We had no idea where the rotters could be hiding. My eyes could see any attack coming our way, but one moment of inattention would turn Tommy into some zombie's meal.

I slid the flashlight back into the pack and settled Tommy's hand on my shoulder. He clutched the shotgun to his chest with his free hand, muttering to himself and rubbing his thumb against the stock like the weapon offered holy protection. His comments had a very different connotation. In fact, I heard my name uttered a few times along with some unkind birthday wishes. I ignored it for the most part, except when I failed to warn Tommy about a low hanging sign on purpose. He cursed me a lot more after that.

Someone on high must've had a soft spot for Tommy because we didn't run into more than a handful of the undead as we cleared the lower levels. I didn't have to fire off a single shot. Every time we ran into one of the dead loitering around the hallways, I'd leave Tommy hugging the wall, tiptoe forward, and take the rotter out with a quick blow to the neck. Didn't matter if it killed them or not. A broken neck meant no communication from brain to body. They could gnash their teeth and gurgle all they wanted to on the floor while we went on our merry way.

I'll admit, I enjoyed myself a little bit. Most of our days involved hunting for supplies or defending our neck of the woods. Here we were on a treasure hunt for a way to end our suffering in this hellhole. Kind of made me nostalgic for my early days in the army. Back then, I thought they'd train me to be a hero, bigger and better than all the rest. I ended up the same as all my peers, which worked back when deploying to a war zone was my biggest concern. Here, I needed to be Tommy's hero, keep him alive, keep him safe, so he could do the same for me.

I did well in my role of seeing-eye hero until the sixth floor. It started with a chair wedged under the door handle of the stairwell entrance. Someone wanted to keep the things on this level locked inside. I agreed with them as soon as I opened the door.

Zombies. Dozens of them spread out through the hallway. More of them wheezed from the open doorways of several lab rooms, just out of sight. I would've been inclined to leave the entire floor well enough alone except for the giant Almesa symbol emblazoned on the wall. Like hanging a sign that said "the shit you want is here." Tommy would've called it the boss level. I made a mental note not to tell Tommy about the symbol.

Very, very quietly, I pulled the door shut, eased the latch back into place and turned around to face Tommy.

"Dammit, I had some light finally! Why'd you shut the door?"

"On the other side of this door is a whole lot of things that want to eat us."

Tommy didn't speak for a second, putting the might of his two brain cells into figuring out the extent of our trouble.

"How many things?"

"Lots."

"Lots lots?"

"Lots lots."

Another beat of silence.

"Yanno, he could've been lying to you. We leave right now, no harm done."

Now I needed to think for a minute. Tommy made a very good point. Basil could've been lying to me. I didn't know what he gained from the lie, but I also didn't know Basil from Tom, Dick, or Harry. If we left now, we'd lose nothing.

Other than what could be our one and only chance at escape.

"No. We're going in."

"You really believe in this thing, huh?"

"I believe we've spent too long running around like idiots. I'm sick of it. I'm sick of their game. This thing, whatever it is, might be what we need to fix this place."

"You're thinking of saving the whole damn town."

"What's left of it."

"I don't know when you became such a bleeding heart, but I kinda like it. Makes you just a little bit hotter."

"Get stuffed." I tried to make my voice sound gruff and angry, which turned out to be a difficult feat when a smile kept trying to escape. I cleared my throat and reminded myself of the hallway of living trip mines waiting for me on the other side of the door. "Alright, put your hand on my shoulder and point your shotgun forward. When I open this door, you stick to my shadow—Tommy?"

"Yeah?"

"That's my ass."

"Yes. Yes it is."

I wrenched his hand into the proper position with a little extra force than necessary and checked the safety on my pistol. Still off. Same as two minutes ago. My heart beat against the inside of my throat like a trapped insect. I did not want to open the door in front of me. I did not want to run a gauntlet of things wanting to eat my face off if I made one wrong step. I did not want to drag Tommy into this mess with me. I also did not want to leave empty-handed.

The latch clicked as I opened the door a second time. Every squeak and creak of the hinges made me wince, expecting one of the rotters to turn our way and call out the charge. They remained immobile and I kept inching forward.

The stench of the undead clung to the air and crawled across my skin. I thought I'd gotten used to it weeks ago, but the concentration levels on this floor rivaled a nuclear stink bomb. Tommy gagged over my shoulder. If he threw up on me, I'd leave him to the zombies, hero-complex be damned.

We made it two feet into the hallway. My hopes rose a little higher. Every zombie I looked at stared back at me with white, unseeing eyes. They didn't move. They didn't so much as blink.

Wait, that one did.

I took another step and it tracked me like a cat following a laser pointer. Moonlight seeped across its pale flesh, filling in the holes where its nose used to be. Half its upper lip hung by a thread of skin, baring its black teeth in a garish grin. A lab coat hung off its bony frame, making a poor attempt to disguise the ravaged remains of its torso. I assumed it had once been a woman, but too many parts were missing to be sure. It cocked its head to the side and blinked again. Then it pounced. One minute it stood stationary, and the next it flew across the hall, arms out-stretched and a hissing shriek issuing from its throat. I reacted on instinct as the others began to respond.

An open door next to me called my name. I shoved Tommy toward it, ignoring his protests, and threw myself in after him. The door slammed shut behind me, pressed against my back. The first zombie to connect with the wood sent a vibration along the length of my spine.

"Cass, I can't see. What the hell is going on?"

I would've loved to respond to him, but the open maw of a rotting corpse two inches from my face stole my attention. I brought my gun up to fire, but the damn thing was too close. It caught my arm as I pressed the pistol to its stomach, twisted, threw off my aim. A shot barked through the humid night air and smacked into the far wall. The zombie yanked me forward, away from the door, right into Tommy's line of sight.

"Twelve o'clock," I shouted. Tommy's shotgun came up, aimed on blind faith and the sound of my voice. I ducked as low as my trapped arm would allow. The shotgun roared and the zombie stumbled back, one arm dangling from a few shreds of meat left on its shoulder. He'd freed my arm but Tommy's shot didn't take the bastard down. It recovered from the blast, released a rattling moan, and stumbled forward again.

"Twelve thirty! Twelve thirty," I cried.

Again, the shotgun roared. This time the zombie's head disappeared. I waited until the body hit the ground before climbing back to my feet and scanning the room.

"Twelve thirty?" Tommy demanded in the aftermath.

"It worked, didn't it?"

While Tommy stumbled blindly over the corpses, I scanned the room. Windows lined the far wall, each one covered by a pull down blind. In between each tall, covered frame sat a tower and monitor, all arranged along one long table. More tables with more computers snaked around the far walls and filled the centre of the room, stopping only once to allow for another door marked "LAB" in big, black letters. Overhead, flat, black screens stared down at us from all angles. There didn't seem to be an inch of the room that didn't support some piece of technology.

Something large thudded against the door.

"Cass, I could really use some vision right about now."

"Give me a second." No time for games then. I navigated my way over to the far wall and started pulling up the blinds. Bit by bit, moonlight flooded into the room.

"Oh sweet, merciful Jesus. It's like Christmas, my birthday, and a private stripper party all in one. I think I'm in heaven."

Alright, so Tommy could see finally.

"Keep it in your pants. We need to block that door, like you said."

Tommy ignored me. He stared at the rows and rows of computers with the same look of longing he often gave my ass when he didn't think I could see him. I discovered that it is possible to be jealous of a bunch of plastic and wires.

"I think I could live here. Cass, we need to move in here. This'll be my room."

The door rattled on its hinges.

"Focus, nerdboy."

Tommy and I dragged a few chairs over to the door and propped them up in the best barricade we could manage. I doubted it would hold for long, but with the tables all bolted to the ground and Tommy protesting using any of the computers as weights, we had nothing else to work with.

"Check everything and do it fast. That barricade won't hold for long."

"Yeah. In a minute." Tommy headed toward the nearest row of computers.

"Tommy, there's no goddamn power. It's not like you can just turn one on and hack into their systems," I called after him.

"I don't need power. I just need to get one of their hard drives. Hell, Cass. I bet it's all here. You want to get out and burn Almesa to the ground, we're going to need proof." Tommy unhooked one of the towers from its numerous cords and spun it around to face me. He thumped the side of the black case like someone petting a beloved dog. "This, right here, is our ticket to Almesa's meltdown."

"It won't give us a cure," I countered, but I'd already lost Tommy. He bent over the tower, muttering to himself and fiddling with the rear of the case. The door shuddered again, echoing with smaller thumps like the aftershocks of an earthquake. We were running out of time.

I left Tommy to caress his technological goddess and headed over to the lab door. Viruses came from labs. It stood to reason that cures would come from one too.

The door slid open at the slightest touch. The sound of splintering wood drew my attention back to the main entrance. Bad idea. The next thing I knew, cool tiles pressed against my face, and on my back, the clawed fingers of a zombie scrabbled at my neck. A small, silver briefcase lay beside me on the ground, jerking and twitching with each move of the zombie's arm. The rotter must've come out of the lab swinging, which would explain the massive ache spreading across the back of my head.

"Cass," Tommy cried. He bolted across the room, but his fastest still left him several feet to cover. The zombie's teeth had inches.

I rolled, throwing the zombie to the side. Broken fingernails dug into my arm and came away wet with my blood. I raised the same arm to slam against the zombie's throat, keeping a mouthful of gnashing teeth away from my cheek.

Tommy's boot connected with the rotter's head. A mess of blonde hair whipped around the creature's face, and then she toppled to the side.

"You okay?" Tommy held out a hand, the other one wrapped tight around a small, black square, hauled me to my feet, and inspected my new battle scar.

"I just got clocked by a twig in a lab coat carrying a briefcase. I think my pride may need to be amputated."

Tommy snorted. "Good. Got too big anyway."

I glowered, but the main door chose that moment to give out. Our barricade stopped it from collapsing into the room right away. Yet with the number of half-rotted hands clawing at the wood and the walls, that wouldn't hold true for long. Tommy and I scrambled into the lab. We pressed against the door together, forced it shut, or most of the way shut. Two feet from the wall, it thudded against something on the floor and refused to budge.

"It's the damn rotter. Get it out of the way," Tommy said.

True enough, the zombie that had brained me with her briefcase lay three-quarters in the room with only her top half sticking through the opening. I grabbed her legs and hauled her the rest of the way through the door, and Tommy slammed it shut.

"Why the hell are you bringing her in here?" he snapped at me as he braced his shoulder against the door.

"Because it was easier than kicking her ass out there. Can you lock the door?"

"No. There's no goddamn lock. Now we're trapped in a room with no exit, with a zombie, and no fucking lock on the door!"

"I'm sorry. I didn't realize I was supposed to ask the zombies to wait for you to finish humping the computer before they tried to eat us alive," I threw back.

"At least I got something useful. You know, what we came here for."

"We came here for the fucking cure, Tommy," I roared. "The cure that is supposed to be somewhere in this building, that we can't search now because we wasted too much time stumbling around in the dark."

"Well how the hell is that my fault? You're the one with the goddamn goggles."

"I'm the one with the goddamn training."

"Fat lot of good that training does us now. We're still trapped."

No, not trapped. I wheeled around and jogged over to the window. It slid open easily enough, but an old frame made keeping it open difficult. A ruler lay on the windowsill, clearly intended for one purpose alone. I jammed it into place and the window stopped attempting to take my fingers off. A cool breeze pressed against my stinging wound.

"Out," I said to Tommy.

He stared at me, his back pressed to the door, and the gears turned in his head.

"You first," he countered.

I shook my head and planted my feet.

"I came here for the cure. I'm going to find it. You go out the window. Climb down, fly down, fall down. I don't give a shit, but don't expect me to follow. I'll catch up once I have what we came here for."

Disbelief lifted his eyebrows into the brim of his hat. Then they came crashing down and he shook his head.

"You have got to be the dumbest, most stubborn, pig-headed, brainless idiot I have ever met. You're gonna get us both killed."

To the untrained ear, those words were an insult. To me, they were a promise of support.

"It's got to be here somewhere." I headed for the nearest drawer.

"Make it fast. I think they've figured out where we are." The door rattled and a low, rasping moan emanated from the other side. Tommy tensed and loaded new shells into his shotgun. "Yep. Definitely figured it out."

I tore through the room, opening every drawer, cupboard, and desk I could find. I overturned tables, knocked equipment aside, turned everything upside down in search of the cure. I didn't even know what it would look like, but I had to find it. The thumping of undead bodies against the door picked up in tempo, matching the racing of my heart.

"Cass, give it up. We'll have to come back later."

"There might not be a later. It's got to be in here."

"It's not here. It might not even exist at all. The only thing we've seen in this whole damn place is computers and zombies. I've got as much as we need from the computers and..." Several thuds in quick succession made Tommy spread himself flat against the door. "And we've got way too many zombies already. Face it, whatever they had in this place is gone."

I pushed my hands through my hair and stared at the room, willing it to cough up something useful. Anything. A sign, a clue, even a hint that the cure existed. I did not come this far for nothing. I dropped to the ground and began to search the tiled floor in desperation. Nothing. No dirt, no loose papers, not even a body remained to inspect. Except for the corpse by the door.

The corpse and its briefcase.

"We're out of time!" The now familiar sound of snapping wood followed Tommy's shout. Tommy threw himself away from the door and whirled to face it with his shotgun. The first face that popped into view ate a mouthful of buckshot.

I scrambled on hands and knees to the former scientist, within arm's reach of the rotters. The briefcase remained fixed in her hand, glued there by rigor mortis. My turn to claw at her, prying her fingers open one by one to the tune of snapping joints. I yanked the handle out of her grasp, spun the case to face myself, and pressed the sliding locks.

"Cass, for fuck's sake, move," Tommy roared, but I didn't answer him. I was transfixed by the sight in front of me. Not papers, as I had suspected, but six syringes filled with vicious, silver liquid. Each glass casing came with a clear imprint of the Almesa logo. A black computer screen took up the top of the case. I wanted more than anything in the world to push the power button.

The shotgun roared a foot away from my head. Another scientist dropped to the floor, half his face now a smoking ruin. I slammed the lid shut, clicked the locks back into place, and thanked God for His good will. Time to go.

"Window," I bellowed, then bolted. The briefcase went out first, landing on the steel grating of the fire escape with a solid clang. I landed beside it and looked behind me.

Tommy hung half in and half out of the window, his attention focused on the horde of undead boiling into the room. I grabbed his arms, planted a foot against the wall, and hauled with all my might. For a few seconds, we remained trapped in a deadly game of tug-of-war. Me on one side, a zombie on the other, and Tommy the unfortunate rope. Then he kicked, and the pressure on the other end broke. Tommy flew through the opening, kicking free the ruler on the way. The window slammed shut. Tommy and I hit the steel grating in a pile. For a minute, we just lay there, breathing.

"This was a lot more fun when there weren't any zombies in the building," he said.

I laughed, or tried to. His weight sat directly on my chest. He smiled down at me, cowboy hat tilted at a drunken angle over one eye. How he kept the damn thing in the middle of a fight for our lives boggled the mind. I pushed it back into place and looked into his eyes. Eyes the colour of the moon, shining with a lust for life.

A hundred warning bells went off in my mind.

"You know there's a window right over our heads, right?"

"More on the way down."

"We should probably go."

"Yeah." Tommy stood up and held out a hand to me. I took it, and he pulled me to my feet. We each collected our gear and started the climb down to the ground. I clutched the case to my chest the entire walk back to the truck.

CHAPTER SIXTEEN

REDBY, NEVADA
August 23, 2021

When we got in to Casa del Grayson, I went for the washroom. I'd been rolling in sewer water and zombie guts for the last few hours. While I washed off the worst of the unidentifiable bits with the minuscule amount of bottled water allotted for bathroom use, Tommy pulled out his laptop. He'd been saving the thing like someone might save a vintage bottle of wine. Conserving the battery, charging it off any MacGyvered pack he could rig together, using it when he had a hope or intuition that he might get a connection outside of the wall. He kept saying he only needed ten seconds with an Internet connection to get us the spotlight we needed. Ten seconds never came.

I came out of the bathroom fifteen minutes later, gauze wrapped around my arm and bandages slapped over every cut and scrape on my body. I did not need to die of gangrene so close to the end.

Tommy sat on the floor amid a sea of boxes, wires, and computer bits, bathed in the pure white light of his laptop. The briefcase lay open on his left, the hard drive on his right, connected to the laptop via a cord and small, black box. Tommy's cowboy hat, beaten, battered, but still whole, sat on the arm of the couch beside him.

I paused for a minute to admire the way he looked when he wasn't staring at my ass. He had a boyish charm about him. All hyper energy and no thought. His short, brown hair stood up in a mess of spikes and cowlicks. One sleeve of his shirt bunched against his elbow instead of holding the tight roll over his bicep that he preferred. He looked like a two-year-old just come in from playing in the mud, except with the arms and chest of a Greek god. Somewhere in the past few weeks, Tommy had lost his roundness and gained a harder, more defined look. He still had the mischievous grin, but now when he said he could handle something, I trusted him.

Huh. I trusted Tommy.

Tommy glanced over his shoulder, alerted to my presence by the creaking of a floorboard. His face lit up with familiar glee when he spotted me.

"Hey, you gotta come see this."

"It can wait until after you're bandaged." I didn't give him a choice in the matter. The minute he tried to squirm away, I put him in an arm lock and attacked his hand with disinfectant.

"I don't need bandages. I barely got—Ow! That stings!"

"I don't need you dying of infection now. Hold still."

"Alright, but you can look at this at the same time."

"What am I looking at?" I glanced up from my work. To be honest, I really wanted to know what our victorious run had netted us.

"This is some of the decrypted information from the smartphone. Extracted it first. It runs off a local connection. Any phone it talks to is on the same network. I think they had some kinda safeguard installed, cause the connection failed when I tried it. Couldn't get it back and couldn't get another. I did get a lot of info though." He said everything in one breath, then drew in a deep one to refill his empty lungs. Excitement could kill him before infection had a chance.

"Like what?"

"Like a map of the tunnel system. Apparently, those delivery guys weren't working off memory. Plus, all the hot spots for restocks. Even if we are stuck here for a while longer, we'll be living like kings. We'll get all the supplies before anyone else even knows they're there."

"And this is?" I pointed at a string of numbers and letters that made no sense in the context of what Tommy had told me so far. All the maps were labelled. These numbers just sat there, like they'd been spewed out after all the important bits were stuffed into the files.

"Codes, I think. Whatever they used to get in and out of the wall itself. The thing's huge. Look here."

I watched Tommy's hands fly over the keyboard. With a few quick clicks, he made the maps and numbers disappear. In their place rose a gridwork outline of the town, all black and glowing blue lines. A thick, impenetrable bar ran around the outside of the city, mimicking the warped bubble shape the wall made. When Tommy clicked another button, the thick bar bloated up to fill the entire screen and hollowed out. I saw floors, stairs, rooms, security check points, and tunnel access points, a massive network riddling the inside of the wall like an ant nest. Forty feet across and a hundred feet high according to the readout.

"That's all in the wall?"

"Yeah. They live inside. Can you believe it? And…" Tommy paused for dramatic effect. He reached across me and tugged the small, plastic ID card I'd taken off Basil out of his backpack. A grin spread across his face as he paired a waggle of the card with his words. "Now we got our own personal invite."

"Wicked." Now we had a complete map of where we wanted to go and free access too. And we hadn't even reached the bottom of thegoodie bag yet. "What about the briefcase?"

"Hard drive first. I was waiting on you before reading too far in. I found the files we need though. By the way, anytime you want to praise me as the world's best hacker, don't hold back. I know I've earned it."

"That only brings you up to even. You're still the world's worst zombie hunter."

"You know, just for that, I'm not giving you the last chocolate bar."

"You ate it already."

"I ate it already."

I gave Tommy's shoulder a half-hearted nudge and he chuckled.

"Alright, alright. Let's find out the meaning to life, the universe, and Redby. Here we go." Tommy tapped a few keys. The grid disappeared, replaced by an official-looking document. At the top of the page were two symbols. One I expected; the blazing circle of Almesa. The other one, the soaring eagle of the president of the United States, came as a bit of a shock.

"Okay, so says here this project was sanctioned by the president herself. Bunch of legal mumbo-jumbo, in this time of war, blah blah blah.

Huh." Tommy trailed off.

I waited. Tommy scrolled through the page faster than I could read. I needed him to tell me the good bits. All I caught before the words blurred and became a new paragraph were bits of alarming information like "population size" and "ideal testing grounds."

"Huh what?" I pressed him.

"Hang on a sec." Tommy scrolled further. Annoyance set in.

"Tommy, either tell me what the hell is going on or slow down. Some of us can't read at the speed of light."

"Hey Cass, you said you served in the Middle East, right?"

"Yeah. Why?"

"What were things like out there?"

I frowned. Thinking about my tour out East tended to bring up bad memories. I suppressed it as much as I could. "Bad. I saw a lot of good people die out there. A lot of friends. I got rotated out six months before being shipped here. When I left, our troops were being pushed back hard. We lost the outpost I'd been stationed at a few days after I got back stateside." I narrowed my eyes at Tommy. He still hadn't answered my question. "Why?"

Tommy turned the laptop toward me. "It's a biological weapon. They designed it for war."

That didn't make any sense. Biological weapons were the trade of the enemy. They poisoned our food, made it so we had to have all our provisions shipped in and inspected before we were allowed to get so much as a glass of water. They hit us with gas bombs and acidic spray, even infected their own people so we would be exposed. Things out East were desperate, but my country would never stoop so low as to fighting fire with fire.

And yet there it sat in plain black and white. A biological weapon designed to turn the enemy's own dead against them. The virus spread through contact, meaning anyone an infected person came in contact with would then become infected themselves. They intended to blanket the East in undead. Nothing would be left alive.

I read the document over twice, stealing the mouse away from Tommy to scroll through paragraph after paragraph of damning details. The government knew about Redby. Hell, they helped set it up. The perfect test site, easy to control and easy to disguise. Everyone was so focused on the conflict overseas, they would never think to look in their own backyard. Even after memorizing the words, I still didn't believe them. I sat back and shook my head.

"There's no way the president would agree to this," I said.

"She did more than agree, according to this. She handed the keys over to Almesa and let them drive. Looks like the contract the mayor signed was for more than just a big, fancy wall and a lot of guards. Looks like it was a consent form."

"You think your mayor sold the town out?"

Tommy shrugged. He refused to look at me when he answered. "Well, I know she went on vacation a week before Day Zero. Kinda incriminating if you ask me."

"So, this whole damn thing was a setup. Almesa, the virus, the wall, they planned everything."

"The soldiers." Tommy muttered the words under his breath and stared at the screen, pretending he hadn't just lumped me and mine in with the bastards running this experiment.

"Captain Stone would never agree to this," I said. I wanted to believe the words. I wanted to think that, if the captain knew anything about this business, he would've ordered the whole company to pack up and ship back to Georgia. I wanted to believe a court-martial would be preferable to this.

"He's a good soldier, right?" Tommy asked.

The words enraged me more than they should have. I ground the anger out between my teeth and fixed Tommy with a look that promised bloody violence if he didn't answer the way I wanted.

"Where are you going with this?"

Tommy shrugged again and looked back to the computer screen. He tapped a few keys on the keyboard, but nothing about the damning words changed. He just didn't want to face me.

"A good soldier follows orders," he said.

I didn't answer. Instead, I read the words on the screen over again, looking for any hint, any loophole that would indicate my company had nothing to do with Almesa. Yet no matter what I wanted to believe, I knew the truth. Soldiers got bad orders all the time. That never changed the outcome.

"Maybe they tried to..." Tommy started, but I cut him off mid-breath.

"Drop it."

Tommy's face fell. Without the shadows of his cowboy hat, the contours of his face had nowhere to hide. When he frowned he looked sad, beaten, and tired. He looked the way I felt inside.

"Cass..." he tried again.

"I said drop it, Tommy," I snapped. The silence weighed on us afterward. It breathed down my neck and glowered at me, shaming me for upsetting Tommy. Never mind the fact that I would've been perfectly happy in my ignorance if he hadn't brought up my company's involvement. Soon enough, the torture became too much and I had to say something just to break the oppression. "Okay, so we're lab rats. How does leaving the cure lying around factor into their grand plan?"

"There's nothing in here about a cure. From the way this reads, they were planning on just dropping the virus over a few cities and forgetting that part of the world exists."

"Right, cause I'm sure it'd just stop spreading at the border."

Tommy's brows came together and his lower lip jutted out. Something about what I said got him thinking. Good, because I had no idea how Almesa's plans didn't end with the whole world eating each other's brains.

"It's part of the test. It has to be. See if they can control the spread," he muttered. I didn't know if he inteded the words for me or not, because instead of waiting for my confused response, he reached across me to power up the screen in the briefcase.

The screen in the lid turned from black to bright white, then calmed down to a sedate grey. The familiar burning yin-yang of Almesa appeared, followed by a woman in a sleek grey business suit.

Something about the woman sent a twinge down my spine. It could have been that her eyes were too blue and her skin too pale. Or the way she sat perfectly still. Perfectly. No one was that motionless. Or it could've been the way Tommy sucked in a breath when he saw her.

"Jesus, I know her. That's my mom's old boss. She came over for dinner a few times."

"She ever mention being pure, concentrated evil?" I asked.

Tommy snorted. Then the woman spoke.

"Hello and welcome to the N41 Toxoplasmosis Nanotech Recovery Program. My name is Melissa Chamberlain, CEO of the Western branch of Almesa Corporation and Director of Operations of the Redby Project."

Melissa Chamberlain. I knew that name. It was the same one I'd seen on the dedication plaque outside the Almesa building. Damn, this woman really did run Redby.

"Within this case you will find six syringes containing the nanobots designed to work in conjunction with the N41 virus as outlined in your introductory booklets. At the beginning of Phase Two, these syringes are to be introduced into the population. Your duty, as blind administrators, is to attach yourself to a suitable group, provide the syringes, and return your findings to the drop points marked on your map. While the syringes carry the official name of N42-NRS, the human resources department has decided that a moniker will allow for easier integration into the project. You will refer to them as Quickening Sticks, or Quicks for short.

"The virus, as you recall, has a ninety-eight percent success rate in lab tests. When moving to human trials, we expect to see the same results. Failure of the virus to propagate in the human host means that when the host dies, it will not reanimate. You must ensure your population sample is not part of the two percent failure rate, or else the Quicks will be rendered useless. Hold a few syringes in spare for re-tests.

"At this phase in the program, we expect the Quicks to show a fifty percent success rate or greater when applied to subjects infected with the N41 virus. Your results will allow us to improve that number. As such, it is important you choose your test subjects carefully. They must prove to be revivable on multiple occasions.

"You have been given a difficult task. There is significant risk in what you do today, but know that without you, this project would fail. You are the key to the greatest breakthrough in medical history. With your help, we will ensure none of our soldiers are ever lost in battle again. Keep that in mind while completing your task, and do not return until you have a significant contribution.

"Destroy this briefcase upon the conclusion of this message. Any information leaks to the test subjects will jeopardize the project and nullify your contract. Succeed and you will be safe. Fail and you will be left behind."

The Almesa logo replaced the image of Melissa Chamberlain, and then the screen faded to black.

Silence swallowed us again, but the weight of it made me miss the quiet of before, back when I'd been pissed and Tommy hurt. Now I felt confused and the rage boiling inside Tommy looked hot enough to set him on fire. He clenched his jaw tight enough to make the grinding of his teeth audible. Then he blinked, and something inside him snapped.

"Nope. That's not it," he said, each word sticking in his throat. He turned back to the laptop, closed the document, and began pulling up each and every file available on the hard drive. Lab reports, video surveillance, and enough medical jargon to make my head hurt flashed across the screen. The more Tommy pulled up, the more he shook with fury.

"Chill," I said, laying a hand on his shoulder.

Tommy shook me off. I tried again.

"Hey, it's okay."

Wrong thing to say, apparently. Tommy turned on me. The shadow of his brows crashing over his eyes turned their stormy grey into a full-blown hurricane of wrath.

"Okay? *Okay*? Nothing is okay, Cass! You don't even know what this is, do you? It's Hell. It's literal Hell on Earth. You die, you get back up, you get a needle and you do it all over again. They've taken a death sentence and turned it into immortality. And for what? To test some sick weapon they're going to throw at the rest of the world. Cause who gives a fuck if everyone else dies so long as America lives on, right? This, all of this," he gestured furiously at the laptop, briefcase, and all the rest of the gadgets that had nearly cost us our lives, "is just someone's idea of the ends justifying the means. They are going to let us die here again and again and again, and when it's all done, they'll write us off as an unfortunate but necessary cost of business. We are the fucking tax at the end of their tab for the war on terrorism. There is no fucking cure, Cass. There never was."

The words dried up. The rage remained, milling about the room like a thick fog, but it stopped growing. Tommy spent what he had in him and fell silent. I should've been trying to calm him down again. I knew what the hate could do to you if it overwhelmed you. I'd learned to control it, but he didn't have the benefit of my childhood. I should have been his guide. Instead I played his words through my head like a broken record.

You die, you get back up, you get a needle, and you do it all over again. A cycle.

You die, you get back up. You get a needle.

Ace and BigMac would get a needle.

I could still save them.

"Fuck this. We're not going to use it. We won't play into their stupid fucking game." Tommy let the words out in a single breath before I'd had time to work them through my brain. He snapped the briefcase shut, stood up, and stormed toward the balcony. I had to throw myself at the air to catch up.

"No!" My hands closed on the case, scraping across the smooth, metal exterior. I dug in and tugged it against my chest. Tommy didn't let go. He just stared at me like I'd stabbed him in the back. I started talking before the words fully formed in my mind. "Don't throw it down there. Someone else will find them and use them and then they'll get what they want anyway. Just... just put it down."

Tommy's expression morphed from hurt to confused to angry in less than a second, and then started the cycle all over again. He fought with himself over what to do. Any second I expected to see smoke coming out of his ears. I needed to distract him.

"It's been a long day. We're both tired and this sure as hell was a shock. But that doesn't change the plan. Tomorrow, we're getting out of here. I mean, yeah we don't have a cure, but all we gotta do is not die. We're good at that. We'll clear out, expose this place, then come back to watch Almesa burn."

Tommy's grip weakened on the case, but it still wasn't enough.

I chose that moment to stop thinking. Trying to come up with a convincing argument got in the way of actually doing it. I leaned into him, pressing my lips to his for a befuddled but passionate kiss. When it ended, I pulled away just enough to look into his eyes and see my own thoughts reflected on his face.

Huh, that was kinda nice.

The case slipped from Tommy's fingers, entirely forgotten as we came together. His lips pressed against my skin, soft and warm and hungry. He moved from my lips to my jaw and back again, hunting for something. I captured his lips with a gentle nip, ending his search.

My hands moved on their own power, wrapping around the back of his neck, yanking him down to my level. The heat of the night air swirled around us, an arctic wind compared to the heat of his body against mine. He pulled me against his chest and for a few blissful moments, the world we lived in ceased to exist.

The kiss ended but neither of us made to pull away. Tommy tilted his head down to rest his forehead against my own and let out a contented sigh. "You always say the sweetest things."

I could not avoid smiling with the tingle of his hot lips still a memory on my skin. This was dangerous. Getting this close to someone left me exposed, vulnerable, open to attack. A little voice in my head screamed at me to run away. If I did that, I'd never get the briefcase. A sacrifice had to be made. A very hot, thoroughly enjoyable sacrifice.

"Come on to bed," I whispered in his ear. Tommy offered no resistance.

Thin rays of sunlight crept across the floor by the time Tommy drifted off to sleep; exhausted, bruised, and deliriously happy judging by the smile on his face. I closed my eyes and lay beside him until I knew he wouldn't wake. Though exhausted myself, I couldn't risk giving in to fatigue now.

As his slow and steady breathing turned to snores, I eased myself up on my elbows and looked at him in the morning light. The dull, grey gloom of a storm stole what little warmth the sunlight might have offered the room. What filtered in through the windows was cold and colourless and cast a dreary pallor over everything. Everything but Tommy. He existed in his own private world of sunlight.

Thunder rumbled in the distance. Some primitive part of me wanted to curl up under the blankets where I felt warm and safe, wrapped in Tommy's arms. He looked so peaceful when he slept, like none of this had affected him at all. No lines marked his brow and no frown turned down the edges of his mouth. His muscles were relaxed, his body completely at ease. He trusted the world to leave him alone while he slept. I wanted to share that peace.

Instead, I slipped out of bed and grabbed my pants off the floor. I had a limited window of time in which to find Ace and BigMac, revive them, and drag them back to the apartment complex. Getting back before Tommy woke meant I could explain everything without freaking anyone out. Then Tommy could accept them into the group. End of story.

I found my shirt and, after a second of hesitation, took my jacket as well. Everything stank of overuse. Though we'd found some spare clothes since joining up, we didn't risk washing anything. Not with water being so scarce.

I tiptoed out of the bedroom and made for the living room. The rain pattered against the windows. I took up the briefcase and unlocked the front door, slipping past the traps and alarms with the care of a barefoot man on hot coals.

When I got to the window leading out to the fire escape, hesitation froze me in place. This was a terrible plan. If it failed, I would die and Tommy would be alone. Ace and BigMac would remain dead. My chances would be better with Tommy along, but I knew what he would say. Ace and BigMac weren't worth the risk. Not to him. He didn't understand how much we'd been through together. How far we'd go to keep each other safe. I wanted to include Tommy in that group, not just start a new one. I needed Ace and

BigMac, and Tommy would just have to accept that.

Besides, if I did this right, Tommy wouldn't even know I'd been gone. Aside from the fact that I'd be soaking wet when I got back. Which I didn't think would be a big deal. Not compared to introducing my two army buddies after he'd declared that we were not to use the Quicks. Wasn't quite sure how I would handle that yet. One issue at a time.

I crawled out the window, shivering as the first few icy drops pelted my exposed neck. Terrible plan or not, it had to work. Ace and BigMac would live again. I could make everything right again. Even if they hated me for getting them killed, it would be alright. I could live with that, just so long as they did too.

I should've listened to my gut.

CHAPTER SEVENTEEN

OAK RIDGE MENTAL HOSPITAL, TEXAS
August 23, 2032

The pinecone pendulum of the cuckoo swung beneath its wooden base, keeping steady rhythm as the seconds ticked by. Loudly. The doc probably didn't even remember that the clock existed right then. I did. This was no quiet background noise for me. I couldn't escape it. Each beat of the pendulum rang like a gong inside my skull, resonating off my splitting headache until my entire body threatened to come apart.

I couldn't understand why people would want a clock that just made noise anyway. There were plenty of quiet clocks out there. This one wasn't even musical. It just ticked. Every second of every day, it ticked. In the room. In my skull. In the damn tapping of the doc's pen on his stupid little pad of paper.

"Cassandra?" The doc's voice jolted me out of my thoughts.

I bolted upright in my chair. My brain slammed against the sides of my skull, weakening the last fragile barrier between my coherence and a fetal position on the floor. Pressing my palms against my temples helped shore up my defences a little bit. As did curling up in the chair with my knees pressed to my chin.

"Cassandra, are you feeling alright?" Honey and sympathy dripped off his tongue. Or I bet that's what he wanted it to sound like. Instead I got needles and searing hot pokers jabbed into my ear lobes.

"No. I'm not. I have a headache and I want to stop," I spit out through gritted teeth.

"We're nearly done. Just a few minutes left in our session. Here, I'll get you some ibuprofen and you can tell me what happened when you went to get Ace and BigMac."

Ace and BigMac. I remembered them. I remembered they were in the room with me right then—Wait. No. That's wrong. They're dead. Had been for years. I'd tried to save them and... and...

Something inside my brain broke. A slow, agonized scream rose in my mind, accented by the ticking of that damned clock.

What had happened to Ace and BigMac? It was important, but trying to think about it scared me. I wanted to run away from the memory. Run where?

Somewhere without clocks. That's for damn sure.

There had been a clock at the bar too. One of those stupid cartoon cat clocks that just ticked. And stared. And ticked. The eyes were broken according to the bartender. Stared at me. Never moved. I wanted to shoot it. I could hear it over everything else. Over the music, the talking, even the douchebag who'd sidled up to sit next to me. The clock kept creeping into my thoughts, distracting me from... from what?

Goddammit! Why couldn't I think? What had happened to Ace and BigMac? What had happened at the bar?

The doc opened his desk. The wood scraped against its rails, a pause, and then the drawer shutting again with a thunderous clap.

"It appears I'm out of ibuprofen. I'll call for some. One moment."

Doc stood up, scraping his chair across the tiled floor. The sound of a jet engine played through my head. I pressed my palms harder against my temples, willing my brain to stay inside my skull.

"These headaches are, unfortunately, a side effect of the sleep medication. I will see about switching to a different prescription. It could be that you've just been on them for too long. A cleansing period might be in order. Nurse, come here please." The doc walked and talked at the same time, his footsteps thundering past my chair, drowning out Tommy's tinny voice.

A song. I remembered a song. It had been playing in the bar. Some old country and western warble. Tommy loved those songs. He had a passable singing voice and sometimes, when we were safe enough, he sang to pass the time. I remembered wanting that song to end in the bar. It reminded me too much of what I'd lost, but that would leave me alone with the ticking clock.

"Tick tock tick tock," Ace mocked, his words whispering across my thoughts. "Come on, Cass, you're running out of time. What is it you don't want to remember?"

"Stop it," I whispered. I couldn't have the doc accidentally overhearing me again.

"You can't keep running forever. You're making progress, remember?" The way Ace whined the last few words made me want to reach over and strangle him. He mocked me, the doc, and everything I'd done since I escaped.

"Did you escape?" Ace pressed. "Did you really get out of there alive?"

No. It wasn't an escape. They let us go. They let us walk away and then I—

"You what, Cass? What did you do?"

The night came back to me in vivid, eye-bleeding colour. The cat clock on the wall ticked out a steady rhythm, its feline eyes staring at me. A drink sat on the counter in front of me. Scotch. I emptied most of it in one gulp. A sour odour of sweat and beer sat down next to me, began talking to me, patronizing me. He wanted to mock me and he didn't even know me. He just saw the scars and assumed. The asshole was so full of himself, so convinced that the laws of society would protect him when he had only one life to spare. And then Tommy started singing over the speakers. Sweet, smiling Tommy who'd watched his whole world burn and still found reason to act like a decent human being. Tommy, who had given everything to keep me safe.

And this asshole thought he had more right to live than Tommy? No.

I broke him inch by inch. People tried to interfere, but I broke them too. Not as badly. Not so they couldn't flee when the panic set in. The douchebag though, I kept him. One bone at a time, one joint at a time, I took him apart like a doll with interchangeable parts. I didn't need weapons. Just my hands. Five pounds of pressure to remove an ear, seven pounds of pressure to shatter a kneecap. Eyes, ribs, fingers, teeth, everything went.

By the time the police arrived, I had taken up my stool again, finishing up the scotch I ordered. The douchebag lay unconscious or dead. I didn't care. The song changed. I'd smashed the clock. The police had no trouble taking me into custody. I did it, Officer. Did I kill him? Damn. Too bad. Yeah, I'll wait until you're done being sick in the corner. Put in a good word for me with the judge, would you?

Voices echoed over my head, through my skull. Voices I once knew, but now their words made no sense. The cat's eyes stared at me. I'd broken them to bits but still they stared. Stop staring at me. Stop. Staring.

A hand closed on my shoulder.

"They're coming for you, Cass. Run," the voices whispered.

NO!

I twisted out of the chair, grabbing the arm off my shoulder as I went. It twisted too, winding around like a rubber band in tandem with my movements. My feet hit the ground and my hand came down on my assailant's elbow. Bone snapped, glass shattered, and someone screamed. I vaulted over the falling body before the scream ended.

A shadow loomed in the doorway. Someone in a dark blue uniform with a stick in his hand. He stepped into the room, headed straight for me. I went sideways, bouncing off the wall and flinging myself at his outstretched arm. His wrist shattered beneath the force of my kick. Another aimed at his knee sent him sprawling to the floor. His body hit the ground with a dull thud and a high-pitched warble that didn't belong in the human vocal range. Behind him stood another shadow.

I couldn't think of anything beyond my need to get out. Everywhere I turned, enemies waited. Every face I saw morphed into someone wanting me dead. I needed to get outside.   Safety waited outside.

I went straight for the door. One jump and I swung off the door frame, flying at the second shadow's chest, knocking him to the ground. His head hit the floor with a resounding crack. I didn't even need to punch him out.

"On your feet, sweetheart. There's more on the way," Tommy whispered.

Yes, couldn't get caught now. Couldn't let them trap me.

I stood and whirled toward the far end of the hall, facing the next obstacle.

Muscle and fat combined into a mountain of raw force as wide as the doorway behind him. I could take the shadow, but it would take time. I didn't have time. I turned and ran down the opposite hall instead.

"Left." Ace appeared in front of me, his arm outstretched in the direction I needed to turn. I didn't question him. I just dodged left at the next hallway. A minute later the alarms blared and footsteps pounded down the hall behind me.

More people appeared to block my path. These men held little black boxes in their hands. Stun guns. I knew them by sight. They wanted to take me alive. I wouldn't let them.

One of them lunged forward, trying to jab me with the business end of the weapon. I twisted sideways, slapping his wrist down as I spun in close to his body. The electrical tool clattered to the ground. The flat of my hand went up into his face, smashing his nose. As he reeled back, blood spurting over his lips and chin, his partner came at me with the other stun gun. I grabbed his arm and use his own momentum against him, tripping him up to make him fall into his friend. The man with the broken nose spasmed as a quick jolt of electricity ran through his body. I curled my hand into a rigid claw and drove two knuckles into the second man's temple. They went down together. I jumped back, gone before they hit the floor.

"Hurry, Cass. They're closing in," Ace urged me. Up ahead, BigMac stood pointing down another hallway. I ran for it, heedless of where it would take me.

Nothing in this hall save for a door at the far end. Probably locked, but I could get around it. If necessary, I'd go back to one of the fallen enemies and take his key. They were sure to have keys on them.

"What if they don't? Don't get trapped here," Ace said.

Right. Forget the locked door. I twisted to the right. Another door stood open, beckoning me. It could lead nowhere, or it could provide me with an escape route. It was a complete unknown, but so long as I had a chance of success, I had to try it.

Someone stepped out of the open doorway before I reached it. He had skin the colour of burnished copper and a long, black braid hanging behind his pastel shirt. A serene smile lit up his face as he stared at me.

Stop. Staring.

I grabbed his arm, ready to fling him aside, and then he got mine.

He held my arm in a vice grip and flung my body across the room. The wall slammed into my spine, spawning an explosion of stars in front of my vision. He slid forward, all snake-like grace, fingers poised like fangs ready to sink into my skin and drain the fight out of me. I slipped under him, away from the wall, and spun around. He stood across from me, a manic grin on his face, his legs braced and hands raised in a defensive pose in front of his face. This was not a fight I could run away from.

We crashed together in a flurry of attacks and blocks, twisting around each other in a dance of lethal force. Every punch I threw, every shuffle of my feet, he met and countered. I did the same to him, turning aside his hands, slipping away from his long reach. I was faster than him, but he moved as if he had ten arms instead of two and eyes in the back of his head. The adrenaline started to wear off, the fatigue of fighting my way here to kick in.

"Cass, the door. You have to go," Ace shouted.

The distraction nearly cost me my head. His hand whipped past my temple, an electric tingle racing along my skin in the absence of his touch. I leaned back, raised an elbow to his chin, and when he moved to counter the feint, I caught his jaw with a quick jab. He reeled back. I disengaged and pelted toward the open doorway. Toward freedom.

His arm closed around my shoulder and I turned to slip away, but he turned with me. He used my momentum against me. He was using my tactic!

We hit the wall together, me pressed to his chest and him pressed to the wall. His long arm locked across my throat, pinching the side of my neck. My fingers wrapped around his arm and applied pressure to his exposed wrist, just like I'd done a hundred times before. The world tilted sideways and my fingers slipped. That wasn't supposed to happen.

Something clattered to the ground. I looked down and saw the needle, devoid of its contents, roll against my foot.

"Shush, Cassandra. It's not time yet," the man whispered in my ear. His voice came out soft as velvet, soothing and terrifying at the same time. It felt like a blanket closed over my head, cutting off my air, and his arm held me trapped beneath it.

"Focus, Cass! You've gotten out of this hold before. Do it again." Ace stood over me, his face blurring.

I tried. I closed my fingers tightly over the stranger's wrist, digging in. I knew I could do this, but I couldn't remember how when the room kept spinning and the lights kept stabbing into my eyes. So bright and fuzzy. Like little balls of fluff drifting down from the ceiling. Everything got kind of wobbly and...

Oh...

Shit...

CHAPTER EIGHTEEN

REDBY, NEVADA
August 24, 2021

Goosebumps marched up and down my arms as I jabbed the truck's key into the ignition, wincing at the growl of the old engine. Tommy's apartment was on the top floor, but in the dead silence of early morning, a pin drop sounded like an explosion. Thunder rolled overhead, drowning out the truck's motor. I edged the beater onto the street and let out the first breath of the day.

This was wrong. I didn't think it; I just knew. Though I'd driven the truck before, Tommy had always been beside me. The briefcase and my ten-ton guilty conscience road shotgun that morning. First I'd distracted him with sex, then snuck out the door, but stealing the truck? That was the sort of bad deed that got you sent to the place of fire and brimstone.

I could make it all better though. I just had to get BigMac and Ace, bring them back to life, explain the situation to them, then sit everyone down for introductions.

Hey, guys! Remember how I said men were stupid and I never wanted to be in anything save a wildly passionate and utterly physical relationship ever again? Well, meet Tommy. My... not boyfriend but attachment sort of thing. Now the four of us are all going to make nice, sneak inside the wall, and pull off an escape from this hellhole by means of some plan that I'm sure will be brilliant when I come up with it.

Yeah, not a good plan. At least they'd be alive again.

The closer I got to downtown, the harder the rain came down. By the time the remains of the Almesa building peeked into view, the windscreen looked like a river. Even with the wipers going full blast. It didn't surprise me at all when I ran into something.

Well, the running into it part scared me. Wasn't expecting a corpse to pop up over the hood and slam into the glass.

I hit the breaks hard enough to nestle the pedal right up against the worn interior carpet. The tires screeched, skidded for purchased on the watery ground, and bounced up over the curb. I hit the ceiling, steering wheel, and headrest of the driver's seat in short order, and took a moment to thank God for not sending me through the windshield to meet my new friend.

Friends. Plural.

They came out of the rain like wraiths, incorporeal until the moment they struck the cab of the truck. Their mangled hands rained blows on the glass, scraping and clawing at the invisible barrier. The driver's side window shivered in its frame. It wouldn't hold for much longer, and every second that ticked past saw more of the undead swarming around the truck. I needed a way out, but the dead blocked the way forward.

The rear window. Tight fit, but I could squeeze through.

I grabbed the case off the passenger seat, slid open the rear window and threw my precious cargo into the empty flatbed. Priorities. For the first time in my life, I felt gratitude for my narrow hips. I wriggled and twisted, kicking against the steering wheel to push myself through the small opening. Just as I cleared the cab, the glass of the driver's window gave way. I had just enough time to yank the sliding screen shut before half a dozen zombie arms occupied the space I'd been moments before.

I grabbed the case, hopped out of the flatbed, and loped a few paces away before I realized something important. Nothing followed me. No moaning, no gnashing of teeth, no grasping arms. All the zombies swarmed around the truck without so much as a thought to the escape of their prey.

To be honest, I felt a little spurned.

I raised an arm and waved it in the air. Not the smartest move, but as it turned out, not stupid either. The zombies didn't respond. Not even a half-hearted moan in my direction. They kept pounding away at the truck, tearing at the hood and chewing on the windshield wipers. I figured it out while watching one of them gnash his teeth against the headlights.

They couldn't see me. Whatever they were now, they used to be human. They had human senses, or at least what remained of them. The rain obscured what they could see and the purr of the truck droned out any noise I made. So long as I didn't go singing and dancing through the street, I was invisible.

Cool.

I decided to take advantage of my good fortune. A quick glance around confirmed my suspicion. I stood maybe ten feet away from the store where I'd last seen Ace and BigMac. Assuming they hadn't wandered off into parts of the town unknown, they'd still be around here. Which left me with the problem of figuring out where around here they were.

A flash of lightning lit up the sky. A dozen faces surrounded me, dead eyes staring straight through me. I recognized a torn summer dress, a woman in a pant suit, and something small and silver dangling from a rotter's neck.

Dog tags. Though his face was mangled and torn, I recognized the figure. Even in death he walked with the same cocky strut, though it looked a little more lopsided now. Ace shambled right past me, heading for the truck.

I held my breath until the group passed me by. Invisible or not, that was damn close. Once they passed, I crouched down on the ground, opened up the case, and took out two needles. One I stashed in my front pocket for BigMac. The other I uncapped and held tight in one hand. Then I did the stupidest thing I have ever done in my life. I went after my zombie buddy.

Ace joined the crowd forming around the truck. He bumped against his fellow rotters, jostling for a position closer to the growling engine. The longer I waited, the more zombies arrived, the further out of my reach Ace got. My skin burned at the thought of getting up close and personal with all those undead, but I had to make my move now or else lose this opportunity forever.

I lifted the needle high, lining it up with the nape of his neck. From the back, he looked almost normal. Thinner and more bloody than usual, but if I squinted and tilted my head sideways, I could almost believe he had

159

just missed a meal or two.

Yeah, if I wanted to fool myself.

"Okay, buddy. Here we go," I whispered as I drew in a steadying breath. No more hesitation. Time to do this.

I took a step forward. Then another. When I stood within a foot of his back, I caught a whiff of his decaying body. Even the rain couldn't dampen that stench. I drew in a deep breath, trapped it in my lungs, then lunged forward and snaked an arm around his throat. The crook of my elbow closed across his windpipe, trapping the surprised gurgle that rattled up his throat. He wrapped his skeletal claws around my arm in exchange and tried to peel the skin off my bones. Excruciating pain ripped down my arm. My jacket provided enough protection to keep me from jerking away, which gave me just enough time to wrestle his head into position and slam the sharp end of the needle into the back of his neck.

The slender stick of metal disappeared into his flesh. When the butt of the needle nestled up against his rotted skin, I pushed down hard on the plunger. The silvery liquid swimming sluggishly around the cylinder exploded with activity. It swirled and burst, snaking round and round the glass tube like trapped fireworks. As the last of it disappeared into Ace's neck, his undead body shuddered and slackened. His hands dropped away from my arm and his slight, bony weight landed squarely on my chest. I dragged Ace back a few feet, into the shadows of an alley, and lowered him to the ground. His head rested on my lap, just as it had when he'd drawn his final breaths. A little part of my brain hoped that he would forget that part.

Seconds ticked past. The rain fell. I didn't notice it anymore, being so thoroughly soaked through that crouching in the mud barely registered on my senses.

The seconds turned into minutes. I started to worry. With each new heartbeat, my brain ran through a list of problems that could be keeping Ace from returning to me. What if the syringes were a lie? What if Ace was too far gone? What if it took hours?

I didn't have hours. An hour, maybe. If the rain let up, less time. All I had right now was a theory that the steady downpour kept me safe from the undead.

"Come on, Ace," I whispered to the motionless corpse. Nothing changed. He looked just as dead as when I'd first found him. This close up, I had a hard time ignoring the damage death caused. Blood drenched his shirt and a good portion of his pants. One half of his face had been shredded to ribbons.

Ace didn't respond to my plea. The rain started to lessen. I found myself willing the sky to open up again, praying the rain lasted the entire day. Then I started praying in earnest, my head bowed over my dead friend and my desperate thoughts reaching out to the one being I knew who could make a miracle happen.

I'd always believed in God. My parents raised me Roman Catholic. Until I entered school, I didn't even know that there was any other sort of religion out there. Even then, the different faiths and beliefs didn't bother me. God was God. He existed whether you believed in Him or not. Which worked for me, since I hated getting up early for Sunday school, fought tooth and nail against my mother for forcing me to wear dresses to church, and never behaved as devout as I should have. Despite all that, I'd never questioned what I believed. It was the one point my father and I could agree on.

I prayed for God to be with me. I prayed for Him to return Ace to me. I prayed because I had nothing left to cling to as the rain petered to a stop and my friend still did not move.

A gentle, probing tug on the corner of my jacket sent my heart soaring. God had answered my prayers. I opened my eyes, ready to greet Ace with a joyous hug and even ready to take whatever punishment he felt I deserved. My joy died the instant his dead eyes met my own. Nothing had changed.

"Ace?" I called tentatively, hoping he was just playing with me. Coming back to life had to leave one looking a little rough around the edges. Maybe the syringe still needed time to work. The zombie opened its mouth and gurgled. Its head lolled to the side, open mouth craning toward my elbow, which it now held in one bony hand. I twisted away and scooted back a few feet on my behind. Some long forgotten, sane part of my brain told me to get my gun. I didn't know why since I didn't plan to shoot Ace again, but I did it anyway.

"Ace, come on. Don't do this, man," I pleaded with my friend. The zombie flipped onto its stomach and began to claw its way across the muddy ground toward me.

My head spun. My chest tightened and each breath I drew in hurt. My limbs felt as if they were attached by silly putty. I just needed enough strength to lift my gun, but every nerve in my body screamed at me not to. I'd already shot him once. I couldn't do it again. I scooted another few inches back.

"Goddammit, Ace. Answer me!" My voice rose to a high, squeaky pitch. This must be panic.

My friend was gone. Forever.

I scrambled to my feet, unable to shoot down the corpse that had once been Ace, even if I knew it would never be him again. The end of the alley met me with a wall of darkness and a giant, looming monster out of my nightmares. Ace and BigMac were never far apart. BigMac had been no more than ten feet from his best friend the entire time.

Ace rasped a broken melody behind me. BigMac, with his missing throat, just gaped at me and hissed.

That was my first death in Redby.

CHAPTER NINETEEN

OAK RIDGE MENTAL HOSPITAL, TEXAS
August 24, 2032

I remember being dead.

It's not something you think would stay with you. Brain shuts down, body cools, nothing left of you. That's the way zombies are supposed to work.

That isn't how the virus works.

I remember it like a dream. A really bad, full sensory input dream. There was no actual thought involved. I just acted. Street; walk it. Zombies; follow them. People… eat them. I can't even say I was disgusted with myself when I came back again, because the zombie never cared, never questioned its biological imperative. And when I woke up, a different kind of survival instinct kicked in.

I lay in my room, dosed out of my mind on drugs. If I moved my focus for even a split second, the entire room tilted on its side and spun me around. At least they had strapped me in tight.

Air rushed in through my nostrils and ripped at my sensitive skin like rusted nails. The coppery tang of its passing filled my throat, leaking into my lungs, my heart, my stomach, everywhere. My chest ached. Same as my arms and legs. I couldn't remember why. Something violent had happened. I suspected I'd lost.

"Your friends are dead."

"Your parents are far away."

Where did that come from?

I tried to turn my head, but a strap held it in place. I swiveled my eyes around instead, gritting my teeth through the upending of the room. The walls swam in pre-dawn grey while darker blotches shifted and danced at the edges of my vision. All of them loitered about the room, sightless eyes fixed on me. The ghosts never left me. Even when the drugs were strong enough to keep me down.

Ace stood beside my bed, his face creased with worry and his hands shoved into the pockets of his cargo pants. He wore that stupid, ratty old red hoodie that he liked so much. He wore it to bed almost religiously back in Basic. His eyes were shadowed from lack of sleep and I imagined that he'd been up half the night looking out for me.

"Hey, Princess," he said in a soft, sorrowful tone. Why was he sad? Was I dying for real this time? Sure, I hurt a little, but I'd died before. This did not feel like lethal pain. His face lightened with the hint of a smile and he answered my questions without me even needing to open my mouth. "No, you're not dying. You're not getting better though."

"Of course I am. That's why I'm here. Wherever here is." The voice did not sound like my own. It undulated through the air, warping in colourful waves before my eyes. I did not like this strange voice, but it echoed my thoughts, so I left it alone.

Ace shook his head. His words echoed through the murk. "This is just like you. Put your head down and push your way through any problem like a damn bull. When are you going to learn that you can't force some problems to fix themselves?"

"Sure I can. Obviously, I'm not pushing hard enough. Watch."

I tried to sit up. The straps held me down.

My heart lurched into my throat and I tried to thrash my way off the bed. The room became a centrifuge, spinning me round and round and forcing me ever harder onto the blankets. I clawed at the soft covers, doing no more damage than a kitten's claws. It took a few minutes for me to figure out that I could not get out of these bindings.

"It's not going to work. Nothing you do here will work." Ace waved off my glare. "You just don't get it, do you, Cass? Me and the rest, we're not trying to torment you. We're trying to help you. This is you trying to help yourself, and you're not listening."

"Bull. You've been nothing but an ass since I got here. That is not helpful."

"I've been an ass because you needed me to be an ass. On some level, you've already figured out what I'm trying to tell you."

"If it's that you're an ass, yeah, I got that."

Ace leaned forward and planted his hands on the pillow to either side of my head. I stared into his eyes. Through his eyes. I could see the ceiling behind him.

"Dammit, you're not listening. Again. You know, I think you listened to me more when I was alive."

"Because I liked you then."

"Because I wasn't part of you then. It's like you're programmed to ignore any sense your brain comes up with."

"I am not. I can be totally sensible."

"All you're being is contrary."

"Am not. And Ace would never use a word like contrary. It's all big and stuff." A childish, high-pitched giggle echoed around the blurred corners of the room.

Ace gave me a patient, if somewhat aggrieved, smile before he started pacing. He never walked out of my line of sight. Just back and forth beside the bed, one hand cupping his elbow while the other pinched the bridge of his nose. "I know things are muddled right now, but I need you to think. Think about what I was to you before you got here. What changed. Why I changed."

I did think about it. Or tried to. I had trouble connecting one thought to another. My brain sloshed around in my head, moving to the rhythm of my rising and falling breaths. Forming a single thought became as difficult as picking a red dye out of a bowl of water. I could put my fingers in the dye, through it, but never separate it from the rest of the liquid. Thinking was hard, so I decided it wasn't important.

"It is important! Focus!" The hiss of Ace's words drove a spike between my eyes.

Pain.

Not just on the physical level. Something deeper lurked in the shadows of my room, buried by the constant onslaught of paranoia and sullenness that made up my everyday life. A shield I'd built to protect myself, make it

165

easier to survive. Cut yourself off from the wounds you can't heal so they don't cripple you later. To survive Redby, I lost the ability to connect to people. I had a crew, not friends. People in my care, not people I cared for. All of it a lie, but a lie that kept me alive.

What had I cut out when they'd sent me to the hospital?

"Why did you come here, Cass?" Ace asked in a hollow whisper.

"To get better."

"Why do you need to get better?"

"So that I can live a normal life."

"What is normal?"

"I…"

I didn't know. A life with a job and a house and a social circle. The things people were supposed to have. That was what most of the world strove for as soon as they realized they couldn't live off their parents forever.

"Do you really think they'll let you have that?"

"What else can they do? I won't be here forever."

"Won't you? How do you know what their definition of normal is? How do you know they won't keep sending you back here saying that you need more therapy?"

"No…" No, that wasn't right. They couldn't keep me here forever. "The doc said I'm improving. Once I've improved enough, he'll let me go. He'll sign the papers and tell me I'm a free woman."

"No, he won't. Why are you really here, Cass?"

"I told you. To get better. To be normal."

"You're lying to yourself. Try again."

Anger flared up from my gut. A chill chased it and when the two met, my stomach threatened to expel itself. I desperately wanted a drink, but there was no one around to help me. Just Ace and his damn questions.

"You've never given up before. Even when you had to run, you always found a way to come back and get the job done. So why did you give up when the police came for you?"

"They would have found me anyway."

"That isn't it and you know it."

"My prints were all over the scene. A dozen witnesses watched me kill the guy. What was I going to do? Find a hole to live in for the rest of my life?"

"Cass, why did you turn yourself in?" Again, the room exploded with a bright white flare that sent a lance of pain through my forehead. This time, I flared back.

"I was fucking scared, alright? Because the world doesn't make any sense. Cars that drive themselves and bots that fly right in through your front fucking window. People are just numbers now. Things to be bought and sold. It's not the world I left behind and it's sure as hell not the world I fought to protect. It's alien and it's cold and I hate every inch of it. I don't belong out there."

"And you think they're going to let you live a normal life in that world?"

Cold understanding slammed into my gut.

"What about us, Cass? Do you honestly think they'll let you keep us?"

A chill ran down my spine. My eyes locked on Ace's face, willing him to be solid and real and eternal. I'd been living with my ghosts for so long that I couldn't imagine life without them. Sure, I'd tried to get rid of them, but all families bicker. Everyone wanted to be rid of their troublesome relatives. Until that possibility materialized. Then you'd give anything just for one more day with them.

"The next time you're in a bar, or a store, or just walking down the street and something goes wrong, they'll find a way to blame you. People that go missing will be your fault. Murders that happen in your home town will be your work. It won't matter if you're involved or not. That's what people will see. They are never going to let you stop being a Red."

Ace's words sank in. Finally. I closed my eyes, let the darkness settle around my trembling thoughts, then opened them and found his face above me, still fixated on me. The others leaned in, Tommy, BigMac, everyone I'd let down. "What am I supposed to do, Ace?"

"Stop fighting yourself. You are a Red. Stop trying to turn yourself into what you think will satisfy them. Being what they want means giving up everything you are. Everything you have fought and died for. You'll lose your family, your memories... Us. You didn't come here to get better. You came here to hide. Long ago, you told me you'd rather die than give up the fight. Whether you like it or not, the fight's not over. You have to pick yourself up and keep going. You can't give up, Cass. You can never give up." Ace's voice rose with anger on the last few words.

I was damaged. That was undeniable. The hospital had drugs and programs that could help me deal with that damage. I'd made some progress working with them, but at what cost? I could become whatever complacent little creature they wanted me to be. Then I could become the scapegoat for everything that went wrong around me.

Redby had been the worst kind of hell I'd ever experienced. Ten years of non-stop death and suffering and loss. Yet through all that, I'd found a reason to keep going, day after day. I'd found my purpose in life.

I wasn't going to have that purpose anymore once the doc finished with me.

"Now you're getting it," Ace whispered. "There is no life for us out there, Cass. You don't have any skills that could get you a normal job. You would need to stop being who you are just to find a home and a community that would accept you. And all of it would disappear the moment anyone discovered your past."

"So, what am I supposed to do? Spend the rest of my life on the streets?"

"No. You find a way to survive. Like we always have." Ace's hand drifted over my own. My skin felt nothing. My mind felt a blaze of warmth where his fingers touched mine. "And we do it on our terms."

"Yeah. Alright. Our terms."

The drugs started to pull me under again. The edges of the room blurred into static as consciousness slipped away. I held onto Ace as long as I could. Just before darkness swarmed over my vision, I made him promise to remind me when I woke up.

I would get better. On my own terms.

CHAPTER TWENTY

REDBY, NEVADA
August 25, 2021

Pain. A lot of it. I didn't think pain existed in purgatory. Unless I'd already been judged and sent to hell. I could see that being possible, what with me killing my teammates and failing to formulate an escape. I really botched our last mission badly. Then there was all that illegal stuff I'd done as a youth. Yeah, I could see myself ending up in hell pretty easily.

As soon as I'd settled on that idea, I began to question why the pain wasn't excruciating. Sure, it ran through my entire body, making even the thought of movement frightful, but I wasn't screaming. My limbs didn't feel like they were being twisted off or roasted while I lay awake and aware of every sensation. Come to think of it, there was no fire at all. Not even a whiff of sulfur. If this was hell, I'd ended up in a pretty lame part of it.

I opened my eyes, convinced I would come face to face with some horrific representation of my failings in life. Demonic versions of Ace and BigMac or bodies twisted in torment hung from a cavern roof. Instead, I stared at a panel of fluorescent lights set in a flat, white ceiling. The lights were dead silent and dark. Except for that one making a high-pitched ringing sound.

No, wait, the ringing came from inside my head.

I tried to sit up even though every part of my body screamed at me to lie still. I ignored it, and it decided to take some vengeance.

The nausea started as a tingling feeling in the back of my throat. Then a tidal wave erupted in my stomach, threw itself up my esophagus, and broke past all my defences. I had half a second to realize I could not stop the flow, twist sideways, and lose my stomach contents on the cold, tiled floor. What came out of my mouth was a sickly grey mess that I couldn't remember ingesting. A metallic taste lingered on my tongue. It took me a minute to connect the odd taste to blood, and then I threw up again.

I lay on the floor in a barely conscious state for what felt like hours, emptying my stomach again and again until I had nothing left to give. Then I lay there and dry heaved until my lungs ached. When my body had finished punishing me, I collapsed into the fetal position and curled my hands over my head, trying to ignore the shivers wracking my body.

Okay, this was hell.

A demon waited nearby, running steel against steel to create a soundtrack for my torture. The sound filled my world after the heaving finished. A steady rhythm that would have been pleasant save for the way it shredded my nerves. It was too loud, too close, and something about the smooth, endless melody felt ominous.

"You done yet?" a familiar voice rasped in my ear. The harsh, gravely tone mixed with the hiss of steel made every nerve in my body tingle as if electrocuted.

I didn't answer. Just curled tighter in on myself and willed the world to stop existing.

"You might wanna speak up. I'm still not sure I shouldn't light you up like a Roman candle."

My stomach bottomed out when the familiar tone finally made its connection. Tommy. He'd found me. He must have dragged me back to his place and… and how did I survive? The last thing I remembered was being torn apart by a dozen hungry undead.

Vivid, painful memories surged to the forefront of my thoughts. Their bony fingers sharp as knives, digging into my flesh. Teeth like saw blades tearing off chunks of my skin, latching into bone and pinning me in place. An endless sea of stinking bodies pressing in, vying for a taste of me. If I'd been able to hurl my actual stomach onto the floor, I would have. Instead, I suffered a few more dry heaves before being able to turn my head enough to catch sight of him.

Tommy sat in a chair beside the kitchen table, sharpening a knife on a slab of stone. The light slanting in from the kitchen window caught on his hat and cast a shadow across everything except his lips. They were set in a scowl, utterly immobile. He put aside the knife and stone when he caught my eye and tipped his hat up enough for me to get a glimpse of his cloudy grey eyes. Angry eyes.

"Losing patience here, sweetheart."

"Tommy?" I croaked. My God, was that my voice? It sounded old and haggard, like I'd lived a hundred years instead of a little over two decades.

"So, you can speak. Good. That's one thing I know the rotters can't do. Now, you mind telling me what the hell you were doing?"

"How'd I get here?" My brain could only process one thing at a time. The taste of bile remained in the back of my throat, threatening to make a reappearance if I thought about it for too long. Turning my head to spit it out allowed me to escape Tommy's searing stare.

"I brought you here after I rescued your ass. Followed the sound of the truck, then had to sacrifice the damn thing to get you out. I think you would've liked the effort. Drove it right into a building and set it on fire. Took out the whole place along with a good chunk of the horde you'd hooked up with. Had to drag you back here on foot, guns blazing the entire time, and then stick you with the needle. Which, by the way, does work. Guess whoever finds the rest of those things is going to be real happy."

"They don't work," I countered. He must've found me before I died because there was no way I would willingly come back to this place. I already knew the Quicks were bogus.

"I'd say you breathing and speaking says otherwise."

I looked up at Tommy. He sat there all smug and convinced he was right. Like he needed to have been the guy who literally brought me back from the dead in order to win. Win at what, I didn't know, but the whole act started to piss me off. I'd lost my best friends twice. Once to death, and once to false hope. Yet he sat there expecting me to kiss his feet in gratitude. I wasn't grateful. I would rather have died than wake up to know the extent of my failure.

"I tried it. Nothing happened." My voice came out as a cold, firm line.

"So that's why you snuck out, huh? To go find some buddy of yours that you thought needed saving?" Tommy leaned forward in his chair and planted his elbows on his knees. A slow, laughing sneer wormed its way across his lips. "Someone important enough to die for?"

"They didn't deserve this."

Then the dam burst.

"Of course they didn't. None of us did. Christ, what do you think this town was before you got here? A haven for murderers and thieves? We were all just normal people. We didn't ask for this shit. Hell, if we had known what Almesa was up to, do you really think we would've invited them into our homes with open arms?" The force of Tommy's words drove him to his feet. He paced back and forth in front of me, his hands flying about to punctuate each new question. "I mean, for Christ's sake, Cass, what the hell were you thinking? After everything I told you, what the hell made you think that was a good idea?"

"It's not like I dragged you along. You could've just left well enough alone," I said.

"Like hell I could have."

"What the hell have you got to be so pissed off about?" I snarled. We were just partners. It wasn't like I'd made a commitment to him.

"You, Cass! You! Christ's sake, do you think you're the only one who had the bright idea to go out and save people? Do you think that wasn't the first thought going through my head? You had what? Army buddies out there? People you thought you needed?"

"They were good men." I wanted to say more, to tell him how important Ace and BigMac were.

His voice bellowed over me before I got another word out. "Who the hell wasn't? In this town, who the hell didn't have people they needed and cared about?" Tommy spent his rage in a roar, then collapsed back into his chair.

When he spoke again, control had returned to his voice. Still brimming with pent up aggression, but at least it wasn't flying in my face anymore. "I had parents here, friends, relatives. Everyone I knew lived here. The first thing that came to mind when we found those damn needles was I could save them. I could bring them all back. First it'd be my mom and dad, then my uncle Charlie. Can't forget his wife and kid too. That's five needles gone already and I haven't even gotten outside the family. And what about the rest, huh? Who would I pick to live and who would stay dead? Undead. Tell me, did you head straight for your good old buddies or did you consider saving any of the civilians you passed along the way? You know, the people you're sworn to protect? I know they weren't anything important to you, but you could've saved them, Cass. Right?"

"Fuck off, Tommy."

Tommy flew to his feet and into my face. He crouched on the floor in front of me and leaned in until we were less than a foot apart. Behind me lay my pool of sick, and then a wall. In front of me, filling the room with his rage, was my partner. I had nowhere to go.

"No, you owe me now, Cass. Not 'cause I saved your ass but because I was right. Those damn things are nothing but a curse. So, you're going to listen to me now whether you like it or not. When we get out of here, and we will, you have something to go back to. You have your parents, or the military, or whatever the hell you choose. You have options. Me? My entire life was here. Everyone I loved and everything that mattered was here. Even if we save the town, it'll never be the same way again. So, you can give me whatever excuse you want for going to your buddies but unless it amounts to calling down God Almighty and turning back the clock, it will mean less than shit. This town was everything to me. Now all I've got is you." He paused to let the words sink in. "You are my everything, and I just about lost you too."

I didn't say anything. I couldn't. My brain shut down. I sat somewhere between admiring this new, dangerous side of Tommy and trying to reconcile the beneficial partnership we had with the deep attachment he'd just thrown at me. Tommy didn't wait for me to overcome my stupor. He stood up and reached into his pocket. Something clattered to the ground beside me. Out of the corner of my eye, I caught a flash of sunlight glinting off two sets of steel tags.

"Take it these guys were your buddies. Got this off them just before everything exploded. They're not coming back."

Then Tommy turned around and stormed off. The door to his bedroom slammed shut, and I knew he wasn't coming back. Good. I needed time to think.

I needed to clean myself up first though. I reeked of rot and vomit and other things I didn't want to think about. My clothes were ruined and my weapons gone, but it didn't matter, we had spares. Assuming I would be around in the evening to ask Tommy for some. A very loud part of my brain told me my best bet was to run out the door and never come back.

Instead, I forced my pain wracked body to lift itself off the floor. After a second of thought, I scraped the dog tags off the tiles and shoved them into my pocket. I hated cleaning, but dealing with my mess meant less time dealing with Tommy. I got some paper towels and got to work. So, did my brain.

In terms of connections, Tommy had a point. He really had only me. He was a social person, but even he wasn't dense enough to go strolling on up to the nearest band of survivors looking for new friends. The survivors of the last few weeks were scarred and hardened people. They were more likely to shoot first and loot later. He'd taken a risk on me. We'd bonded since then. That much I could understand. The suicidal run to rescue my undead ass was the mind-boggling part. Only people who were stupidly in love with each other did that sort of stuff. Tommy hadn't fallen...

Oh hell. Had he fallen? Was that the key that I didn't have?

The full meaning of Tommy's words hit me like a sledgehammer. My legs turned to jelly and my weight collapsed on itself. I hit the ground hard enough to send a jolt up my spine.

Tommy had fallen in love with me.

Oh God. Tommy had fallen in love with me.

What the hell was I still doing there? I didn't want some love-sick puppy following me around. He would get us both killed.

Never mind how I'd already done that myself. Chasing after people I cared about too much to lose.

Right. I should leave. I stood up and looked at the door. I willed myself to move. Nothing happened. I sat down again.

This was stupid. I was being stupid. I didn't get attached to people. There were too many dangers. Going through Basic, I'd encouraged the Gutter Princess nickname. The less people wanted to know about me, the safer I could be. So, the smart thing to do would be walk out on Tommy before things got complicated.

But I couldn't walk out. Every time I looked at the door, Tommy's face filled my vision. Tommy with his stupid steely grey eyes and even stupider cowboy hat, and that especially stupid grin. Much as I hated to admit it to myself, he was all I had left too.

I needed to talk to Tommy. It was possible, very remotely possible, that I'd just misinterpreted his actions. It could be that he only rescued me because he still found me useful. Barging into his room and accusing him of falling in love with me would turn into a very awkward situation if that was the case.

First, I needed to change my clothes. I washed up in the bathroom sink and caught a glimpse of myself in the mirror. Ashen skin, matted hair, and pink, puckered lines left by healing scars. Dressed in civilian clothes, a simple black t-shirt and blue jeans, I could barely recognize myself. I pulled my tags out from under my shirt and held them over my heart. Those, at least, were unchanged. I was still Cassandra Saratores; soldier. I pulled Ace and BigMac's tags out of my pocket and examined them in the light. Mud encrusted the steel. I flicked it off with the edge of my fingernail and ran my thumb over the indentations. Sebastian Montana and Mackenzie Hobbs. Dead and gone. I pulled the chains over my head and settled the tags next to my own. The weight of them burned against my skin. Then I took a deep breath and headed to Tommy's room.

The door opened after one knock. Tommy went back to the bed and sat on the edge. He glanced at me once, like he had to make sure I hadn't knocked and dashed off, and then he went back to his busy work. A cleaning rag and pistol occupied his hands while I stood in the doorway, trapped on the threshold.

"Hey," I said in a small voice.

"Hey," he answered. The rag moved in a steady rhythm over the gun in the stillness that followed.

Once again, I found my voice failing me. I knew exactly what I had to say, but I didn't want to. I didn't want to allow that final acknowledgement of what I'd discovered. Like I could make it not real by saying nothing. We could go back to being just partners. I could go back to being ignorant of how people who were not raised to be loners operated. Instead, I forced my lips to open, my throat to work, and sound stuttered out.

"Tommy, do you…"

"Love you? Yeah."

A single long breath whooshed out of my lungs, followed by actual words. "That's why you came for me then."

"It's why you went out there to save your army buddies, right?"

I stared at him in shock.

"What? No. I didn't love Ace and BigMac. They were just… They were…" My hand closed over the tags. What were they? My friends. My teammates. I didn't feel love for them, not like what Tommy felt for me, but I had been willing to risk my life to save them. Just like I accused Tommy of doing for me.

"Your family. I get it," he said.

Good, because I didn't.

Ace and BigMac were not my family. My parents were my family. Ace and BigMac were the people I depended on to keep me alive. I needed them to watch my back. I trusted them. I trusted Tommy too but there was something Ace and BigMac could give me that he couldn't. They grounded me. Having them alive and by my side let me know that we had a way to go back to how things used to be. The three of us, looking out for each other, protecting each other. Keeping each other sane.

"I needed them. The way you need me," I said after a few minutes.

"You could need me too, you know."

"No, I can't. It's not that easy, Tommy." Pressure built behind my eyes. My brain couldn't handle all this new information, let alone process it. I raised a hand to pinch the bridge of my nose and dug out what bits of information I needed for this discussion. "Look, I need you as a partner and… Yeah, I like you. Things are a little too crazy for me to think about anything other than that just yet."

"It's not something you need to think about, Cass. Is it there or not?"

I said nothing. I didn't even look up. Several more minutes passed before he spoke again, resignation in his tone. "Okay. That's okay. I can wait."

"That's not an option."

"Why not?"

Because it would be crazy? Because he would throw his life away waiting for something that wasn't going to happen? Because a million reasons that all seemed perfectly logical in my head but I couldn't voice. I picked one, the most rational one, and looked him in the eye to deliver it. "Because once we get out of here I'll need to report this. I'll go back to the military."

"And I'll go with you."

"No, Tommy. I mean, I'll go back. For good." I paused a second to let that sink in. Not many people chose to go career military. Fewer still chose to dedicate their lives to those people. "The military's the only thing in my life that's ever been stable. I won't leave them. Even after all this."

"Then I'll wait."

I let out a sudden, exasperated sigh.

Tommy didn't like that. He came to his feet, his voice filling the room just as it had in the kitchen. "Jesus, Cass, I'm not stupid. You keep treating me like some kinda special needs kid you have to lead around by the hand. I don't need a sugar coating. I've saved your life near as often as you've saved mine. I know how to handle a gun. I know what's going to happen once we get to the other side. More running, hiding, searching for the right way out of this goddamn mess. Less zombies, but hell, I kinda like them better than the Almesa assholes at this point."

He paused, sucking in a breath to refill the vacuum left by the sudden storm of words. "It won't be any easier than what we've been doing here and I get that. What I'm feeling ain't a part time thing though. I'm not going to wake up tomorrow and decide I want to love a supermodel instead. I know what love is and what it means. I love you. And I'll wait for you."

There he went again, breaking me. I couldn't think of a reason to turn him down anymore, even though I was still convinced this was a terrible idea. He could vow to be loyal all he wanted. Following through would not be possible on the outside. The only thing keeping us together was a mutual need to survive. Soon as we got out, he'd see that and be gone. He wouldn't even have time to see the mess of my life.

"You have no idea what you're getting mixed up in," I muttered in defeat.

A grin broke across Tommy's face. He crossed the room in two steps, his hands on my shoulders and his wide-brimmed hat brushing the top of my hair.

"A month ago, I had no idea how to kill zombies. I think I'll get by." Then he kissed me.

His lips were warm and soft and inviting. I lost myself to the moment. I don't know how long. I stopped trying to count the seconds or make sense of what went on around me. It hurt too much. As long as I stood in the doorway with Tommy, time froze. Nothing existed outside the circle of his arms.

When he pulled away, the world snapped back into focus. I was about to escape an impenetrable fortress of undead doom with nothing but a handful of weapons and an insane boyfriend. I may not have been ready to love him yet, but I wanted to make damn sure he lived to see tomorrow. Even if that meant I had to die.

Again.

"Come on," he whispered in my ear, his lips brushing my jaw. I found myself grinning back, his contagious excitement bleeding over my hesitation. He tugged me away from the wall and out into the hallway. "We have a wall to storm."

CHAPTER TWENTY-ONE

OAK RIDGE MENTAL HOSPITAL, TEXAS
August 25, 2032

They didn't remove the restraints for another full day. I drifted in and out of a drug haze while orderlies fed me my meals and changed my clothes. I'm sure I would've been indignant if I knew what they were doing for me.

Ace, Tommy, and all the rest stopped visiting. I still saw their shadows drifting across the wall, swimming through a world I could neither touch nor hear. Bit by bit, they became more distant and indistinct until nothing remained but the memory of their presence.

And the promise.

The first thing I did upon finally being able to string together an entire, coherent thought was recall as much as I could of my time under sedation. Most of my memories were choppy or so disjointed as to make no sense at all. I went through them one at a time until I came to the memory of Ace. Our entire conversation played out in my mind, fresh as if we had it two seconds ago. Everything was intact. Good. I would not forget my promise to him.

The second thing I did involved finding out my damage tally for this episode. Five staff members injured, three of them needing hospital care, including my doctor. One patient dead. Not my fault. Not directly. She'd died in the confusion caused by my breakout. Something about a drug overdose and inappropriate care. Whatever they said, they thought I was responsible. Just like Ace said they would.

I got breakfast in my room. That worked fine for me as it gave me time to go over some of my more confusing memories. Such as the one that involved Zeke and floating, fuzzy lights. He was the man in the hallway.

The one who drugged me. No one else at the hospital came near to matching his height or unique looks. Having come to that conclusion, I was left with the very troubling question of why he wanted to stop me. And what he meant when he said it wasn't time yet.

I needed to talk to him.

I asked for a shower after lunch. The guard outside my door, a sour-faced woman with more girth than height, obliged me. Of course, they'd give me a female guard. That way she could follow me into the washroom.

Privacy is dead.

Thirty seconds after entering the washroom, someone started screaming in the hallway. I came out of the stall in time to see my guard stick her head out the door and begin cursing up a storm. She pulled her head back in, gave me a shrewd-eyed glare, and waggled a finger in my face.

"Stay right there. Right. There." Her finger jabbed at the spot on the floor, just before the row of sinks across from the toilets. I pointed at the same spot and gave her my most innocent expression.

"Right here?"

"Right. There." Then she was gone.

As she commanded, I did not move. I towelled off my hair, wrapped the towel around my shoulders and started examining how long my nails had grown since I'd last cut them when the door opened again. I expected my guard. In fact, I would've been happy to see her face. Instead I got Zeke.

"Hello Cassandra." He greeted me with a serpentine smile, as if we had just met by chance in the rec room once more.

"You," I snarled back. The only thing keeping me from leaping forward and clawing his eyes out was a stubborn need to disrupt whatever low expectations my guard had of me. I just knew she would be smug as hell if I stood anywhere but exactly where she left me when she returned.

"I suppose you have a few questions for me." Zeke took a few steps forward. I balled my hands into fists to make sure he knew I was ready for him. He stopped walking, holding his hands up in surrender.

"Damn straight. Who the hell are you?"

"I am Ezekiel Okayama. We have already been over this."

"You know what I mean."

"Yes. Yes, I do." The smile grew wider. Most people got a twinkle in their eye when they were as delighted as he looked. His eyes remained flat and dark and calculating. "I am a mercenary. I was sent here to retrieve you."

Puzzle pieces started to fall into place. The sneakiness, the constant vigilance, the casual approach. Zeke was more than a mercenary. He was a professional. The kind that cared only about the money and nothing about the people hurt along the way. The kind of person Almesa liked.

"I hate mercs."

"I know. As does my employer. He believed it would be useful in gaining your attention." Again the smile twitched at his lips, like a snake trying to escape a closed sack. "It worked."

"What the hell does your employer want with me?"

"That is not something I have been briefed on. You would have to ask him." Another step forward. I did not move. Not even an inch.

"Bullshit. He wouldn't send you in here with half a plan. Answer the question, or I start screaming." Screaming was the one advantage I had. Every guard within hearing distance would be in the room in seconds. Standard response to a patient freak-out.

"You wouldn't do that. It would be too much like calling for help." Another step forward.

"Try me."

Zeke shot forward faster than I'd ever seen anyone move. Faster than the snake he seemed so keen on emulating. His arm snapped out to catch my wrist as I raised it in defence, his body sliding in to pin me to the wall. I recognized the move a second before it hit me. Just long enough to shift my weight sideways and slide out of his grasp. My hand came up to shove his head into the wall and give a quick end to the fight. He saw it, expected it, jerked his head back just in time. I caught his chin instead. He twisted at the waist and slipped a leg between mine to upset my balance. It worked, but only because I wanted it to. I already had his neck and shoulders in a lock when I started to go to the ground. He came with me. We hit the tiles together, rolling, fighting for dominance, switching tactics from the quick strikes we both favoured to a test of strength.

In the end, I came up on top, slamming his chest against the cold, tiled floor and twisting one arm around behind his back. I held it straight out behind him with one foot planted on his shoulder blade to keep him immobile. He had an out, if he wanted to dislocate his own shoulder. He struggled for a few seconds before going limp. Then, to my frustration, he laughed.

"You are much better at this when you are focused."

"I'm still waiting for your answer." I gave his arm a little twist.

"Release my arm and I will tell you what I know."

"Nope. Think I like this angle better." Another twist. His lips peeled back in a grimace. I didn't think anyone would be dense enough to harm themselves in an attempt to win a fight. Other than me. I really should've spent more time getting to know Zeke.

A short jolt ran down his arm and through my hands. I had a split second to realize what he'd done before he used the extra few inches of mobility to knock me off my feet. I rolled back, came up in a crouch, and got to my feet in tandem with him.

We launched at each other a second time. Zeke kept his dislocated arm close to his chest. I took advantage of the weakness, circling around him, always on his bad side. We worked our way around the room, never allowing each other to get close enough to any of the stalls or sinks to use them as props. No normal human could bend the way he did, arching backward whenever I threw a punch, sliding sideways to keep me from pinning him to the wall. If his arm gave him a disadvantage, he didn't show it. I would've had better luck fighting a wall of water.

The fight began to take its toll. Despite the exercise yard, I didn't have much time to work out. Air stuck in my lungs, never enough to fill them. I started looking for a quick way to end the battle. Zeke beat me to it.

His leg shot out of nowhere, appearing in my peripheral vision one second too late. His foot connected with my head and I went flying.

I hit the wall hard, stars bursting before my eyes. Instinct drove me to cling to the sink beside me to keep my balance. When the stars cleared, Zeke stood a few inches away. He held his dislocated arm against his side.

With the same lightning quick speed he'd used to attack me, he turned to the wall, slammed his shoulder against it, and reset his arm.

"Ow," he said, as if he'd just stubbed his toe. I tried to slip past him while he was distracted.

"Enough." His good arm came up across my throat and drove me back against the wall. Stars again, but this time they came from a sudden lack of oxygen. I wrapped my hands around his arm, but with no air filling my lungs, Zeke having all the leverage, and the sink refusing to give me a few inches in which to move, I couldn't make him budge. Zeke leaned in close to my face. "Calm yourself, woman."

"Fuck you."

I brought a knee up, but he deflected it against his leg before I could reach his groin.

"Do you want answers or not?" His voice took on an edge of irritation.

"So now you're willing to talk, huh?"

"I was always willing to talk. What I need is for you to cease squirming and listen."

Darkness crept in at the edge of my vision. I would be able to breathe better if I stopped struggling, but then I would be admitting defeat to Zeke.

"You are literally choking the life out of me. What part of this is supposed to convince me you're not just here to kill me?" I rasped beneath desperate gulps of air.

The pressure disappeared. Air rushed back into my lungs. Zeke stepped back and swept his hands out to his sides, as if waiting for applause at the end of a magic trick.

"Better?" he asked.

"Okay, talk. But if I don't like what I hear, I call for help. Or punch you in the throat. We'll see how I'm feeling."

"Someone on the outside wants you delivered alive."

"Yeah. Think I'll go with punching."

"My employer..."

I threw a punch before Zeke could finish his sentence. He caught my fist two inches from his face and let out an exasperated breath. I would enjoy beating the smug look right off his face. Then he said three words that sucker punched the fight out of me.

"…is Thomas Grayson."

CHAPTER TWENTY-TWO

"So, what's the plan?" Tommy asked as we stood over his arsenal of odds and ends. In preparation for the battle to come, he'd pulled out every gadget, weapon, gardening tool, and random piece of crap he owned and piled them in the middle of the living room floor. Boxes marched around the outside of the pile like a cardboard fort, marshalling the chaos of equipment into a kind of order.

"Well we can't just go waltzing in there. They probably got defences of some kind. We'll need a distraction." I picked up a rake wrapped in colourful wires and held it out to Tommy.

"Electric back scratcher," he supplied. He took the rake and leaned it against the couch in the "potential weapons" stack we'd started. "What're you thinking? Pizza delivery?"

"I wish. Pizza'd be great right about now."

The truth was, I had no idea what the hell we were going to do. Getting out through the wall was great in theory, but it came with the price tag of still being alive on the other side. That would be the tricky part.

I frowned at the mess of gear as I mulled the issue over. Tommy sure had a hell of a lot of electrical gadgets. Putting them together filled his free hours before I arrived, or so he claimed. Personally, I think he did a lot more pole pulling during those days than he cared to admit.

I bent to retrieve something shiny from the bottom of the stack. After a few tugs, I held a small, silver lighter in my hand. An intricate tracing of a skull and snake writhed across one side. I flicked the top and gave the flint a roll with my thumb. A tiny, orange-yellow flame leapt to life before my eyes and sparked a matching flame in my mind.

"Hey Tommy, you remember if there was a sprinkler system down in the tunnels?"

"Huh? Oh, yeah. I think there was. I mean, I remember seeing some kinda sprinkler type thing hanging off the pipes. Might not be any fresh water flowing in, but should still have some saved up in the pipes." He waited a beat. I flicked the lighter shut. "Why?"

"I think I got an idea. You got any gadgets designed to make a lot of noise?"

"Well, yeah. I got the Screamer. Supposed to be an early warning system. Damn thing kept going off in the middle of the night though." Silence. "Why?"

"How's it fare if it gets wet?"

This time, Tommy rolled his eyes.

"Like all mechanical shit that gets messed with. Goes up in a giant fireball. What do you think happens? It stops working."

I stood up and smiled at my partner, tucking the lighter into my pocket.

"Think you can keep it alive long enough to attract a horde?"

Tommy smiled and started to laugh. When I didn't laugh with him, the smile dripped off his face like ink running down a drain.

"You're not serious."

I didn't say a word.

Tommy took my shoulders in his hands and held me at arm's length. "Cass, tell me you are not serious."

I was totally serious.

We headed into the tunnels ready for bear season. Guns, knives, flashlights, body armour—made primarily from old coats and kitchenware—backpacks full of ammunition, and enough of Tommy's toys to start our own rave. We got past the sewer opening by blasting our way through the throngs of undead using Basil's fancy energy weapon. A flashlight placed at the top of the manhole ensured that even if the first group didn't get back up in time, we'd still have plenty of zombies for our plan.

Then came set up. To give us enough time, we barricaded the door to the secret tunnels. Even if they broke through, we'd have warning before they were on top of us. Finding the doorway into the wall itself proved easier than either of us expected. The smartphone led us right to it. No detours, no traps, not even a security camera.

Tommy set the Screamer in its place of honour right before the door and I headed back to the barricade to begin phase two.

Phase two was not as clean cut as phase one. As I stared at the flimsy pieces of wood blocking off the door to the sewer tunnels, all outlined in green thanks to my goggles, I had to wonder how much of my sanity really had gone down the drain. Even Ace would've balked at this plan. I had no safety net or back up. My only connection to Tommy existed in a little two-way radio attached to my shoulder. Hit the button too late and I'd be zombie food. Too soon, I'd be zombie food. Hell, if I tripped, I'd be zombie food. I had no wiggle room with this plan.

A few months back, the worst of my worries involved running over a faulty IED. Now I found myself wishing for those carefree days.

I drew in a deep breath and pried off the first board blocking the sewer door. The undead moaned from the other side, awakened to my presence like a cat called by a can opener. The second board came away and crashed to the ground. The zombies pounded on the door, making it shiver against its hinges. Just before pulling off the last piece of the barricade, I kicked the debris out of the way, set my feet facing the other way, and counted to three.

Later in my life I would have to question my choice of what to scream in a moment of dramatic tension. At the time, as soon as that door flew open, all I could think of was "Boo!"

And then I ran.

The undead came screaming into the secret tunnels, their gurgling cries echoing off the pitch-black walls, filling every nook and cranny until the floor itself vibrated to the sound of the hunt. I didn't bother checking to see how big of a following I'd gathered.

The first corridor flew past. Two more and I threw myself down a side tunnel. Another turn, another inch lost to the rampaging horde. A twisted thought flitted through my mind, painting an image of myself as some sort of insane Pied Piper. Dude had it easy. Rats only gave you the plague.

I started to laugh. I couldn't help myself. I didn't have to worry about how crazy I looked because no one in their right mind would be leading a legion of zombies to assault the secret, underground entrance to a hollow wall anyway.

There! A piece of reflective tape torn off a work vest. Tommy's signal to let me know when to start phase three. I hit the button on my walkie-talkie.

"Now!" I screamed, then waited for the fireworks.

Another turn. I had little hallway left. No explosion. No fireworks. No water.

Oh shit.

"Tommy!" The radio answered with static. A door stared at me from the end of the hall. "Tommy, answer me you son of a bitch!"

He never did. I did get my fireworks though.

They started with a short whistle, and then a bang. The end of the hall lit up with a million puffs of flame, increasing in intensity the closer I got. The sprinklers stuttered and began to spit water onto my head. I didn't see the door at the end of the hall open, but I heard it clunk against the wall. Someone started yelling from the other side. The Screamer drowned them out. The Screamer drowned everything out.

White noise, shrill and piercing, blasted down the hall. Shrieks and static and whooping alarms rang through my skull until I thought my ears would bleed. No wonder Tommy called it the Screamer.

The blinding white brilliance of the fireworks began to fade, allowing green, fuzzy edges to fade in across my vision. An arm hooked around my midsection and yanked me down a maintenance shaft. Just in time too. Whoever started shouting from the other side of the door opened up with a barrage of gunfire into the wave of hungry undead.

Tommy didn't let go until we squeezed behind a wall of thick, steel pipes. We were soaking wet, out of breath, and less than twenty feet away from a battle for the ages, but we were alive.

I slammed a fist into his arm. "Your radios are shit!"

"Ow! Don't blame me for the shitty reception down here."

"Oh, I blame you."

The Screamer made a noise like a strangled cat and went silent. Gunfire and zombie screams continued.

"Think it worked?" Tommy asked.

"We only need a few to get through. Whichever way they go, we go opposite."

The plan, in all its brilliance, was to use Almesa's creations against them. Force a horde into the sewers and sic 'em on the entrance to the wall. The soldiers would take care of the horde, the horde would take care of the soldiers, and we could waltz in once the air cleared. I didn't like the idea of sacrificing the people who used to be my peers, but they abandoned me first. I just wanted to survive.

When the gunfire died down to a muted rattle deep in the bowels of the wall, I stuck my head out to check the tunnel.

"Coast is clear." I motioned Tommy to stick to my shadow as we made our way up to the entrance. The Screamer lay on the ground just inside the door, the nucleus of a sea of dead bodies and spent ammunition. Blue smoke trickled into the air from numerous bullet holes riddling its flimsy tin shell.

Tommy took off his hat and held it to his chest. "Poor little guy. He died well."

"Christ, you are such a nerd. Put your hat back on and get your gun. I don't want you fumbling around like an idiot when we run into trouble."

"Love you too, schnookums."

"Oh, gag me."

Tommy stashed his flashlight and my goggles in the backpack. We didn't need them inside the wall. The soft, white glow of fluorescent lights filled every inch of the entrance with all the comfort of a hospital waiting room. Or it would if not for the pulsating beat of a red light silently announcing our presence. The garish splatter of blood painting the once pristine white walls looked less menacing in the alarm's flashing light. Though it did nothing good for the multitude of bodies littering the floor.

"Which way?" Tommy whispered.

"You're the one with the damn map."

"Oh, yeah."

Tommy fished the phone out of his pocket but before he could plot us a course, the little device exploded in his hands. He let out a cry as blood welled between his fingers. I grabbed him by the collar, dragging him to the ground seconds before a bullet tore through the air above us.

"Halt!"

Shit. Backup.

Men in black body armour pounded down a stairwell from the left, their faces concealed by black helmets. Half a dozen assault rifles pointed our way. They swarmed around us in precise order, ready to fire if we so much as twitched the wrong way.

"Well, it was worth a shot. Nice knowing you." Tommy flashed me a pained grin. He gave up too easy.

"Hands in the air," one of the clone soldiers shouted. Tommy raised his bloody palms to the sky. I moved slower, shifting my weight so Basil's space weapon sat within easy reach. I only needed one second of distraction.

It came in the form of more backup. This time from the opposite team. I never would've thought I'd be thanking a zombie for saving my life, but as the undead creature threw itself on the back of one of the unsuspecting soldiers, I said a quiet thank you.

"Shoot them! Goddammit, shoot them all!"

The soldiers turned on the advancing horde. The second, slower wave of our initial invasion. I drew Basil's   stun gun from my back pocket.

"Down!"

Tommy flattened himself to the floor. I hit the button, unleashing a wave of blue light into the skirmish. Soldiers and zombies went flying across the room like rag dolls, and for a few seconds, the way cleared.

No time to get our bearings now. I grabbed Tommy's arm and hauled him to his feet. The soldiers came from the left. We went right.

"Which way?" I shouted as we tore toward the end of the hall. Not many options awaited us. One doorway leading straight on and a stairwell to our left.

"I don't know! This place is a goddamn maze. Without the map, we're sunk."

"Tommy, we did not come this far to go back now. Pick a direction."

"Up!"

I veered toward the stairwell, taking the steps two at a time. Tommy stumbled after me.

"Why the hell are we going up?" I demanded. The next level appeared first as a wash of red light spilling over the cement stairs. I dove through the opening while shouts of pursuit echoed from the bottom of the stairs.

"We're still underground right now. We gotta get to ground level to find the gate, but to do that, we gotta go up and over," Tommy said.

"Why?"

"Because I like detours. It's a goddamn maze. I already told you that."

"So what? We're looking for stairs until you say otherwise?"

"Right!"

"Okay—"

"No, right!" Tommy hooked a hand around my elbow and yanked me down an adjoining corridor as bullets filled the hallway. I stumbled, found my feet, and kept running. If God was with us, the stairs would be at the end of this hall.

I didn't realize Tommy wasn't right behind me until I heard something clatter to the ground. My heart stopped a second before my feet.

"Tommy!" I turned, expecting to find him sprawled on the ground. Instead, I faced a wall of smoke. Tommy's shotgun roared in the murk and a thick, dark shadow shuffled toward me.

"Go, go," he shouted as the shotgun roared again.

"What the hell was that?"

"Smoke bomb. Where are the stairs?"

I answered by yanking him into the stairwell and not letting go until we were halfway up to the next floor. It took him that long to regain his balance.

"We can slow down a little, you know. It'd be a damn shame to come this far and be offed by you throwing me into a wall."

"This place is crawling with zombies and soldiers, both of which want us dead. And you want to slow down?"

"I wanna live, dammit."

"That's what I'm trying—" Again I got cut off. At the top of the stairs, a trio of soldiers waited with guns raised. I caught a glimpse of their buggy, black helmets seconds before bullets screamed through the air over my head. I ducked down on the cement stairs, caught between one level and the next with Tommy pressed against my side. Without a second thought, I raised the stun gun and pressed the button.

Nothing.

No beep, no whoosh, no wave of blue energy throwing everything aside. I pressed the button again.

Still nothing.

I shook the damn thing and considered throwing it at one of the soldiers. "This damn thing is broken."

"It's not broken. It's recharging. Dammit, I told you, it's gotta build up a charge."

"Yeah, you told me. Doesn't mean I listened."

"We've got them cornered," one of the soldiers shouted.

"Like fuck you do," I snarled back, snatching something small and round off Tommy's belt. I hurled the thing in the air, expecting a wall of smoke to conceal our retreat.

Instead, I got a shower of shrapnel ripping through the soft joints in the soldiers' armour and narrowly missing our own exposed flesh. As the soldiers screamed and writhed on the top step, I grabbed Tommy by the arm and hauled him past their legs.

"What the hell are you doing throwing a grenade over our heads?" he screamed as we pelted down yet another hallway.

"What the hell are you doing making grenades?!"

"Booby-traps!"

Christ. Glad I never tripped any of his alarms by accident.

We hauled ass to the next set of stairs, shouts and tromping feet chasing us every step of the way. Just like before, these stairs lead up. I took them two at a time. Tommy hesitated.

"Tommy, come on! We don't got time to wait around."

"This is wrong," he said, staring at the steps as if they'd turned to quick sand.

"What the hell do you mean wrong? They're stairs. We need stairs. Besides, you said we had to go up before we could get out, right?"

"Yeah but there was supposed to be a down part. I'm pretty sure—"

Gunshots ricocheted off the doorway.

"Tommy, move!"

He did, finally. We made our way to the next level where I began to understand Tommy's hesitation. Something about this floor felt wrong. Maybe it was the absolute silence after the frantic chase. Or maybe it was the sterile white rooms beyond the sterile white doors. Or even the abundance of key card locks everywhere I looked. The longer we raced down the empty halls, the more uneasy my stomach felt. When we reached the end of the hall where the stairwell usually waited, that sense of dread became a full fledged panicked scream in the back of my mind.

A door blocked our way. A door with a key card lock. And we'd lost our key card.

"Shit." Tommy stared at the card reader in disbelief. "Shit! No, no this isn't happening. We're too damn close." He raised his shotgun and nestled the muzzle against the card reader. I ducked for cover behind him, grabbing my pistol to cover our rears. Tommy pulled the trigger to a cry of "This always works in the movies."

The gun roared and the card reader exploded in a shower of broken plastic and sparks. Tommy threw himself against the door, hauling on the handle with all his might, but it didn't budge. He let out an inarticulate roar and kicked it. The door remained steadfast.

"Okay, we're not out yet. There's got to be more stairs, right?"

Silence. I looked over my shoulder at my partner.

"Tommy! There's got to be more stairs, right?"

"Yeah." No fight remained in his voice. His shoulders slumped. Dread returned as curdled milk spoiling in my stomach. "Two levels down."

Two levels down meant going back through all the soldiers we'd just dodged. By now, they would have set up barricades and established choke points. They'd be dealing with the zombies too, but I didn't have high hopes the zombies had made it in far enough to distract them when we came rushing back down the stairs. We might as well have painted targets on our faces for the easy pickings we'd be. No wonder they hadn't chased us up the stairs. No need to expend the effort when we'd have to come down eventually.

"Okay. Okay, we can figure this out."

"Cass, there is no figuring this out. We're stuck. All because I couldn't hold on to the damn key card." Tommy kicked the door again.

"You said it yourself. We're too close to give up. There's got to be another way."

"There is no other way," Tommy exploded. "Every goddamn room on this floor is locked down, which means no access to ventilation shafts, no secret back exits, nothing. There is nothing but the way we came and that's swarming with your goddamn people!"

"Don't go turning this shit around on me. They left me down here to die, same as you."

"And if you hadn't gotten stuck on the wrong side of the wall, you'd be one of them!"

"Hey!" I rounded on Tommy. "I don't know where the hell this is coming from, but it needs to stop right the hell now. None of us knew what we were getting into."

"Yeah, and I can see how they all just hate themselves for going along with it."

My vision turned red. Sure I bitched about how the military abandoned me after years of loyal service all the time, but I had that right. I'd earned it through blood, sweat, and tears. Tommy didn't know them, didn't know what military life was like. He had no right. My hand balled into a fist.

The door opened. Once again, Tommy and I were on the same side. We both raised our guns, stood shoulder to shoulder, and stared down the barrels of three sub-machine guns.

"Stand down." Three soldiers faced us, all wearing the same black suit and helmet as Basil. The same as every soldier we'd passed so far. I couldn't see the speaker's face, but his voice sounded oddly familiar.

"Like hell," Tommy barked. His finger twitched toward the trigger. Before it connected, I slammed the nose of his shotgun down. He stared at me with betrayal in his eyes. Until I nodded to the soldiers, who were also pointing their guns at the ground. The command hadn't been for us.

"Corporal Saratores," the lead soldier said.

"Captain," I replied.

CHAPTER TWENTY-THREE

OAK RIDGE MENTAL HOSPITAL, TEXAS
August 25, 2032

"You're lying." I stood my ground, staring down the merc, as the whole world spun around me.

"He said you would be paranoid. He also said he is still waiting for you to come back for him." Zeke frowned and cocked his head to the side. The next comment came out as a question. "And he mentioned a cowboy hat."

My stomach fell out. I couldn't breathe, and I no longer had Zeke's stranglehold as an excuse. I stumbled back. The wall caught me before my legs gave way.

"Tommy's dead." I hadn't directed the words at Zeke. More to the dark splotches hovering on the edge of my vision. The mercenary replied anyway.

"So were you. It does not seem to be a permanent ailment."

"No, Tommy is dead. I'm sure of it. He died in the wall. Almesa killed him. For good." I knew this to be true. I hadn't actually seen him die, hadn't seen a body, but I knew he died there in the wall around Redby. To believe otherwise, that he'd been locked away in some Almesa test facility for ten goddamn years while I gave up on him, was too much for me to handle.

"Did they tell you that?" Zeke shrugged, and that damn smug smile made a comeback. "Perhaps you haven't noticed, but they are prone to lying."

Lies. Everything I knew, a lie. I couldn't believe anything to be true anymore, which meant I couldn't believe Zeke.

"So are you," I said.

Zeke let out a short, impatient sigh. His hands moved and I tensed, waiting for another fight. Instead, he tugged something out from beneath his shirt and handed it to me. A letter, neatly folded and a little wrinkled. I had to wonder how long he'd been carrying the damn thing.

"I am not going to stand here and debate life and death with you, Cassandra. I have been given a job and I will complete it. This is from Thomas. It explains everything. Take it, read it, and decide. Either you come with me, or you stay here. In which case, I wish you all the best with your recovery."

Zeke stepped back and stared at me. I stared back. His eyes, often half-lidded as if I'd caught him mid-nap, looked at me and through me with perfect clarity. I saw the colour of his irises then. Not quite black, but the darkest shade of brown imaginable. Calm, dark eyes. The eyes of a professional. He inclined his head to me, and then turned toward the door.

I had only a second to gather my thoughts.

"Where the hell are you going?"

Zeke paused at the door, one hand on the handle. He no longer wore the smug smile when he spoke. "Group therapy. I will come for you tomorrow morning, Cassandra. Have your decision made by then."

And then he disappeared out the door as if he'd never been there, leaving me with a sore throat and a sore head to remind me of his presence. And a letter.

I turned my attention to the folded piece of paper. It looked like any other piece of paper, white and rectangular and roughly palm-sized. I passed a finger over the edge, willing the contents to be blank. Life would be so much easier to sort out if that paper turned out to be blank.

I unfolded the letter. Flowing black ink danced across the page and stabbed at my eyes. Not blank at all.

Hey beautiful,

The words echoed through my skull in surround sound. I jerked my head up and glowered at the ghostly image of Tommy standing in front of me.

"Stop it," I growled at him.

Tommy shrugged, the corner of his mouth turned up in a lop-sided grin.

"Can't help it. You're reading it in my voice."

I glowered harder, but he had a point. Even if I tried to shut out the ghost, I would still hear the letter in his voice. So, I bent my head and focused on the script, and let the memory of the Tommy I knew read out the words of a Tommy I had yet to meet.

Hey beautiful,

Did you miss me? Cause I've missed you. Probably wondering if this is all real still. Let me break it down for you.

You met me in a convenience store. I was the one looking all rugged and handsome as I saved your ass. Your birthday is August twenty-third. I gave you a pair of night vision goggles. You still got them? Damn, those were nice. You got a scar on your neck from the time you got yourself killed, a tight ass, and a cute little birthmark just above your tailbone. A little over ten years ago, I told you to come back for me. You've been taking your sweet ass time, so here's a little incentive.

You and me, we got unfinished business.

After you fell off the wall all those years back, Almesa got me. I'm not going to go into the nitty-gritty of what happened next, but it sucked. Turns out not everyone on the inside was all happy about what they were doing there. One of their own broke me out. I went to that dude your captain talked about, but they got to him first. Killed him. Made it look like a heart attack.

This shit Almesa's into, it's more than just military weapons testing. It's big. Like apocalypse big. They've been making people disappear for years. Half the people in the government belong to them, and the other half aren't long for this world. And whatever they're really planning, it's coming to a head soon. I've been doing my damnedest to stay on top of them for years. Got some help. Finally had a breakthrough a year ago, when someone pulled back the curtain on Redby.

All those weird pictures and stories of a missing town the media talked about? Yeah, that was yours truly. Though I'll tell you something, watching you walk out of those walls on national television was greater than anything I could've hoped for.

Thought I would be doing this on my own. I mean, not all on my own, but being one of the tinfoil hat wearing good guys operating in the shadows isn't the same as being part of a kick-ass zombie hunting dynamic duo.

We made a promise to take down Almesa. We need to finish what we started.

Zeke's a good guy. Real professional. I'd have come myself, but Almesa's got eyes everywhere. If you don't trust Zeke, then trust me. I'm still here waiting for you. So get a move on, beautiful.

Your man,

Tommy

I stared at the last line of the letter, the way the ink swirled around the Y in his name and speared off to the side, like he wasn't happy unless he filled every inch of blank space on that page. Just like Tommy, filling up the whole damn world with his presence.

He still stood in front of me, cowboy hat tilted over his steel grey eyes. He smiled, and the room came alive around him.

Tommy. Alive. The whisper ran through my brain like a current, dragging me down every time I thought I had escaped it. Alive and waiting for me. We could finish what we started. After ten years of living and dying and losing my fucking mind, this was the moment I came back to. Picking up exactly where I left off.

But hell, wasn't that what I wanted? After all, I made a promise.

The door handle rattled, interrupting my train wreck of a thought process. I had just enough time to hop back to my spot, finger-comb my hair back into place, and effect boredom before the door opened and my guard's squinty, accusing eyes locked onto me. For a moment, she seemed disappointed to find me where she left me. Then she growled something about being late for group therapy and told me to hurry up.

We made the rest of the trip in silence. I thought about Tommy and what he had in mind for Almesa, and my guard glowered at me every time I twitched. I had no idea how Zeke planned to get us out of there, but it had to be better than storming the wall with a horde of zombies on my heels.

CHAPTER TWENTY-FOUR

REDBY, NEVADA
August 25, 2021

We stared at each other in silence for a while. Three soldiers against two ragged, dirty, desperate survivors. I couldn't count myself as one of the soldiers anymore. They were aliens dressed in strange uniforms, bearing unfamiliar guns and guarding a world I knew nothing about. My dog tags weighed heavily against my neck.

Captain Stone broke the silence. "Where are your shadows? Where's Miller?"

Shit. I'd completely forgotten about Steve. We were supposed to find him. Then everything went to hell. I shook my head.

"Dead. Miller too, I'd wager."

"Damn." Captain bowed his head as if offering up a silent prayer, then jerked his chin at the stairwell behind him. "Come on. I know the way out."

"Oh, hell no," Tommy interjected. "We are not trusting you. We're not trusting them, right, Cass?"

I opened my mouth to respond, but only empty air came out.

Captain Stone had seen me through some of the worst shit in my life. He dragged me back to base after an IED claimed our sergeant, he put my name up for promotion. I once swore I would follow the man into hell itself and meant every word. We found hell this time, but I never promised I would follow him out again.

"You abandoned us." My voice sounded thick and heavy against my ears. I swallowed the lump rising in my throat and shook off the little voice screaming at me to shut up and obey orders.

"Saratores, we don't have time for this shit. Get your ass up those stairs."

Sir, yes— No! I squeezed my eyes shut and shook my head. Tommy shifted beside me. The fabric of his sleeve brushed past my arm as he raised his gun. My heart lurched into my throat and I grabbed the weapon away from him.

"Don't you fucking dare!" The words tumbled out of my mouth faster than the shouts of the soldiers to drop the weapon.

"Cass, those fuckers are the only thing between us and freedom. Let go."

"Son, that is a stupid move. She just saved your life." Captain raised his gun, slow and deliberate, like he had all the time in the world to line up his shot.

"These are the people trying to kill us," Tommy growled, yanking on the butt of the shotgun.

I refused to let go of Tommy's gun and stepped between the two men to keep them from killing each other. "Both of you shut the hell up."

Silence answered me.

The two soldiers behind Captain exchanged a glance, or at least it looked like they did. Couldn't read a thing off their faces behind those damned helmets. "Sir, we've come a long way to break out of this hellhole and I will go through you if I have to."

"I am trying to help you."

"You left me out there to die."

Captain grabbed me by the front of my shirt and dragged me within an inch of his faceless mask. "Listen here, you little shit. If I'd had the option, I would've personally gone out there and rounded up every last one of you sorry assholes. Hell, I would've cleared out this whole fucking town. But it's not up to me. For some goddamn reason I can't figure out, the brass is in bed with Almesa. Brass says listen to them, I listen to them. I still got more than a hundred men this side of the wall I have to look out for, so save me the fucking betrayal speech. Now collect your fucking balls, pick up the goddamn puppy you got trailing after you, and get your ass up those stairs!"

A chill ran down my spine as Captain released me. I felt like a grunt in Basic all over again and this was the last exercise of the day. Complete it and I could rest. I took a step toward the stairs.

"No. No! Cass, we can't trust them. He's just waiting for a chance to shoot us in the back." Tommy raised the shotgun again, nestling it against his shoulder like he could coax a better shot out of the barrel if he coddled it enough.

"Son, the only thing keeping you alive right now is my good mood. I suggest you do not tarnish it."

"I'm thinking the only thing keeping me alive is this here shotgun. Cass, we're finding another way around."

"How? Back the way you came? Back there is an ambush. Even if you get through that one, there's another at the next stairwell, and the one after that. You won't make it past the first goddamn floor and even if you do, Almesa's locked the exit down tight." Captain lifted his gun and pointed at the stairs behind him. "This is the only way out. I don't need your trust to get you out of here alive. I just need your cooperation."

"Why the hell would you be interested in helping us?"

"Because I can't do shit about the men I've lost to this place already, but you can." No one spoke for a while. No one on our floor anyway. A distant river of noise threaded through the air, reminding us of how little space we had. People shouted orders back and forth, equipment rattled, the noose closed around our necks. "Time's running out, son. Up or down?"

Tommy said nothing.

"Suit yourself. Saratores, move out." Captain turned to go.

I remained rooted to the spot, glued there by crippling indecision. I couldn't leave without Tommy, but Captain Stone wouldn't wait forever. "I trust him, Tommy." A shot in the dark. Tommy still looked suspicious, but he trusted me. God, I hope he trusted me.

For a minute, I believed he would run. His eyes darted back down the hallway, counting the steps to the last flight of stairs. Then he let out a shaky breath, tilted his hat low over his eyes, and jogged past me, muttering along the way. "We're so gonna get shot in the back."

A hundred feet of stairs is a long way to run. We remained silent for a good portion of it. Part saving our breath and part being too afraid to speak lest we attract attention. On every new floor, we caught glimpses of soldiers running one way or another. Never in our direction except for one patrol, which quickly about-faced at a gesture from the captain.

The signs on the wall read "Level A 52." We were near the top. Captain Stone broke the silence as we charged up the next flight of stairs. "Saratores, I assume the zombies were your idea."

"Yes, sir."

"Started a whole shit-storm on the lower levels. Good for a breach, bad for a cover. They got the whole damn place on lockdown now. Every door, every floor."

"So why the hell aren't we running into problems?" Tommy piped up between huffs and puffs and clattering equipment.

Captain spared a quick glance over his shoulder. "I may have to answer to Almesa, but my men answer to me. We got a window of ten minutes to make it to the catwalk."

"Whoa, wait. Catwalk? Like up at the tippy top kind of catwalk? What the hell are we going up there for?"

"Shut up. From there, you'll be able to get down and around to the front gate. Gate itself is locked up tight, but there's a service door for bringing in supplies. Only leads out. I got a man waiting at the door. Once you're out, you go to Sergeant Major Tim Hammond. Lives in D.C. Works for the inspector general. He's an old friend of mine. You don't speak to anybody else before you reach him, got it?"

"Yes, sir," I answered. A little part of my soul regrew with those simple words.

"Corporal, you find out what these sons of bitches are up to and you shut them down. Here's the roof. I'll have to double back to make it look like we missed you. Make this count." Captain Stone slammed open the heavy steel door blocking our path.

"Yes, s—"

Bang.

The shot reverberated through my skull. Nothing more than a tiny pop amid the howling wind, but in my mind, a nuclear warhead detonated. I looked down at myself. No blood. I looked at Tommy. Clean. Then Captain Stone stumbled into me.

"You," he rasped. A rattling breath wheezed through his mask. "I'm going to have you court-martialed so fucking fast, your great-grandchildren will be too disgraced to show their faces in public."

"Again," a low, feminine voice commanded.

The gun barked obediently. Captain's body jerked in response. He stumbled, started to fall, one hand reaching for the crenellations marching along the edge of the wall. His hand missed. A strangled noise escaped my throat. I dove to catch him.

I missed.

Captain Stone looked at me as his body tilted sideways. Blood trickled across the glossy black armour of his suit. The armour remained undamaged, but the soft fabric covering his neck, giving him mobility, showed a gaping hole. For one long second, we stared at each other, my eyes reflected in his black mask. Then he toppled off the wall, out of sight. If not for Tommy's arm around my midsection, I would've gone after him.

"Congratulations on your promotion, Lieutenant," the feminine voice said.

"It's Captain now, ma'am." The soldier checked the chamber of his weapon, then lifted it to his shoulder and pointed the barrel at me.

"Of course. My apologies, Captain."

I took stock of my audience for the first time. A barricade of people lined up from one side of the wall to the other, all of them dressed in the same black uniform. The woman stood out. Nothing different about her attire, but the way she stood, hands clasped behind her back, like an actor waiting on a script to play itself out.

The man beside her, the one who shot the captain, towered over her. Only one lieutenant I knew of that height.

"Wickers," I snarled. "What the fuck do you think you're doing? You killed your commanding officer."

"Just following orders." Not a hint of remorse in his voice.

I wanted to rip his head off. He stood between me and the other soldiers. I could get to him in time. I twisted in Tommy's grasp. He held tight. Good thing he did, because seconds later, the last of the captain's men were overrun by more soldiers coming up the stairs. I caught a glimpse of our two silent escorts dropping their weapons and placing their hands on their heads before they were swallowed by more black uniforms bristling with guns. Now the barricade of black armoured enemies stretched all around us.

"Don't get upset," the woman said. "You've already stressed your systems enough. We'll have to sedate you in order to get our base readings, and that just won't do."

"I don't know who the fuck you think you are but—"

"Director of Operations, Melissa Chamberlain. This," she paused and swept a hand out across the wall, over the city, and then laid it to rest on Wickers' shoulder, "is mine. You are mine. You are standing here now because I commanded it. I needed test subjects."

"Well hey there, Mel. Long time no see. You coming over for dinner again any time soon?" Tommy asked, his tone all sing-song and chipper. When Melissa didn't reply, he smacked himself in the forehead. "Right. Stupid me. You can't come over anymore. You killed my parents." He levelled the shotgun at her face.

The soldiers gave an immediate response. All around us, weapons turned their dark mouths in Tommy's direction.

"I remember you now," the woman in the mask said. "You're Irene's boy. Pity she didn't survive. She had a brilliant mind. Too much of a moral stick up her ass to be brought into the fold though."

This time I held Tommy back instead of the other way around. He surged forward, but I planted my feet and pressed my hands against his shoulders.

"You would have been safe if she had just stopped probing," Melissa continued. "She always had questions. Always wanted to see more than she was allowed. I took personal interest in making sure she did not survive the initial release. And my agents made sure she could not be brought back."

"You fucking whore," Tommy snarled. "I am going to kill you and everyone you love. I am going to burn your fucking life to ashes, and then I'm going to piss on those ashes. I am not going to rest until I ruin you."

Melissa Chamberlain let out a long-suffering sigh and tilted her head to the side.

"Are you done? Good. Thomas, I will be frank. I liked your mother, but she could never see the big picture. Science demands sacrifice. Some things can only be learned by dissection, deconstruction. In other words, death. The deaths suffered in Redby will guarantee long lives for men and women who are willing to sacrifice. Who choose to sacrifice. And in doing so, secure the futures of so many innocent lives. For that reward, isn't a little sacrifice worth it?"

"You don't have to give us the sales pitch," I snarled. "We've already heard it. You invent immortality, and the first thing you do is find a way to weaponize it."

Melissa tilted her head in the opposite direction, regarding me the way a dog regards an insect it's about to eat. "Is that so surprising? If you think about it, every great invention has its roots in military research. In a few years time, they will be using this research to save lives that would otherwise be lost. Just as we will as we secure America's dominance in the field of battle."

"Keep her talking," Tommy whispered in my ear.

I didn't understand until I felt the slight pressure on my hip. Right next to the stun gun.

"I've had enough of this. Take their weapons and take them downstairs," Melissa ordered.

I had to think fast. I pointed my pistol at Wickers, then the soldier beside him, then another. There were too many, and they were all advancing in a steady, unbreakable line. Even if I killed a few, they would soon overwhelm us and claim our weapons. So, I did some outside the box thinking instead. I put the gun to my own head.

"Stop," I bellowed. "Stop or I blow my brains out. Then you don't get your test subject, right? That'd put a damper on your plans."

Melissa paused, raised a hand to halt the soldiers, and let out an aggravated sigh

"A little bit. Yes," she said.

"Tell me why," I demanded. I had to keep her talking. Just a little bit longer.

"Why what?"

"Why Redby."

"I thought you read the file. It was all in there. If we tried this anywhere else in the world, we'd have to deal with foreign politics and investigations and all that troublesome legal stuff. Here, no one looks in their backyard for trouble. No one would expect this sort of operation to be happening on their own soil. Even though we've done it before. It's because we've done it before that we know it works. Redby is secluded, has an acceptable population size, and has never done anything noteworthy. It is invisible in the public eye. So, it provides the best example of a controlled testing environment. I chose it because it is perfectly in control. My control."

"Guess you like control, huh?"

Melissa clasped her hands behind her back and drew in a breath. She looked like a crow puffing out its chest with pride.

"I have overseen every single aspect of this project from beginning to end. This is my life's work. I am Redby. And I'm done debating it with a lab rat." Melissa took a step back and waved a hand, as if unpausing the soldiers. "If she kills herself, wait for her to turn, then give her the injection. We know it works on her at least."

Okay, Cass, moment of truth. Are you woman enough to pull the trigger? I stared into the lightless pit of Wickers' helmet and curled my finger around the trigger.

Tommy leaned in close to my ear, his breath hot on my neck, and whispered, "Time to blow this popsicle stand."

Tommy drew the weapon and shot from the hip, filling the air with a bubble of sizzling blue light. The second he moved, I did too, flinging myself at Melissa's exposed back. The heat and energy of the weapon picked me up off my feet, propelled me forward. I dropped the gun and stretched my hands toward her shoulders. She looked up, and for the briefest of seconds, the sunlight caught her mask at just the right angle to give me a dusky image of her face beneath. Wide eyes stared up at me, full of understanding.

My hands locked around Melissa's shoulders and dragged her with me as the energy blast flung me away from Tommy. We lurched sideways in the air and I caught a fleeting glimpse of a dozen soldiers spread across the skyline like blackbirds in flight. Then the world tilted upside down and the edge of the wall rushed up to meet me.

I released Melissa and stretched out a hand, willing myself to catch the ledge. My fingers scraped across solid concrete. A fingernail tore off on the unforgiving stone, but I held on. Searing warmth blossomed all down my arm. Melissa hung on to my other hand like a goddamn barnacle, her gloved fingers wrapped around my wrist. Below us stretched the webwork of paved streets that made up Redby's industrial district.

At the very least, I could've died on the side of freedom. But no, I had to fall over the edge on the wrong side of the damn wall. I looked down at Melissa, swinging from the end of my arm and making little chirps of distress. At least I could still take her out with me.

"Don't," Melissa cried, as if reading my mind. "Let go and we both die."

"That's kinda the idea," I shot back.

"I can save you! I can save your entire family. Not just from Redby, but from what's coming."

"Let me guess. All I have to do is pull you up and let you continue your research."

"It's for a good cause," she cried.

"They always say that." The pain in my arm grew to a wildfire raging through my shoulders and back. I wanted to let go, if only to lessen the agony.

A cowboy hat fluttered past my vision, skating on the strong winds down to Redby.

Tommy appeared above me, blood trailing down his face from a cut on his forehead. His strong, warm hands took my wrist and hauled back.

"Let me go," I screamed at him.

"Not a chance in hell." He spoke through gritted teeth. Pulling up the dead weight of one person was hard enough. Two made it nearly impossible.

"Tommy," I waited until he opened his eyes and looked down at me. "Tommy, let me go."

The remaining soldiers stirred. They shouted to each other, calling for backup, calling for someone to grab Tommy.

A bullet chewed a bite out of the crenellation beside Tommy's head. He ducked instinctively, shielding his face with his shoulder. One glance back and the remaining colour in his face drained away. Yet when he looked at me, he smiled.

"Come back for me," Tommy shouted.

He let go.

I fell. Melissa screamed and her grip on my wrist disappeared. Black hands appeared behind Tommy's head, closing around him, dragging him away. I kept watching, waiting for him to reappear. This couldn't be the end for us. We'd come so far.

Then I hit the ground.

That was my second death in Redby.

CHAPTER TWENTY-FIVE

OAK RIDGE MENTAL HOSPITAL, TEXAS
August 26, 2032

I stared at the last full page in my journal. It stared back with its blotchy script and stick figure drawings of me falling to my death, and Melissa splattered on the ground beneath me. That death marked the end of my time with Tommy. We might've won a small victory that day, but I lost him. I never did find Tommy again. Not in Redby.

"Maybe it's time to change that." Tommy materialized beside my bed, cowboy hat sitting askew over his grey eyes and hands shoved into the pockets of his faded jeans.

I looked at him. Really looked at him. Like I hadn't done in years. Much as I clung to my ghosts, I never liked seeing them. They were reminders of everything I had failed to do.

"You didn't fail, Cass. You survived," Tommy said.

"I gave up." I spat the words out. They tasted as vile as the kitchen's concept of pudding.

"If you'd given up, you'd be dead. Just like the other Reds." Tommy took a step closer. "Come on, Cass. Let's fix this."

I looked away, but when I did BigMac materialized at the foot of my bed and Ace appeared between him and Tommy. I was surrounded.

"We thought we fixed this years ago. That didn't fucking work. I got trapped there for ten years." I rounded on Tommy. "Hell, you've been trying to fix this on your own according to your letter. Not even sure I believe it yet."

To my eternal irritation, he smiled.

"Even if you don't, you really going to choose to sit here and rot instead? That don't sound like you, Cass."

No, it sure as hell didn't. Especially after the talk I had with Ace. I wanted to get better, but my way. With my mind intact. Or at least glued back together the way I liked it. Ghosts and all.

"How long are you going to debate this, Cass? You know what your decision is already," Ace said.

"I don't trust him. Zeke, I mean."

"So kill him." Tommy shrugged. "Just try to wait until after he gets you back to me. Kinda, yanno, important to keep the guide alive this time."

"Cass, you've got an opportunity not many people get. You can make this right." Ace moved closer, sliding through the bed and into my personal space. I saw him as he used to be, all cocksure and full of life, but faded. Like a photograph left in the sun too long. "Maybe not everything, but the important things. Someone's got to take Almesa down before more people get hurt."

"I don't give a fuck about other people."

"You care about your people. You care about Tommy, and if he's in the world, Almesa's going after him."

I turned my head and looked at Tommy. The sunlight filtered through him, cutting away the bright colours of his shirt. God, I wanted to touch him again. I wanted to touch anyone who wasn't there just to jab a needle in my arm or remind me of how I no longer fit in the world.

At least I fit in Tommy's world. And if he was alive, then I had to find him. I had to save what little I had left. Ace was right. I'd already made up my mind.

I swore under my breath and flipped to the first page of my journal to look at the name tag stuck to the inside cover. Cassandra Isabella Saratores, resident of Oak Ridge Mental Hospital. In a fit of childishness, I crossed out the hospital's name and wrote underneath; Redby.

"'Atta girl," Tommy crowed.

"You better damn well be alive, asshole," I growled at him.

Then I leaned back in bed and waited.

Screams echoed through my head. No wait, they weren't in my head. They were outside of it. Out in the hall. I sat up and turned my ear toward the door, straining for every hint of noise. Ace, BigMac, and Tommy turned with me.

There! The sound came through distant and muffled, but carrying the undeniable high pitched, erratic quality of terror. Shouts joined the screams. Not the familiar calls for backup or calm or quiet the guards often used. Footsteps pelted past my doorway, and with them went a strangled cry for help.

"The hell is going on out there," Tommy muttered.

The fire alarm started up, its grating ring echoing through my skull. My heart beat a little faster.

"Sounds like an evacuation," Ace said.

"Sounds like they're leaving us behind," Tommy added.

"The hell they are." I swung my legs over the side of the bed and stood up. Ace, BigMac, and Tommy came to stand beside me.

"This is part of Zeke's plan, right?" Tommy asked, a thread of tension running through his voice.

The screaming continued, getting louder as it moved down my hallway. Another person thundered past my door. Through the little square window, I saw a blur of dark hair and wide, terrified eyes. An underlying sound became more distinct as the screaming person moved away. A low, monotonous moan that made my blood run cold.

"I'm gonna go with yes." Though the knowledge that Zeke's plan included panic and fire alarms did not provide me with much comfort. Effective plan though.

More footsteps in the hallway. This time they skidded to a halt outside my room. Zeke had finally arrived.

Doc Brown burst through the door, his thin, wispy hair standing on end as if he'd been struck by lightning. His eyes loomed large as baseballs behind his thick glasses. I remained frozen in a moment of confusion as he slammed the door shut behind him, then promptly dropped his keys.

As my aging doctor bent to retrieve them, I realized it wasn't fear making his hands shake. Well, not fear alone. One plaster-wrapped arm pressed against his stomach, held there by a sling.

Right. I'd broken his arm.

"Uh..." I said by way of greeting.

213

"You have to help me," he shrieked.

"I...what?"

"Help me," he pleaded again.

"Why?"

"Wh—why?" the Doc sputtered. His eyes slipped into focus and found my face. "It's the zombies, Cassandra. They're here. They've taken the hospital. They're everywhere. I barely escaped alive. I can't get out. You can though. It's what you do, right? You kill zombies." A fevered light filled the doc's eyes and sweat stood out on his forehead. The metallic tang of blood filled the air. If it hadn't been for that smell, I could've passed his intense stare off as desperation. I knew the signs of blood loss and shock though. All too well.

One quick look over the doc told me all the little missing details of his story. He hadn't just barely escaped alive. He'd been caught and bitten. Ravaged, really. I couldn't see how bad the damage was because his cast nestled against the open wound on his stomach. The blood told enough. It stained his shirt from chest to groin and dyed the white plaster of his cast a sickly pink.

A loud bang resounded on the door. The doc screamed and jumped away, scrambling to hide behind me. I balled my fists and raised them for a fight, but the tension left me as soon as the door opened.

"You're late," I said to Zeke.

The merc looked different than the last time we'd met. He'd tossed the hospital scrubs and donned an old pair of jeans and a white t-shirt in their place. Sleek, black glasses concealed his eyes. The braid hadn't changed, though it looked a little slicker and glossier than before. An old duffel bag rested against his hip, supported by a frayed strap. He stepped into the room and shut the door behind himself, then threw the duffel onto the bed and nodded past me to the doctor.

"What's he doing here?"

"Me? What are you doing here?" Doc Brown demanded. Scared out of his wits and bleeding from a gut wound, and still the man balked at the slightest hint of derision.

I didn't answer Zeke. Instead, I smiled. "So zombies, huh?"

"It would appear Almesa is not content to let you sit and stew any longer. I thought they would merely send someone here to finish you. They had other plans."

"Zombies are kinda the wrong way to go about it. I know how to deal with them," I said.

"Whether you survive or not is immaterial at this point."

That caught me off guard.

"Why?"

Zeke stepped closer to the door and peered through the little window into the hall. He spared me a short glance over his shoulder.

"Because regardless of what happens to you now, they can blame you for the outbreak. They have unleashed the virus into the world, and you are the new Patient Zero."

"Well that sucks," I quipped.

"What do you mean Patient Zero? What's going on here?" Doc Brown looked from me to Zeke and back again.

Zeke ignored him and motioned to the bag on the bed. "Get changed. We need to leave."

"Leave where? Where are you going?" Doc demanded. He reached for me, but I shook him off and moved to the bag. The faded green canvas sagged and bulged around its contents, worn so thin in some places it could almost pass for see-through.

Though the outside of the bag looked tattered and frayed, the inside looked like a treasure chest. Everything I had on my person when I'd been taken into custody jumbled together on one side of the duffel. The other half contained an assortment of weapons, both makeshift and illegal. Enough to make an arms dealer giggle.

I dug out my old clothes first. The battered white tank top worn so often the collar had turned permanently yellow, the old cargo pants "donated" by an army surplus store, and the heavy black boots that had marched straight out of Redby. I shrugged out of my hospital clothes without a thought to the presence of the two men and wriggled into my old duds. The moment the threadbare fabric touched my skin, my life returned to normal. I drew in a deep breath, held it, savoured the sense of wholeness, then let it out and peered at the weapons left behind. A pistol, a shotgun, a couple boxes of bullets, a couple shivs, brass knuckles, and then...

Jesus H. Christ.

My weapons.

My weapons!

I pulled them both out and clutched them to my chest. Clangy, the old, scratched and dented crowbar whose paint had once been blue and Mona, the nicked bowie knife with her name carved into the handle. My best friends. My most trusted and reliable companions. My babies. My babies were home.

Last of all, I snagged the mess of dog tags sitting at the bottom of the bag and pulled them out. I held them up to the light, examining the names etched into their steel surfaces. Then I laid them around my neck one by one.

"Cassandra, please. Tell me what is going on." The doc gave up on demands. He looked at me with the terrified eyes of a child, so out of place on a man who had impressed on me just how big and important he was with every word he spoke. Finally, I got to see the real man.

"Long story short, Doc, I'm checking myself out. Almesa's found a way to resurrect the zombie virus, so I'm going to go ahead and clear myself for duty. Zeke here's my ride home."

"And me. You're saving me, right?" the doc asked in a quavering voice.

"Sure," I said just before I put the muzzle of the pistol to his head and pulled the trigger.

Doc probably hadn't wanted my brand of salvation. Unfortunately for him, it was all I had to give. He'd already died. He just hadn't known it yet. At least this way he wouldn't come back.

"Are we ready now?" Zeke asked, impatience in his tone.

"Give me a minute," I replied.

I tucked the pistol into the back of my belt, slung the shotgun over my shoulder and moved back to the bed. The journal with its glossy green cover stared at me from the bedsheets. I picked it up, flipped to my dog-eared page, wrote a few final words, and tossed it into the duffel bag. Then I stripped the bed of fabric and used it to wrap the doc's body. After a moment of regret, I upended a flask taken from the duffel onto the pile. Half a litre of an unknown alcohol splashed over the old sheets. I returned the empty flask to the bag, pulled out my lighter and lit the cocoon on fire.

The duffel settled on my shoulder with a familiar weight and bulkiness, the old canvas kissing the butt of the shotgun. Smoke curled up from the funeral pyre, mingling with the blood and fear permeating the hospital. Zeke inclined his head and I stepped out into the hallway ahead of him, stepped into my future. Same as my past but hell, I'd grown to like that past.

My name is Cassandra Isabella Saratores. For ten years, I lived and died in Hell, but today?

Today is going to be a good day.

ACKNOWLEDGEMENTS

Like most authors I know, I have conceived, begun, and then abandoned more projects than I can count. When I began this book, I imagined it would turn out the same. The reason this book exists today is due to the difference people in my life made, and the promise I wove into my main character.

When I thought up Cassandra, I wrote her with a very specific motto in mind. I made her stubborn, and thick skulled, and aggressive, but above all else, I made her persistent. Cass lives by the code of *"not 'til the last breath leaves my body."* She will not give up. She will not be persuaded out of a goal, and she will literally choose death over defeat. Which is easy to say when you know resurrection is on the table, but still.

The reason I am including this explanation in my acknowledgements is because I needed that same drive to carry me along to the end of this novel. Conceiving of a book is easy. Translating that masterpiece in your mind onto paper often leaves one feeling like a child struggling to grasp the intricacies of neuroscience. There are always too many pages to fill, too much white void ahead of you, and too much for you to learn to ever consider yourself a halfway decent author. Sheer, stubborn persistence is the only reason any book ever reaches "The End."

So this book is written on behalf of all the people who told me they loved my writing when I could not. To all the authors who inspired me and caused me to despair that I could ever reach their level. To all of my fellow NaNocrats and local writers who glowingly crowed over their literary accomplishments while I wallowed in half-finished rough drafts. To all the editors and agents who told me they loved the story, but they couldn't sell it. To my friends and family, who encouraged me to continue, often without ever seeing a hint of my written works. And finally, to the publisher who looked me in the eye and said he wanted my novel, when I had all but given up on ever letting this book see the light of day.

To all of you, I say thank you, and I hope none of you ever give up on your goals either. Let's keep fighting until that last damn breath.

ABOUT THE AUTHOR

Kaitlin Caul has three great loves in life; writing, drawing, and dragons. She is also a gigantic geek and grew up on a healthy diet of *Star Trek: Voyager*, *Buffy the Vampire Slayer*, and *Dragonlance*. As such, she has developed a fascination with awesome stories, quippy characters, and things that go bump in the night.

Kaitlin was born in Toronto and proceeded to live in various places across southern Ontario during her youth. She grew up with two younger siblings, both of whom she loves dearly now that they've moved to the other side of the country. She shares her father's love of dissecting movies for their intellectual parts, and her mother's love of jumping into adventure without looking first. When not staring in abject terror at the empty pages on her computer screen, she spends her free time assisting her best friends with the Ottawa NaNoWriMo group, writing up campaign maps and stories for her gaming group, or assessing the quality of the latest batch of local brews.

www.ingramcontent.com/pod-product-compliance
Lightning Source LLC
Chambersburg PA
CBHW072354020726
47506CB00004B/1104